Red Money

Fergus Hume

Red Money

Copyright © 2024 Indo-European Publishing

All rights reserved

The present edition is a reproduction of previous publication of this classic work. Minor typographical errors may have been corrected without note; however, for an authentic reading experience the spelling, punctuation, and capitalization have been retained from the original text.

ISBN: 979-8-88942-472-7

CONTENTS

Chapter I	The Drama of Little Things	1
Chapter II	In the Wood	11
Chapter III	An Unexpected Recognition	21
Chapter IV	Secrets	30
Chapter V	The Woman and the Man	40
Chapter VI	The Man and the Woman	50
Chapter VII	The Secretary	60
Chapter VIII	At Midnight	69
Chapter IX	Afterwards	79
Chapter X	A Difficult Position	89
Chapter XI	Blackmail	99
Chapter XII	The Conspiracy	109
Chapter XIII	A Friend in Need	119
Chapter XIV	Miss Greeby, Detective	128
Chapter XV	Guesswork	138
Chapter XVI	The Last Straw	148
Chapter XVII	On the Trail	158
Chapter XVIII	An Amazing Accusation	168
Chapter XIX	Mother Cockleshell	178
Chapter XX	The Destined End	188
Chapter XXI	A Final Surprise	200

CHAPTER I

THE DRAMA OF LITTLE THINGS

"Gypsies! How very delightful! I really must have my fortune told. The dear things know all about the future."

As Mrs. Belgrove spoke she peered through her lorgnette to see if anyone at the breakfast-table was smiling. The scrutiny was necessary, since she was the oldest person present, and there did not appear to be any future for her, save that very certain one connected with a funeral. But a society lady of sixty, made up to look like one of forty (her maid could do no more), with an excellent digestion and a constant desire, like the Athenians of old, for "Something New!" can scarcely be expected to dwell upon such a disagreeable subject as death. Nevertheless, Mrs. Belgrove could not disguise from herself that her demise could not be postponed for many more years, and examined the faces of the other guests to see if they thought so too. If anyone did, he and she politely suppressed a doubtful look and applauded the suggestion of a fortune-telling expedition.

"Let us make up a party and go," said the hostess, only too thankful to find something to amuse the house-party for a few hours. "Where did you say the gypsies were, Garvington?"

"In the Abbot's Wood," replied her husband, a fat, small round-faced man, who was methodically devouring a large breakfast.

"That's only three miles away. We can drive or ride."

"Or motor, or bicycle, or use Shanks' mare," remarked Miss Greeby rather vulgarly. Not that any one minded such a speech from her, as her vulgarity was merely regarded as eccentricity, because she had money and brains, an exceedingly long tongue, and a memory of other people's failings to match.

Lord Garvington made no reply, as breakfast, in his opinion, was much too serious a business to be interrupted. He reached for the marmalade, and requested that a bowl of Devonshire cream should be passed along. His wife, who was lean and anxious-looking even for an August hostess, looked at him wrathfully. He never gave her any assistance in entertaining their numerous guests, yet always insisted that the house should be full for the shooting season. And being poor for a titled pair, they could not afford to entertain even a shoeblack, much less a crowd of hungry sportsmen and a horde of frivolous women, who required to be amused expensively. It was really too bad of Garvington.

At this point the reflections of the hostess were interrupted by Miss Greeby, who always had a great deal to say, and who always tried, as an American would observe, "to run the circus." "I suppose you men will go out shooting as usual?" she said in her sharp, clear voice.

The men present collectively declared that such was their intention, and that they had come to "The Manor" for that especial purpose, so it was useless to ask them, or any one of them, to go on a fortune-telling expedition when they could find anything of that sort in Bond Street. "And it's all a lot of rot, anyhow," declared one sporting youth with obviously more muscle and money than brains; "no one can tell my fortune."

"I can, Billy. You will be Prime Minister," flashed out Miss Greeby, at which there was a general laugh. Then Garvington threw a bombshell.

"You'd better get your fortunes told to-day, if you want to," he grunted, wiping his mustache; "for to-morrow I'm going to have these rotters moved off my land straight away. They're thieves and liars."

"So are many other people," snapped Miss Greeby, who had lost heavily at bridge on the previous night and spoke feelingly.

Her host paid no attention to her. "There's been a lot of burglaries in this neighborhood of late. I daresay these gypsies are mixed up in them."

"Burglaries!" cried Mrs. Belgrove, and turned pale under her rouge, as she remembered that she had her diamonds with her.

"Oh, it's all right! Don't worry," said Garvington, pushing back his chair. "They won't try on any games in this house while I'm here. If any one tries to get in I'll shoot the beast."

"Is that allowed by law?" asked an army officer with a shrug.

"I don't know and I don't care," retorted Garvington. "An Englishman's house is his castle, you know, and he can jolly well shoot any one who tries to get into it. Besides, I shouldn't mind potting a burglar. Great sport."

"You'd ask his intentions first, I presume," said Lady Garvington tartly.

"Not me. Any one getting into the house after dark doesn't need his intentions to be asked. I'd shoot."

"What about Romeo?" asked a poetic-looking young man. "He got into Juliet's house, but did not come as a burglar."

"He came as a guest, I believe," said a quiet, silvery voice at the end of the table, and every one turned to look at Lady Agnes Pine, who had spoken.

She was Garvington's sister, and the wife of Sir Hubert Pine, the millionaire, who was absent from the house party on this occasion. As a rule, she spoke little, and constantly wore a sad expression on her pale and beautiful face. And Agnes Pine really was beautiful, being one of those tall, slim willowy-looking women who always look well and act charmingly. And, indeed, her undeniable charm of manner probably had more to do with her reputation as a handsome woman than her actual physical grace. With her dark hair and dark eyes, her Greek features and ivory skin faintly tinted with a tea-rose hue, she looked very lovely and very sad. Why she should be, was a puzzle to many women, as being the wife of a superlatively rich man, she had all the joys that money could bring her. Still it was hinted on good authority—but no one ever heard the name of the authority—that Garvington being poor had forced her into marrying Sir Hubert, for whom she did not care in the least. People said that her cousin Noel Lambert was the husband of her choice, but that she had sacrificed herself, or rather had been compelled to do so, in order that Garvington might be set on his legs. But Lady Agnes never gave any one the satisfaction of knowing the exact truth. She moved through the social world like a gentle ghost, fulfilling her duties admirably, but apparently indifferent to every one and everything. "Clippin' to look at," said the young men, "but tombs to talk to. No sport at all." But then the young men did not possess the key to Lady Agnes Pine's heart. Nor did her husband apparently.

Her voice was very low and musical, and every one felt its charm. Garvington answered her question as he left the room. "Romeo or no Romeo, guest or no guest," he said harshly, "I'll shoot any beast who tries to enter my house. Come on, you fellows. We start in half an hour for the coverts."

When the men left the room, Miss Greeby came and sat down in a vacant seat near her hostess. "What did Garvington mean by that last speech?" she asked with a significant look at Lady Agnes.

"Oh, my dear, when does Garvington ever mean anything?" said the other woman fretfully. "He is so selfish; he leaves me to do everything."

"Well," drawled Miss Greeby with a pensive look on her masculine features, "he looked at Agnes when he spoke."

"What do you mean?" demanded Lady Garvington sharply.

Miss Greeby gave a significant laugh. "I notice that Mr. Lambert is not in the house," she said carelessly. "But some one told me he was near at hand in the neighborhood. Surely Garvington doesn't mean to shoot him."

"Clara." The hostess sat up very straight, and a spot of color burned on either sallow cheek. "I am surprised at you. Noel is staying in the Abbot's Wood Cottage, and indulging in artistic work of some sort. But he can come and stay here, if he likes. You don't mean to insinuate that he would climb into the house through a window after dark like a burglar?"

"That's just what I do mean," retorted Miss Greeby daringly, "and if he does, Garvington will shoot him. He said so."

"He said nothing of the sort," cried Lady Garvington, angrily rising.

"Well, he meant it. I saw him looking at Agnes. And we know that Sir Hubert is as jealous as Othello. Garvington is on guard I suppose, and—"

"Will you hold your tongue?" whispered the mistress of the Manor furiously, and she would have shaken Miss Greeby, but that she had borrowed money from her and did not dare to incur her enmity. "Agnes will hear you; she is looking this way; can't you see?"

"As if I cared," laughed Miss Greeby, pushing out her full lower lip in a contemptuous manner. However, for reasons best known to herself, she held her peace, although she would have scorned the idea that the hint of her hostess made her do so.

Lady Garvington saw that her guests were all chattering with one another, and that the men were getting ready to leave for the day's shooting, so she went to discuss the dinner in the housekeeper's room. But all the time she and the housekeeper were arguing what Lord Garvington would like in the way of food, the worried woman was reflecting on what Miss Greeby had said. When the menu was finally settled—no easy task when it concerned the master of the house—Lady Garvington sought out Mrs. Belgrove. That juvenile ancient was sunning herself on the terrace, in the hope of renewing her waning vitality, and, being alone, permitted herself to look old. She brisked up with a kittenish purr when disturbed, and remarked that the Hengishire air was like champagne. "My spirits are positively wild and wayward," said the would-be Hebe with a desperate attempt to be youthful.

"Ah, you haven't got the house to look after," sighed Lady Garvington, with a weary look, and dropped into a basket chair to pour out her woes to Mrs. Belgrove. That person was extremely discreet, as years of society struggling had taught her the value of silence. Her discretion in this respect brought her many confidences, and she was renowned for giving advice which was never taken.

"What's the matter, my dear? You look a hundred," said Mrs. Belgrove, putting up her lorgnette with a chuckle, as if she had made an original observation. But she had not, for Lady Garvington always appeared worn and weary, and sallow, and untidy. She was the kind of absent-minded person who depended upon pins to hold her garments together, and who would put on her tiara crookedly for a drawing-room.

"Clara Greeby's a cat," said poor, worried Lady Garvington, hunting for her pocket handkerchief, which was rarely to be found.

"Has she been making love to Garvington?"

"Pooh! No woman attracts Garvington unless she can cook, or knows something about a kitchen range. I might as well have married a soup tureen. I'm sure I don't know why I ever did marry him," lamented the lady, staring at the changing foliage of the park trees. "He's a pauper and a pig, my dear, although I wouldn't say so to every one. I wish my mother hadn't insisted that I should attend cooking classes."

"What on earth has that to do with it?"

"To do with what?" asked Lady Garvington absentmindedly. "I don't know what you're talking about, I'm sure. But mother knew that Garvington was fond of a good dinner, and made me attend those classes, so as to learn to talk about French dishes. We used to flirt about soups and creams and haunches of venison, until he thought that I was as greedy as he was. So he married me, and I've been attending to his meals ever since. Why, even for our honeymoon we went to Mont St. Michel. They make splendid omelettes there, and Garvington ate all the time. Ugh!" and the poor lady shuddered.

Mrs. Belgrove saw that her companion was meandering, and would never come to the point unless forced to face it, so she rapped her knuckles with the lorgnette. "What about Clara Greeby?" she demanded sharply.

"She's a cat!"

"Oh, we're all cats, mewing or spitting as the fit takes us," said Mrs. Belgrove comfortably. "I can't see why cat should be a term of opprobrium when applied to a woman. Cats are charmingly pretty animals, and know what they want, also how to get it. Well, my dear?"

"I believe she was in love with Noel herself," ruminated Lady Garvington.

"Who was in love? Come to the point, my dear Jane."

"Clara Greeby."

Mrs. Belgrove laughed. "Oh, that ancient history. Every one who was anybody knew that Clara would have given her eyes—and very ugly eyes they are—to have married Noel Lambert. I suppose you mean him? Noel isn't a common name. Quite so. You mean him. Well, Clara wanted to buy him. He hasn't any money, and as a banker's heiress she is as rich as a Jew. But he wouldn't have her."

"Why wouldn't he?" asked Lady Garvington, waking up—she had been reflecting about a new soup which she hoped would please her husband. "Clara has quite six thousand a year, and doesn't look bad when her maid makes her dress in a proper manner. And, talking about maids, mine wants to leave, and—"

"She's too like Boadicea," interrupted Mrs. Belgrove, keeping her companion to the subject of Miss Greeby. "A masculine sort of hussy. Noel is far too artistic to marry such a maypole. She's six foot two, if she's an inch, and her hands and feet—" Mrs. Belgrove shuddered with a gratified glance at her own slim fingers.

"You know the nonsense that Garvington was talking; about shooting a burglar," said the other woman vaguely. "Such nonsense, for I'm sure no burglar would enter a house filled with nothing but Early Victorian furniture."

"Well? Well? Well?" said Mrs. Belgrove impatiently.

"Clara Beeby thought that Garvington meant to shoot Noel."

"Why, in heaven's name! Because Noel is his heir?"

"I'm sure I can't help it if I've no children," said Lady Garvington, going off on another trail—the one suggested by Mrs. Belgrove's remark. "I'd be a happier woman if I had something else to attend to than dinners. I wish we all lived on roots, so that Garvington could dig them up for himself."

"My dear, he'd send you out with a trowel to do that," said Mrs. Belgrove humorously. "But why does Garvington want to shoot Noel?"

"Oh, he doesn't. I never said he did. Clara Greeby made the remark. You see, Noel loved Agnes before she married Hubert, and I believe he loves her still, which isn't right, seeing she's married, and isn't half so good-looking as she was. And Noel stopping at that cottage in the Abbot's Wood painting in water-colors. I think he is, but I'm not sure if it isn't in oils, and the—"

"Well? Well? Well?" asked Mrs. Belgrove again.

"It isn't well at all, when you think what a tongue Clara Greeby has," snapped Lady Garvington. "She said if Noel came to see Agnes by night, Garvington, taking him for a burglar, might shoot him. She insisted that he looked at Agnes when he was talking about burglars, and meant that."

"What nonsense!" cried Mrs. Belgrove vigorously, at last having arrived at a knowledge of why Lady Garvington had sought her.

"Noel can come here openly, so there is no reason he should steal here after dark."

"Well, he's romantic, you know, dear. And romantic people always prefer windows to doors and darkness to light. The windows here are so insecure," added Lady Garvington, glancing at the facade above her untidy hair. "He could easily get in by sticking a penknife in between the upper and lower sash of the window. It would be quite easy."

"What nonsense you talk, Jane," said Mrs. Belgrove, impatiently. "Noel is not the man to come after a married woman when her husband is away. I have known him since he was a Harrow schoolboy, so I have every right to speak. Where is Sir Hubert?"

"He is at Paris or Pekin, or something with a 'P,'" said Lady Garvington in her usual vague way. "I'm sure I don't know why he can't take Agnes with him. They get on very well for a married couple."

"All the same she doesn't love him."

"He loves her, for I'm sure he's that jealous that he can't scarcely bear her out of his sight."

"It seems to me that he can," remarked Mrs. Belgrove dryly. "Since he is at Paris or Pekin and she is here."

"Garvington is looking after her, and he owes Sir Hubert too much, not to see that Agnes is all right."

Mrs. Belgrove peered at Lady Garvington through her lorgnette. "I think you talk a great deal of nonsense, Jane, as I said before," she observed. "I don't suppose for one moment that Agnes thinks of Noel, or Noel of Agnes."

"Clara Greeby says—"

"Oh, I know what she says and what she wishes. She would like to get Noel into trouble with Sir Hubert over Agnes, simply because he will not marry her. As to her chatter about burglars—"

"Garvington's chatter," corrected her companion.

"Well, then, Garvington's. It's all rubbish. Agnes is a sweet girl, and—"

"Girl?" Lady Garvington laughed disdainfully. "She is twenty-five."

"A mere baby. People cannot be called old until they are seventy or eighty. It is a bad habit growing old. I have never encouraged it myself. By the way, tell me something about Sir Hubert Pine. I have only met him once or twice. What kind of a man is he?"

"Tall, and thin, and dark, and—"

"I know his appearance. But his nature?"

"He's jealous, and can be very disagreeable when he likes. I don't know who he is, or where he came from. He made his money out of penny toys and South African investments. He was a member of Parliament for a few years, and helped his party so much with money that he was knighted. That's all I know of him, except that he is very mean."

"Mean? What you tell me doesn't sound mean."

"I'm talking of his behavior to Garvington," explained the hostess, touching her ruffled hair, "he doesn't give us enough money."

"Why should he give you any?" asked Mrs. Belgrove bluntly.

"Well, you see, dear, Garvington would never have allowed his sister to marry a nobody, unless—"

"Unless the nobody paid for his footing. I quite understand. Every one knows that Agnes married the man to save her family from bankruptcy. Poor girl!" Mrs. Belgrove sighed. "And she loved Noel. What a shame that she couldn't become his wife!"

"Oh, that would have been absurd," said Lady Garvington pettishly. "What's the use of Hunger marrying Thirst? Noel has no money, just like ourselves, and if it hadn't been for Hubert this place would have been sold long ago. I'm telling you secrets, mind."

"My dear, you tell me nothing that everybody doesn't know."

"Then what is your advice?"

"About what, my dear?"

"About what I have been telling you. The burglar, and—"

"I have told you before, that it is rubbish. If a burglar does come here I hope Lord Garvington will shoot him, as I don't want to lose my diamonds."

"But if the burglar is Noel?"

"He won't be Noel. Clara Greeby has simply made a nasty suggestion which is worthy of her. But if you're afraid, why not get her to marry Noel?"

"He won't have her," said Lady Garvington dolefully.

"I know he won't. Still a persevering woman can do wonders, and Clara Greeby has no self-respect. And if you think Noel is too near, get Agnes to join her husband in Pekin."

"I think it's Paris."

"Well then, Paris. She can buy new frocks."

"Agnes doesn't care for new frocks. Such simple tastes she has, wanting to help the poor. Rubbish, I call it."

"Why, when her husband helps Lord Garvington?" asked Mrs. Belgrove artlessly.

Lady Garvington frowned. "What horrid things you say."

"I only repeat what every one is saying."

"Well, I'm sure I don't care," cried Lady Garvington recklessly, and rose to depart on some vague errand. "I'm only in the world to look after dinners and breakfasts. Clara Greeby's a cat making all this fuss about—"

"Hush! There she is."

Lady Garvington fluttered round, and drifted towards Miss Greeby, who had just stepped out on to the terrace. The banker's daughter was in a tailor-made gown with a man's cap and a man's gloves, and a man's boots—at least, as Mrs. Belgrove thought, they looked like that—and carried a very masculine stick, more like a bludgeon than a cane. With her ruddy complexion and ruddy hair, and piercing blue eyes, and magnificent figure—for she really had a splendid figure in spite of Mrs. Belgrove's depreciation—she looked like a gigantic Norse goddess. With a flashing display of white teeth, she came along swinging her stick, or whirling her shillalah, as Mrs. Belgrove put it, and seemed the embodiment of coarse, vigorous health.

"Taking a sun-bath?" she inquired brusquely and in a loud baritone voice. "Very wise of you two elderly things. I am going for a walk."

Mrs. Belgrove was disagreeable in her turn. "Going to the Abbot's Wood?"

"How clever of you to guess," Miss Greeby smiled and nodded. "Yes, I'm going to look up Lambert"; she always spoke of her male friends in this hearty fashion. "He ought to be here enjoying himself instead of living like a hermit in the wilds."

"He's painting pictures," put in Lady Garvington. "Do hermits paint?"

"No. Only society women do that," said Miss Greeby cheerfully, and Mrs. Belgrove's faded eyes flashed. She knew that the remark was meant for her, and snapped back. "Are you going to have your fortune told by the gypsies, dear?" she inquired amiably. "They might tell you about your marriage."

"Oh, I daresay, and if you ask they will prophesy your funeral."

"I am in perfect health, Miss Greeby."

"So I should think, since your cheeks are so red."

Lady Garvington hastily intervened to prevent the further exchange of compliments. "Will you be back to luncheon, or join the men at the coverts?"

"Neither. I'll drop on Lambert for a feed. Where are you going?"

"I'm sure I don't know," said the hostess vaguely. "There's lots to do. I shall know what's to be done, when I think of it," and she drifted along the terrace and into the house like a cloud blown any way by the wind. Miss Greeby looked after her limp figure with a contemptuous grin, then she nodded casually to Mrs. Belgrove, and walked whistling down the terrace steps.

"Cat, indeed!" commented Mrs. Belgrove to herself when she saw Miss Greeby's broad back disappear behind the laurels. "Nothing half so pretty. She's like a great Flanders mare. And I wish Henry VIII was alive to marry her," she added the epithet suggesting that king, "if only to cut her head off."

CHAPTER II

IN THE WOOD

Miss Greeby swung along towards her destination with a masculine stride and in as great a hurry as though she had entered herself for a Marathon race. It was a warm, misty day, and the pale August sunshine radiated faintly through the smoky atmosphere. Nothing was clear-cut and nothing was distinct, so hazy was the outlook. The hedges were losing their greenery and had blossomed forth into myriad bunches of ruddy hips and haws, and the usually hard road was soft underfoot because of the penetrating quality of the moist air. There was no wind to clear away the misty greyness, but yellow leaves without its aid dropped from the disconsolate trees. The lately-reaped fields, stretching on either side of the lane down which the lady was walking, presented a stubbled expanse of brown and dim gold, uneven and distressful to the eye. The dying world was in ruins and Nature had reduced herself to that necessary chaos, out of which, when the coming snow completed its task, she would build a new heaven and a new earth.

An artist might have had some such poetic fancy, and would certainly have looked lovingly on the alluring colors and forms of decay. But Miss Greeby was no artist, and prided herself upon being an aggressively matter-of-fact young woman. With her big boots slapping the ground and her big hands thrust into the pockets of her mannish jacket, she bent her head in a meditative fashion and trudged briskly onward. What romance her hard nature was capable of, was uppermost now, but it had to do strictly with her personal feelings and did not require the picturesque autumn landscape to improve or help it in any way. One man's name suggested romance to bluff, breezy Clara Greeby, and that name was Noel Lambert. She murmured it over and over again to her heart, and her hard face flushed into something almost like beauty, as she remembered that she would soon behold its owner. "But he won't care," she said aloud, and threw back her head defiantly: then after a pause, she breathed softly, "But I shall make him care."

If she hoped to do so, the task was one which required a great amount of skill and a greater amount of womanly courage, neither of which qualities Miss Greeby possessed. She had no skill in managing a man, as her instincts were insufficiently feminine, and her courage was of a purely rough-and-tumble kind. She could have endured hunger and thirst and cold: she could have headed a forlorn hope: she could have held to a sinking ship: but she had no store of that peculiar feminine courage which men don't understand and which women can't explain, however much they may exhibit it. Miss Greeby was an excellent comrade, but could not be the beloved of any man, because of the very limitations of semi-masculinity upon which she prided herself. Noel Lambert wanted a womanly woman, and Lady Agnes was his ideal of what a wife should be. Miss Greeby had in every possible way offered herself for the post, but Lambert had never cared for her sufficiently to endure the thought of passing through life with her beside him. He said she was "a good sort"; and when a man says that of a woman, she may be to him a good friend, or even a platonic chum, but she can never be a desirable wife in his eyes. What Miss Greeby lacked was sex, and lacking that, lacked everything. It was strange that with her rough common sense she could not grasp this want. But the thought that Lambert required what she could never give—namely, the feminine tenderness which strong masculine natures love—never crossed her very clear and mathematical mind.

So she was bent upon a fool's errand, as she strode towards the Abbot's Wood, although she did not know it. Her aim was to capture Lambert as her husband; and her plan, to accomplish her wish by working on the heart-hunger he most probably felt, owing to the loss of Agnes Pine. If he loved that lady in a chivalrous fashion—and Miss Greeby believed that he did—she was absolutely lost to him as the wife of another man. Lambert would never degrade her into a divorce court appearance. And perhaps, after all, as Miss Greeby thought hopefully, his love for Sir Hubert's wife might have turned to scorn that she had preferred money to true love. But then, again, as Miss Greeby remembered, with a darkening face, Agnes had married the millionaire so as to save the family estates from being sold. Rank has its obligation, and Lambert might approve of the sacrifice, since he was the next heir to the Garvington title. "We shall see what his attitude is," decided Miss Greeby, as she entered the Abbot's Wood, and delayed arranging her future plans until she fully understood his feelings towards the woman he had lost. In the meantime, Lambert would want a comrade, and Miss Greeby was prepared to sink her romantic feelings, for the time being, in order to be one.

The forest—which belonged to Garvington, so long as he paid the interest on the mortgage—was not a very large one. In the old days it had been of greater size and well stocked with wild animals; so well stocked, indeed, that the abbots of a near monastery had used it for many hundred years as a hunting ground. But the monastery had vanished off the face of the earth, as not even its ruins were left, and the game had disappeared as the forest grew smaller and the district around became more populous. A Lambert of the Georgian period—the family name of Lord Garvington was Lambert—had acquired what was left of the monastic wood by winning it at a game of cards from the nobleman who had then owned it. Now it was simply a large patch of green in the middle of a somewhat naked county, for Hengishire is not remarkable for woodlands. There were rabbits and birds, badgers, stoats, and suchlike wild things in it still, but the deer which the abbots had hunted were conspicuous by their absence. Garvington looked after it about as much as he did after the rest of his estates, which was not saying much. The fat, round little lord's heart was always in the kitchen, and he preferred eating to fulfilling his duties as a landlord. Consequently, the Abbot's Wood was more or less public property, save when Garvington turned crusty and every now and then cleared out all interlopers. But tramps came to sleep in the wood, and gypsies camped in its glades, while summer time brought many artists to rave about its sylvan beauties, and paint pictures of ancient trees and silent pools, and rugged lawns besprinkled with rainbow wild flowers. People who went to the Academy and to the various art exhibitions in Bond Street knew the Abbot's Wood fairly well, as it was rarely that at least one picture dealing with it did not appear.

Miss Greeby had explored the wood before and knew exactly where to find the cottage mentioned by Lady Garvington. On the verge of the trees she saw the blue smoke of the gypsies' camp fires, and heard the vague murmur of Romany voices, but, avoiding the vagrants, she took her way through the forest by a winding path. This ultimately led her to a spacious glade, in the centre of which stood a dozen or more rough monoliths of mossy gray and weather-worn stones, disposed in a circle. Probably these were all that remained of some Druidical temple, and archaeologists came from far and near to view the weird relics. And in the middle of the circle stood the cottage: a thatched dwelling, which might have had to do with a fairy tale, with its whitewashed walls covered with ivy, and its latticed windows, on the ledges of which stood pots of homely flowers. There was no fence round this rustic dwelling, as the monoliths stood as guardians, and the space between the cottage walls and the gigantic stones was planted thickly with fragrant English flowers. Snapdragon, sweet-william, marigolds, and scented clove carnations, were all to be found there: also there was thyme, mint, sage, and other pot-herbs. And the whole perfumed space was girdled by trees old and young, which stood back from the emerald beauty of untrimmed lawns. A more ideal spot for a dreamer, or an artist, or a hermit, or for the straying prince of a fairy tale, it would have been quite impossible to find. Miss Greeby's vigorous and coarse personality seemed to break in a noisy manner—although she did not utter a single word—the enchanted silence of the solitary place.

However, the intruder was too matter-of-fact to trouble about the sequestered liveliness of this unique dwelling. She strode across the lawns, and passing beyond the monoliths, marched like an invader up the narrow path between the radiant flower-beds. From the tiny green door she raised the burnished knocker and brought it down with an emphatic bang. Shortly the door opened with a pettish tug, as though the person behind was rather annoyed by the noise, and a very tall, well-built, slim young man made his appearance on the threshold. He held a palette on the thumb of one hand, and clutched a sheaf of brushes, while another brush was in his mouth, and luckily impeded a rather rough welcome. The look in a pair of keen blue eyes certainly seemed to resent the intrusion, but at the sight of Miss Greeby this irritability changed to a glance of suspicion. Lambert, from old associations, liked his visitor very well on the whole, but that feminine intuition, which all creative natures possess, warned him that it was wise to keep her at arm's length. She had never plainly told her love; but she had assuredly hinted at it more or less by eye and manner and undue hauntings of his footsteps when in London. He could not truthfully tell himself that he was glad of her unexpected visit. For quite half a minute they stood staring at one another, and Miss Greeby's hard cheeks flamed to a poppy red at the sight of the man she loved.

"Well, Hermit." she observed, when he made no remark. "As the mountain would not come to Mahomet, the prophet has come to the mountain."

"The mountain is welcome," said Lambert diplomatically, and stood aside, so that she might enter. Then adopting the bluff and breezy, rough-and-ready-man-to-man attitude, which Miss Greeby liked to see in her friends, he added: "Come in, old girl! It's a pal come to see a pal, isn't it?"

"Rather," assented Miss Greeby, although, woman-like, she was not entirely pleased with this unromantic welcome. "We played as brats together, didn't we?

"Yes," she added meditatively, when following Lambert into his studio, "I think we are as chummy as a man and woman well can be."

"True enough. You were always a good sort, Clara. How well you are looking—more of a man than ever."

"Oh, stop that!" said Miss Greeby roughly.

"Why?" Lambert raised his eyebrows. "As a girl you always liked to be thought manly, and said again and again that you wished you were a boy."

"I find that I am a woman, after all," sighed the visitor, dropping into a chair and looking round; "with a woman's feelings, too."

"And very nice those feelings are, since they have influenced you to pay me a visit in the wilds," remarked the artist imperturbably.

"What are you doing in the wilds?"

"Painting," was the laconic retort.

"So I see. Still-life pictures?"

"Not exactly." He pointed toward the easel. "Behold and approve."

Miss Greeby did behold, but she certainly did not approve, because she was a woman and in love. It was only a pictured head she saw, but the head was that of a very beautiful girl, whose face smiled from the canvas in a subtle, defiant way, as if aware of its wild loveliness. The raven hair streamed straightly down to the shoulders—for the bust of the model was slightly indicated—and there, bunched out into curls. A red and yellow handkerchief was knotted round the brows, and dangling sequins added to its barbaric appearance. Nose and lips and eyes, and contours, were all perfect, and it really seemed as though the face were idealized, so absolutely did it respond to all canons of beauty. It was a gypsy countenance, and there lurked in its loveliness that wild, untamed look which suggested unrestricted roamings and the spacious freedom of the road.

The sudden, jealous fear which surged into Miss Greeby's heart climbed to her throat and choked her speech. But she had wisdom enough to check unwise words, and glanced round the studio to recover her composure. The room was small and barely furnished; a couch, two deep arm-chairs, and a small table filled its limited area. The walls and roof were painted a pale green, and a carpet of the same delicate hue covered the floor. Of course, there were the usual painting materials, brushes and easel and palettes and tubes of color, together with a slightly raised platform near the one window where the model could sit or stand. The window itself had no curtains and was filled with plain glass, affording plenty of light.

"The other windows of the cottage are latticed," said Lambert, seeing his visitor's eyes wander in that direction. "I had that glass put in when I came here a month ago. No light can filter through lattices—in sufficient quantity that is—to see the true tones of the colors."

"Oh, bother the window!" muttered Miss Greeby restlessly, for she had not yet gained command of her emotions.

Lambert laughed and looked at his picture with his head on one side, and a very handsome head it was, as Miss Greeby thought. "It bothered me until I had it put right, I assure you. But you don't seem pleased with my crib."

"It's not good enough for you."

"Since when have I been a sybarite, Clara?"

"I mean you ought to think of your position."

"It's too unpleasant to think about," rejoined Lambert, throwing himself on the couch and producing his pipe. "May I smoke?"

"Yes, and if you have any decent cigarettes I'll join you. Thanks!" She deftly caught the silver case he threw her. "But your position?"

"Five hundred a year and no occupation, since I have been brought up to neither trade nor profession," said Lambert leisurely. "Well?"

"You are the heir to a title and to a large property."

"Which is heavily mortgaged. As to the title"—Lambert shrugged his shoulders—"Garvington's wife may have children."

"I don't think so. They have been married ten years and more. You are certain to come in for everything."

"Everything consists of nothing," said the artist coolly.

"Well," drawled Miss Greeby, puffing luxuriously at her cigarette, which was Turkish and soothing, "nothing may turn into something when these mortgages are cleared off."

"Who is going to clear them off?"

"Sir Hubert Pine."

Lambert's brows contracted, as she knew they would when this name was mentioned, and he carefully attended to filling his pipe so as to avoid meeting her hard, inquisitive eyes. "Pine is a man of business, and if he pays off the mortgages he will take over the property as security. I don't see that Garvington will be any the better off in that case."

"Lambert," said Miss Greeby very decidedly, and determined to know precisely what he felt like, "Garvington only allowed his sister to marry Sir Hubert because he was rich. I don't know for certain, of course, but I should think it probable that he made an arrangement with Pine to have things put straight because of the marriage."

"Possible and probable," said the artist shortly, and wincing;

"but old friend as you are, Clara, I don't see the necessity of talking about business which does not concern me. Speak to Garvington."

"Agnes concerns you."

"How objectionably direct you are," exclaimed Lambert in a vexed tone. "And how utterly wrong. Agnes does not concern me in the least. I loved her, but as she chose to marry Pine, why there's no more to be said."

"If there was nothing more to be said," observed Miss Greeby shrewdly, "you would not be burying yourself here."

"Why not? I am fond of nature and art, and my income is not enough to permit my living decently in London. I had to leave the army because I was so poor. Garvington has given me this cottage rent free, so I'm jolly enough with my painting and with Mrs. Tribb as housekeeper and cook. She's a perfect dream of a cook," ended Lambert thoughtfully.

Miss Greeby shook her red head. "You can't deceive me."

"Who wants to, anyhow?" demanded the man, unconsciously American.

"You do. You wish to make out that you prefer to camp here instead of admitting that you would like to be at The Manor because Agnes—"

Lambert jumped up crossly. "Oh, leave Agnes out of the question. She is Pine's wife, so that settles things. It's no use crying for the moon, and—"

"Then you still wish for the moon," interpolated the woman quickly.

"Not even you have the right to ask me such a question," replied Lambert in a quiet and decisive tone. "Let us change the subject."

Miss Greeby pointed to the beautiful face smiling on the easel. "I advise you to," she said significantly.

"You seem to have come here to give me good advice."

"Which you won't take," she retorted.

"Because it isn't needed."

"A man's a man and a woman's a woman."

"That's as true as taxes, as Mr. Barkis observed, if you are acquainted with the writings of the late Charles Dickens. Well?"

Again Miss Greeby pointed to the picture. "She's very pretty."

"I shouldn't have painted her otherwise."

"Oh, then the original of that portrait does exist?"

"Could you call it a portrait if an original didn't exist?" demanded the young man tartly. "Since you want to know so much, you may as well come to the gypsy encampment on the verge of the wood and satisfy yourself." He threw on a Panama hat, with a cross look. "Since when have you come to the conclusion that I need a dry nurse?"

"Oh, don't talk bosh!" said Miss Greeby vigorously, and springing to her feet. "You take me at the foot of the letter and too seriously. I only came here to see how my old pal was getting on."

"I'm all right and as jolly as a sandboy. Now are you satisfied?"

"Quite. Only don't fall in love with the original of your portrait."

"It's rather late in the day to warn me," said Lambert dryly, "for I have known the girl for six months. I met her in a gypsy caravan when on a walking tour, and offered to paint her. She is down here with her people, and you can see her whenever you have a mind to."

"There's no time like the present," said Miss Greeby, accepting the offer with alacrity. "Come along, old boy." Then, when they stepped out of the cottage garden on to the lawns, she asked pointedly, "What is her name?"

"Chaldea."

"Nonsense. That is the name of the country."

"I never denied that, my dear girl. But Chaldea was born in the country whence she takes her name. Down Mesopotamia way, I believe. These gypsies wander far and wide, you know. She's very pretty, and has the temper of the foul fiend himself. Only Kara can keep her in order."

"Who is Kara?"

"A Servian gypsy who plays the fiddle like an angel. He's a crooked-backed, black-faced, hairy ape of a dwarf, but highly popular on account of his music. Also, he's crazy about Chaldea, and loves her to distraction."

"Does she love him?" Miss Greeby asked in her direct fashion.

"No," replied Lambert, coloring under his tan, and closed his lips firmly. He was a very presentable figure of a man, as he walked beside the unusually tall woman. His face was undeniably handsome in a fair Saxon fashion, and his eyes were as blue as those of Miss Greeby herself, while his complexion was much more delicate. In fact, she considered that it was much too good a complexion for one of the male sex, but admitted inwardly that its possessor was anything but effeminate, when he had such a heavy jaw, such a firm chin, and such set lips. Lambert, indeed, at first sight did indeed look so amiable, as to appear for the moment quite weak; but danger always stiffened him into a dangerous adversary, and his face when aroused was most unpleasantly fierce. He walked with a military swing, his shoulders well set back and his head crested like that of a striking serpent. A rough and warlike life would have brought out his best points of endurance, capability to plan and strike quickly, and iron decision; but the want of opportunity and the enervating influences of civilized existence, made him a man of possibilities. When time, and place, and chance offered he could act the hero with the best; but lacking these things he remained innocuous like gunpowder which has no spark to fire it.

Thinking of these things, Miss Greeby abandoned the subject of Chaldea, and of her possible love for Lambert, and exclaimed impulsively, "Why don't you chuck civilization and strike the out-trail?"

"Why should I?" he asked, unmoved, and rather surprised by the change of the subject. "I'm quite comfortable here."

"Too comfortable," she retorted with emphasis. "This loafing life of just-enough-to-live-on doesn't give you a chance to play the man. Go out and fight and colonize and prove your qualities."

Lambert's color rose again, and his eyes sparkled. "I would if the chance—"

"Ah, bah, Hercules and Omphale!" interrupted his companion.

"What do you mean?"

"Never mind," retorted Miss Greeby, who guessed that he knew what she meant very well. His quick flush showed her how he resented this classical allusion to Agnes Pine. "You'd carry her off if you were a man."

"Chaldea?" asked Lambert, wilfully misunderstanding her meaning.

"If you like. Only don't try to carry her off at night. Garvington says he will shoot any burglar who comes along after dark."

"I never knew Garvington had anything to do with Chaldea."

"Neither did I. Oh, I think you know very well what I mean."

"Perhaps I do," said the young man with an angry shrug, for really her interference with his affairs seemed to be quite unjustifiable. "But I am not going to bring a woman I respect into the Divorce Court."

"Respect? Love, you mean to say."

Lambert stopped, and faced her squarely. "I don't wish to quarrel with you, Clara, as we are very old friends. But I warn you that I do possess a temper, and if you wish to see it, you are going the best way to get what you evidently want. Now, hold your tongue and talk of something else. Here is Chaldea."

"Watching for you," muttered Miss Greeby, as the slight figure of the gypsy girl was seen advancing swiftly. "Ha!" and she snorted suspiciously.

"Rye!" cried Chaldea, dancing toward the artist. "Sarishan rye."

Miss Greeby didn't understand Romany, but the look in the girl's eyes was enough to reveal the truth. If Lambert did not love his beautiful model, it was perfectly plain that the beautiful model loved Lambert.

"O baro duvel atch' pa leste!" said Chaldea, and clapped her slim hands.

CHAPTER III

AN UNEXPECTED RECOGNITION

"I wish you wouldn't speak the calo jib to me, Chaldea," said Lambert, smiling on the beautiful eager face. "You know I don't understand it."

"Nor I," put in Miss Greeby in her manly tones. "What does Oh baro devil, and all the rest of it mean?"

"The Great God be with you," translated Chaldea swiftly, "and duvel is not devil as you Gorgios call it."

"Only the difference of a letter," replied the Gentile lady good-humoredly. "Show us round your camp, my good girl."

The mere fact that the speaker was in Lambert's company, let alone the offensively patronizing tone in which she spoke, was enough to rouse the gypsy girl's naturally hot temper. She retreated and swayed like a cat making ready to spring, while her black eyes snapped fire in a most unpleasant manner.

But Miss Greeby was not to be frightened by withering glances, and merely laughed aloud, showing her white teeth. Her rough merriment and masculine looks showed Chaldea that, as a rival, she was not to be feared, so the angry expression on the dark face changed to a wheedling smile.

"Avali! Avali! The Gorgios lady wants her fortune told."

For the sake of diplomacy Miss Greeby nodded and fished in her pocket. "I'll give you half a crown to tell it."

"Not me—not me, dear lady. Mother Cockleshell is our great witch."

"Take me to her then," replied the other, and rapidly gathered into her brain all she could of Chaldea's appearance.

Lambert had painted a very true picture of the girl, although to a certain extent he had idealized her reckless beauty. Chaldea's looks had been damaged and roughened by wind and rain, by long tramps, and by glaring sunshine. Yet she was superlatively handsome with her warm and swarthy skin, under which the scarlet blood circled freely. To an oval face, a slightly hooked nose and two vermilion lips, rather full, she added the glossy black eyes of the true Romany, peaked at the corners. Her jetty hair descended smoothly from under a red handkerchief down to her shoulders, and there, at the tips, became tangled and curling. Her figure was magnificent, and she swayed and swung from the hips with an easy grace, which reminded the onlookers of a panther's lithe movements. And there was a good deal of the dangerous beast-of-prey beauty about Chaldea, which was enhanced by her picturesque dress. This was ragged and patched with all kinds of colored cloths subdued to mellow tints by wear and weather. Also she jingled with coins and beads and barbaric trinkets of all kinds. Her hands were perfectly formed, and so doubtless were her feet, although these last were hidden by heavy laced-up boots. On the whole, she was an extremely picturesque figure, quite comforting to the artistic eye amidst the drab sameness of latterday civilization.

"All the same, I suspect she is a sleeping volcano," whispered Miss Greeby in her companion's ear as they followed the girl through the camp.

"Scarcely sleeping," answered Lambert in the same tone. "She explodes on the slightest provocation, and not without damaging results."

"Well, you ought to know. But if you play with volcanic fire you'll burn more than your clever fingers."

"Pooh! The girl is only a model."

"Ha! Not much of the lay figure about her, anyway."

Lambert, according to his custom, shrugged his shoulders and did not seek to explain further. If Miss Greeby chose to turn her fancies into facts, she was at liberty to do so. Besides, her attention was luckily attracted by the vivid life of the vagrants which hummed and bustled everywhere. The tribe was a comparatively large one, and—as Miss Greeby learned later—consisted of Lees, Loves, Bucklands, Hernes, and others, all mixed up together in one gypsy stew. The assemblage embraced many clans, and not only were there pure gypsies, but even many diddikai, or half-bloods, to be seen. Perhaps the gradually diminishing Romany clans found it better to band together for mutual benefit than to remain isolated units. But the camp certainly contained many elements, and these, acting co-operatively, formed a large and somewhat reckless community, which justified Garvington's alarm. A raid in the night by one or two, or three, or more of these lean, wiry, dangerous-looking outcasts was not to be despised. But it must be admitted that, in a general way, law and order prevailed in the encampment.

There were many caravans, painted in gay colors and hung round with various goods, such as brushes and brooms, goat-skin rugs, and much tinware, together with baskets of all sorts and sizes. The horses, which drew these rainbow-hued vehicles, were pasturing on the outskirts of the camp, hobbled for the most part. Interspersed among the travelling homes stood tents great and small, wherein the genuine Romany had their abode, but the autumn weather was so fine that most of the inmates preferred to sleep in the moonshine. Of course, there were plenty of dogs quarrelling over bones near various fires, or sleeping with one eye open in odd corners, and everywhere tumbled and laughed and danced, brown-faced, lithe-limbed children, who looked uncannily Eastern. And the men, showing their white teeth in smiles, together with the fawning women, young and handsome, or old and hideously ugly, seemed altogether alien to the quiet, tame domestic English landscape. There was something prehistoric about the scene, and everywhere lurked that sense of dangerous primeval passions held in enforced check which might burst forth on the very slightest provocation.

"It's a migrating tribe of Aryans driven to new hunting grounds by hunger or over-population," said Miss Greeby, for even her unromantic nature was stirred by the unusual picturesqueness of the scene. "The sight of these people and the reek of their fires make me feel like a cave-woman. There is something magnificent about this brutal freedom."

"Very sordid magnificence," replied Lambert, raising his shoulders. "But I understand your feelings. On occasions we all have the nostalgia of the primitive life at times, and delight to pass from ease to hardship."

"Well, civilization isn't much catch, so far as I can see," argued his companion. "It makes men weaklings."

"Certainly not women," he answered, glancing sideways at her Amazonian figure.

"I agree with you. For some reason, men are going down while women are going up, both physically and mentally. I wonder what the future of civilized races will be."

"Here is Mother Cockleshell. Best ask her."

The trio had reached a small tent at the very end of the camp by this time, snugly set up under a spreading oak and near the banks of a babbling brook. Their progress had not been interrupted by any claims on their attention or purses, for a wink from Chaldea had informed her brother and sister gypsies that the Gentile lady had come to consult the queen of the tribe. And, like Lord Burleigh's celebrated nod, Chaldea's wink could convey volumes. At all events, Lambert and his companion were unmolested, and arrived in due course before the royal palace. A croaking voice announced that the queen was inside her Arab tent, and she was crooning some Romany song. Chaldea did not open her mouth, but simply snapped her fingers twice or thrice rapidly. The woman within must have had marvellously sharp ears, for she immediately stopped her incantation—the songs sounded like one—and stepped forth.

"Oh!" said Miss Greeby, stepping back, "I am disappointed."

She had every reason to be after the picturesqueness of the camp in general, and Chaldea in particular, for Mother Cockleshell looked like a threadbare pew-opener, or an almshouse widow who had seen better days. Apparently she was very old, for her figure had shrivelled up into a diminutive monkey form, and she looked as though a moderately high wind could blow her about like a feather. Her face was brown and puckered and lined in a most wonderful fashion. Where a wrinkle could be, there a wrinkle was, and her nose and chin were of the true nutcracker order, as a witch's should be. Only her eyes betrayed the powerful vitality that still animated the tiny frame, for these were large and dark, and had in them a piercing look which seemed to gaze not at any one, but through and beyond. Her figure, dried like that of a mummy, was surprisingly straight for one of her ancient years, and her profuse hair was scarcely touched with the gray of age. Arrayed in a decent black dress, with a decent black bonnet and a black woollen shawl, the old lady looked intensely respectable. There was nothing of the picturesque vagrant about her. Therefore Miss Greeby, and with every reason, was disappointed, and when the queen of the woodland spoke she was still more so, for Mother Cockleshell did not even interlard her English speech with Romany words, as did Chaldea.

"Good day to you, my lady, and to you, sir," said Mother Cockleshell in a stronger and harsher voice than would have been expected from one of her age and diminished stature. "I hope I sees you well," and she dropped a curtsey, just like any village dame who knew her manners.

"Oh!" cried Miss Greeby again. "You don't look a bit like a gypsy queen."

"Ah, my lady, looks ain't everything. But I'm a true-bred Romany—a Stanley of Devonshire. Gentilla is my name and the tent my home, and I can tell fortunes as no one else on the road can."

"Avali, and that is true," put in Chaldea eagerly. "Gentilla's a bori chovihani."

"The child means that I am a great witch, my lady," said the old dame with another curtsey. "Though she's foolish to use Romany words to Gentiles as don't understand the tongue which the dear Lord spoke in Eden's garden, as the good Book tells us."

"In what part of the Bible do you find that?" asked Lambert laughing.

"Oh, my sweet gentleman, it ain't for the likes of me to say things to the likes of you," said Mother Cockleshell, getting out of her difficulty very cleverly, "but the dear lady wants her fortune told, don't she?"

"Why don't you say dukkerin?"

"I don't like them wicked words, sir," answered Mother Cockleshell piously.

"Wicked words," muttered Chaldea tossing her black locks. "And them true Romany as was your milk tongue. No wonder the Gentiles don't fancy you a true one of the road. If I were queen of—"

A vicious little devil flashed out of the old woman's eyes, and her respectable looks changed on the instant. "Tol yer chib, or I'll heat the bones of you with the fires of Bongo Tem," she screamed furiously, and in a mixture of her mother-tongue and English. "Ja pukenus, slut of the gutter," she shook her fist, and Chaldea, with an insulting laugh, moved away. "Bengis your see! Bengis your see! And that, my generous lady," she added, turning round with a sudden resumption of her fawning respectability, "means 'the devil in your heart,' which I spoke witchly-like to the child. Ah, but she's a bad one."

Miss Greeby laughed outright. "This is more like the real thing."

"Poor Chaldea," said Lambert. "You're too hard on her, mother."

"And you, my sweet gentleman, ain't hard enough. She'll sell you, and get Kara to put the knife between your ribs."

"Why should he? I'm not in love with the girl."

"The tree don't care for the ivy, but the ivy loves the tree," said Mother Cockleshell darkly. "You're a good and kind gentleman, and I don't want to see that slut pick your bones."

"So I think," whispered Miss Greeby in his ear. "You play with fire."

"Aye, my good lady," said Mother Cockleshell, catching the whisper—she had the hearing of a cat. "With the fire of Bongo Tern, the which you may call The Crooked Land," and she pointed significantly downward.

"Hell, do you mean?" asked Miss Greeby in her bluff way.

"The Crooked Land we Romany calls it," insisted the old woman. "And the child will go there, for her witchly doings."

"She's too good-looking to lose as a model, at all events," said Lambert, hitching his shoulders. "I shall leave you to have your fortune told, Clara, and follow Chaldea to pacify her."

As he went toward the centre of the camp, Miss Greeby took a hesitating step as though to follow him. In her opinion Chaldea was much too good-looking, let alone clever, for Lambert to deal with alone. Gentilla Stanley saw the look on the hard face and the softening of the hard eyes as the cheeks grew rosy red. From this emotion she drew her conclusions, and she chuckled to think of how true a fortune she could tell the visitor on these premises. Mother Cockleshell's fortune-telling was not entirely fraudulent, but when her clairvoyance was not in working order she made use of character-reading with good results.

"Won't the Gorgios lady have her fortune told?" she asked in wheedling tones. "Cross Mother Cockleshell's hand with silver and she'll tell the coming years truly."

"Why do they call you Mother Cockleshell?" demanded Miss Greeby, waiving the question of fortune-telling for the time being.

"Bless your wisdom, it was them fishermen at Grimsby who did so. I walked the beaches for years and told charms and gave witchly spells for fine weather. Gentilla Stanley am I called, but Mother Cockleshell was their name for me. But the fortune, my tender Gentile—"

"I don't want it told," interrupted Miss Greeby abruptly. "I don't believe in such rubbish."

"There is rubbish and there is truth," said the ancient gypsy darkly. "And them as knows can see what's hidden from others."

"Well, you will have an opportunity this afternoon of making money. Some fools from The Manor are coming to consult you."

Mother Cockleshell nodded and grinned to show a set of beautifully preserved teeth. "I know The Manor," said she, rubbing her slim hands. "And Lord Garvington, with his pretty sister."

"Lady Agnes Pine?" asked Miss Greeby. "How do you know, her?"

"I've been in these parts before, my gentle lady, and she was good to me in a sick way. I would have died in the hard winter if she hadn't fed me and nursed me, so to speak. I shall love to see her again. To dick a puro pal is as commoben as a aushti habben, the which, my precious angel, is true Romany for the Gentile saying, 'To see an old friend is as good as a fine dinner.' Avali! Avali!" she nodded smilingly. "I shall be glad to see her, though here I use Romany words to you as doesn't understand the lingo."

Miss Greeby was not at all pleased to hear Lady Agnes praised; as, knowing that Lambert had loved her, and probably loved her still, she was jealous enough to wish her all possible harm. However, it was not diplomatic to reveal her true feelings to Mother Cockleshell, lest the old gypsy should repeat her words to Lady Agnes, so she turned the conversation by pointing to a snow-white cat of great size, who stepped daintily out of the tent. "I should think, as a witch, your cat ought to be black," said Miss Greeby. Mother Cockleshell screeched like a night-owl and hastily pattered some gypsy spell to avert evil. "Why, the old devil is black," she cried. "And why should I have him in my house to work evil? This is my white ghost." Her words were accompanied by a gentle stroking of the cat. "And good is what she brings to my roof-tree. But I don't eat from white dishes, or drink from white mugs. No! No! That would be too witchly."

Miss Greeby mused. "I have heard something about these gypsy superstitions before," she remarked meditatively.

"Avo! Avo! They are in a book written by a great Romany Rye. Leland is the name of that rye, a gypsy Lee with Gentile land. He added land to the lea as he was told by one of our people. Such a nice gentleman, kind, and free of his money and clever beyond tellings, as I always says. Many a time has he sat pal-like with me, and 'Gentilla,' says he, 'your're a bori chovihani'; and that, my generous lady, is the gentle language for a great witch."

"Chaldea said that you were that," observed Miss Greeby carelessly.

"The child speaks truly. Come, cross my hand, sweet lady."

Miss Greeby passed along half a crown. "I only desire to know one thing," she said, offering her palm. "Shall I get my wish?"

Mother Cockleshell peered into the hands, although she had already made up her mind what to say. Her faculties, sharpened by years of chicanery, told her from the look which Miss Greeby had given when Lambert followed Chaldea, that a desire to marry the man was the wish in question. And seeing how indifferent Lambert was in the presence of the tall lady, Mother Cockleshell had no difficulty in adjusting the situation in her own artful mind. "No, my lady," she said, casting away the hand with quite a dramatic gesture. "You will never gain your wish."

Miss Greeby looked angry. "Bah! Your fortune-telling is all rubbish, as I have always thought," and she moved away.

"Tell me that in six months," screamed the old woman after her.

"Why six months?" demanded the other, pausing.

"Ah, that's a dark saying," scoffed the gypsy. "Call it seven, my hopeful-for-what-you-won't-get, like the cat after the cream, for seven's a sacred number, and the spell is set."

"Gypsy jargon, gypsy lies," muttered Miss Greeby, tossing her ruddy mane. "I don't believe a word. Tell me—"

"There's no time to say more," interrupted Mother Cockleshell rudely, for, having secured her money, she did not think it worth while to be polite, especially in the face of her visitor's scepticism. "One of our tribe—aye, and he's a great Romany for sure—is coming to camp with us. Each minute he may come, and I go to get ready a stew of hedgehog, for Gentile words I must use to you, who are a Gorgio. And so good day to you, my lady," ended the old hag, again becoming the truly respectable pew-opener. Then she dropped a curtsey—whether ironical or not, Miss Greeby could not tell—and disappeared into the tent, followed by the white cat, who haunted her footsteps like the ghost she declared it to be.

Clearly there was nothing more to be learned from Mother Cockleshell, who, in the face of her visitor's doubts, had become hostile, so Miss Greeby, dismissing the whole episode as over and done with, turned her attention toward finding Lambert. With her bludgeon under her arm and her hands in the pockets of her jacket, she stalked through the camp in quite a masculine fashion, not vouchsafing a single reply to the greetings which the gypsies gave her. Shortly she saw the artist chatting with Chaldea at the beginning of the path which led to his cottage. Beside them, on the grass, squatted a queer figure.

It was that of a little man, very much under-sized, with a hunch back and a large, dark, melancholy face covered profusely with black hair. He wore corduroy trousers and clumsy boots—his feet and hands were enormous—together with a green coat and a red handkerchief which was carelessly twisted round his hairy throat. On his tangled locks—distressingly shaggy and unkempt—he wore no hat, and he looked like a brownie, grotesque, though somewhat sad. But even more did he resemble an ape—or say the missing link—and only his eyes seemed human. These were large, dark and brilliant, sparkling like jewels under his elf-locks. He sat cross-legged on the sward and hugged a fiddle, as though he were nursing a baby. And, no doubt, he was as attached to his instrument as any mother could be to her child. It was not difficult for Miss Greeby to guess that this weird, hairy dwarf was the Servian gypsy Kara, of whom Lambert had spoken. She took advantage of the knowledge to be disagreeable to the girl.

"Is this your husband?" asked Miss Greeby amiably.

Chaldea's eyes flashed and her cheeks grew crimson. "Not at all," she said contemptuously. "I have no rom."

"Ah, your are not married?"

"No," declared Chaldea curtly, and shot a swift glance at Lambert.

"She is waiting for the fairy prince," said that young gentleman smiling. "And he is coming to this camp almost immediately."

"Ishmael Hearne is coming," replied the gypsy. "But he is no rom of mine, and never will be."

"Who is he, then?" asked Lambert carelessly.

"One of the great Romany."

Miss Greeby remembered that Mother Cockleshell had also

spoken of the expected arrival at the camp in these terms. "A kind of king?" she asked.

Chaldea laughed satirically. "Yes; a kind of king," she assented; then turned her back rudely on the speaker and addressed Lambert: "I can't come, rye. Ishmael will want to see me. I must wait."

"What a nuisance," said Lambert, looking annoyed. "Fancy, Clara. I have an idea of painting these two as Beauty and the Beast, or perhaps as Esmeralda and Quasimodo. I want them to come to the cottage and sit now, but they will wait for this confounded Ishmael."

"We can come to-morrow," put in Chaldea quickly. "This afternoon I must dance for Ishmael, and Kara must play."

"Ishmael will meet with a fine reception," said Miss Greeby, and then, anxious to have a private conversation with Chaldea so as to disabuse her mind of any idea she may have entertained of marrying Lambert, she added, "I think I shall stay and see him."

"In that case, I shall return to my cottage," replied Lambert, sauntering up the pathway, which was strewn with withered leaves.

"When are you coming to The Manor?" called Miss Greeby after him.

"Never! I am too busy," he replied over his shoulder and disappeared into the wood. This departure may seem discourteous, but then Miss Greeby liked to be treated like a comrade and without ceremony. That is, she liked it so far as other men were concerned, but not as regards Lambert. She loved him too much to approve of his careless leave-taking, and therefore she frowned darkly, as she turned her attention to Chaldea.

The girl saw that Miss Greeby was annoyed, and guessed the cause of her annoyance. The idea that this red-haired and gaunt woman should love the handsome Gorgio was so ludicrous in Chaldea's eyes that she laughed in an ironical fashion. Miss Greeby turned on her sharply, but before she could speak there was a sound of many voices raised in welcome. "Sarishan pal! Sarishan ba!" cried the voices, and Chaldea started.

"Ishmael!" she said, and ran toward the camp, followed leisurely by Kara.

Anxious to see the great Romany, whose arrival caused all this commotion, Miss Greeby plunged into the crowd of excited vagrants. These surrounded a black horse, on which sat a slim, dark-faced man of the true Romany breed. Miss Greeby stared at him and blinked her eyes, as though she could not believe what they beheld, while the man waved his hand and responded to the many greetings in gypsy language. His eyes finally met her own as she stood on the outskirts of the crowd, and he started. Then she knew. "Sir Hubert Pine," said Miss Greeby, still staring. "Sir Hubert Pine!"

CHAPTER IV

SECRETS

The scouting crowd apparently did not catch the name, so busy were one and all in welcoming the newcomer. But the man on the horse saw Miss Greeby's startled look, and noticed that her lips were moving. In a moment he threw himself off the animal and elbowed his way roughly through the throng.

"Sir Hubert," began Miss Greeby, only to be cut short hastily.

"Don't give me away," interrupted Pine, who here was known as Ishmael Hearne. "Wait till I settle things, and then we can converse privately."

"All right," answered the lady, nodding, and gripped her bludgeon crosswise behind her back with two hands. She was so surprised at the sight of the millionaire in the wood, that she could scarcely speak.

Satisfied that she grasped the situation, Pine turned to his friends and spoke at length in fluent Romany. He informed them that he had some business to transact with the Gentile lady who had come to the camp for that purpose, and would leave them for half an hour. The man evidently was such a favorite that black looks were cast on Miss Greeby for depriving the Romany of his society. But Pine paid no attention to these signs of discontent. He finished his speech, and then pushed his way again toward the lady who, awkwardly for him, was acquainted with his true position as a millionaire. In a hurried whisper he asked Miss Greeby to follow him, and led the way into the heart of the wood. Apparently he knew it very well, and knew also where to seek solitude for the private conversation he desired, for he skirted the central glade where Lambert's cottage was placed, and finally guided his companion to a secluded dell, far removed from the camp of his brethren. Here he sat down on a mossy stone, and stared with piercing black eyes at Miss Greeby.

"What are you doing here?" he demanded imperiously.

"Just the question I was about to put to you," said Miss Greeby amiably. She could afford to be amiable, for she felt that she was the mistress of the situation. Pine evidently saw this, for he frowned.

"You must have guessed long ago that I was a gypsy," he snapped restlessly.

"Indeed I didn't, nor, I should think, did any one else. I thought you had nigger blood in you, and I have heard people say that you came from the West Indies. But what does it matter if you are a gypsy? There is no disgrace in being one."

"No disgrace, certainly," rejoined the millionaire, leaning forward and linking his hands together, while he stared at the ground. "I am proud of having the gentle Romany blood. All the same I prefer the West Indian legend, for I don't want any of my civilized friends to know that I am Ishmael Hearne, born and bred in a tent."

"Well, that's natural, Pine. What would Garvington say?"

"Oh, curse Garvington!"

"Curse the whole family by all means," retorted Miss Greeby coolly.

Pine looked up savagely, "I except my wife."

"Naturally. You always were uxorious."

"Perhaps," said Pine gloomily, "I'm a fool where Agnes is concerned."

Miss Greeby quite agreed with this statement, but did not think it worth while to indorse so obvious a remark. She sat down in her turn, and taking Lambert's cigarette case, which she had retained by accident, out of her pocket, she prepared to smoke. The two were entirely alone in the fairy dell, and the trees which girdled it were glorious with vivid autumnal tints. A gentle breeze sighing through the wood, shook down yew, crisp leaves on the woman's head, so that she looked like Danae in a shower of gold. Pine gazed heavily at the ground and coughed violently. Miss Greeby knew that cough, and a medical friend of hers had told her several times that Sir Hubert was a very consumptive individual. He certainly looked ill, and apparently had not long to live. And if he died, Lady Agnes, inheriting his wealth, would be more desirable as a wife than ever. And Miss Greeby, guessing whose wife she would be, swore inwardly that the present husband should look so delicate. But she showed no sign of her perturbations, but lighted her cigarette with a steady hand and smoked quietly. She always prided herself on her nerve.

The millionaire was tall and lean, with a sinewy frame, and an oval, olive-complexioned face. It was clean-shaven, and with his aquiline nose, his thin lips, and brilliant black eyes, which resembled those of Kara, he looked like a long-descended Hindoo prince. The Eastern blood of the Romany showed in his narrow feet and slim brown hands, and there was a wild roving look about him, which Miss Greeby had not perceived in London.

"I suppose it's the dress," she said aloud, and eyed Pine critically.

"What do you say, Miss Greeby?" he asked, looking up in a sharp, startled manner, and again coughing in a markedly consumptive way.

"The cowl makes the monk in your case," replied the woman quietly. "Your corduroy breeches and velveteen coat, with that colored shirt, and the yellow handkerchief round your neck, seem to suit you better than did the frock coats and evening dress I have seen you in. You did look like a nigger of sorts when in those clothes; now I can tell you are a gypsy with half an eye."

"That is because you heard me called Ishmael and saw me among my kith and kin," said the man with a tired smile. "Don't tell Agnes."

"Why should I? It's none of my business if you chose to masquerade as a gypsy."

"I masquerade as Sir Hubert Pine," retorted the millionaire, slipping off the stone to sprawl full-length on the grass. "I am truly and really one of the lot in the camp yonder."

"Do they know you by your Gentile name?"

Pine laughed. "You are picking up the gypsy lingo, Miss Greeby. No. Every one on the road takes me for what I am, Ishmael Hearne, and my friends in the civilized world think I am Sir Hubert Pine, a millionaire with colored blood in his veins."

"How do you come to have a double personality and live a double life?"

"Oh, that is easily explained, and since you have found me out it is just as well that I should explain, so that you may keep my secret, at all events from my wife, as she would be horrified to think that she had married a gypsy. You promise?"

"Of course. I shall say nothing. But perhaps she would prefer to know that she had married a gypsy rather than a nigger."

"What polite things you say," said Pine sarcastically. "However, I can't afford to quarrel with you. As you are rich, I can't even bribe you to silence, so I must rely on your honor."

"Oh, I have some," Miss Greeby assured him lightly.

"When it suits you," he retorted doubtfully.

"It does on this occasion."

"Why?"

"I'll tell you that when you have related your story."

"There is really none to tell. I was born and brought up on the road, and thinking I was wasting my life I left my people and entered civilization. In London I worked as a clerk, and being clever I soon made money. I got hold of a man who invented penny toys, and saw the possibilities of making a fortune. I really didn't, but I collected enough money to dabble in stocks and shares. The South

African boom was on, and I made a thousand. Other speculations created more than a million out of my thousand, and now I have over two millions, honestly made."

"Honestly?" queried Miss Greeby significantly.

"Yes; I assure you, honestly. We gypsies are cleverer than you Gentiles, and we have the same money-making faculties as the Jews have. If my people were not so fond of the vagrant life they would soon become a power in the money markets of the world. But, save in the case of myself, we leave all such grubbing to the Jews. I did grub, and my reward is that I have accumulated a fortune in a remarkably short space of time. I have land and houses, and excellent investments, and a title, which," he added sarcastically, "a grateful Government bestowed on me for using my money properly."

"You bought the title by helping the political party you belonged to," said Miss Greeby with a shrug. "There was quite a talk about it."

"So there was. As if I cared for talk. However, that is my story."

"Not all of it. You are supposed to be in Paris, and—"

"And you find me here," interrupted Pine with a faint smile. "Well you see, being a gypsy, I can't always endure that under-the-roof life you Gentiles live. I must have a spell of the open road occasionally. And, moreover, as my doctor tells me that I have phthisis, and that I should live as much as possible in the open air, I kill two birds with one stone, as the saying is. My health benefits by my taking up the old Romany wandering, and I gratify my nostalgia for the tent and the wild. You understand, you und—" His speech was interrupted by a fresh fit of coughing.

"It doesn't seem to do you much good this gypsying," said Miss Greeby with a swift look, for his life was of importance to her plans. "You look pretty rocky I can tell you, Pine. And if you die your wife will be free to—" The man sat up and took away from his mouth a handkerchief spotted with blood. His eyes glittered, and he showed his white teeth. "My wife will be free to what?" he demanded viciously, and the same devil that had lurked in Mother Cockleshell's eye, now showed conspicuously in his.

Miss Greeby had no pity on his manifest distress and visible wrath, but answered obliquely: "You know that she was almost engaged to her cousin before you married her," she hinted pointedly.

"Yes, I know, d—— him," said Pine with a groan, and rolled over to clutch at the grass in a vicious manner. "But he's not at The Manor now?"

"No."

"Agnes doesn't speak of him?"

"No."

Pine drew a deep breath and rose slowly to his feet, with a satisfied nod.

"I'm glad of that. She's a good woman is Agnes, and would never encourage him in any way. She knows what is due to me. I trust her."

"Do you? When your secretary is also stopping at The Manor?"

"Silver!" Pine laughed awkwardly, and kicked at a tuft of moss. "Well I did ask him to keep an eye on her, although there is really no occasion. Silver owes me a great deal, since I took him out of the gutter. If Lambert worried my wife, Silver would let me know, and then—"

"And then?" asked Miss Greeby hastily.

The man clenched his fists and his face grew stormy, as his blood untamed by civilization surged redly to the surface. "I'd twist his neck, I'd smash his skull, I'd—I'd—I'd—oh, don't ask me what I'd do."

"I should keep my temper if I were you," Miss Greeby warned him, and alarmed by the tempest she had provoked. She had no wish for the man she loved to come into contact with this savage, veneered by civilization. Yet Lambert was in the neighborhood, and almost within a stone's throw of the husband who was so jealous of him. "Keep your temper," repeated Miss Greeby.

"Is there anything else you would like me to do?" raged Pine fiercely.

"Yes. Leave this place if you wish to keep the secret of your birth from your wife. Lady Garvington and Mrs. Belgrove, and a lot of people from The Manor, are coming to the camp to get their fortunes told. You are sure to be spotted."

"I shall keep myself out of sight," said Pine sullenly and suspiciously.

"Some of your gypsy friends may let the cat out of the bag."

"Not one of them knows there is a cat in the bag. I am Ishmael Hearne to them, and nothing else. But I shan't stay here long."

"I wonder you came at all, seeing that your wife is with her brother."

"In the daring of my coming lies my safety," said Pine tartly. "I know what I am doing. As to Lambert, if he thinks to marry my wife when I am dead he is mistaken."

"Well, I hope you won't die, for my sake!"

"Why for your sake?" asked Pine sharply.

"Because I love Lambert and I want to marry him."

"Marry him," said the millionaire hoarsely, "and I'll give you thousands of pounds. Oh! I forgot that you have a large income. But marry him, marry him, Miss Greeby. I shall help you all I can."

"I can do without assistance," said the woman coolly. "All I ask you to do is to refrain from fighting with Lambert."

"What?" Pine's face became lowering again. "Is he at The Manor? You said—"

"I know what I said. He is not at The Manor, but he is stopping in the cottage a stone's throw from here."

Pine breathed hard, and again had a spasm of coughing. "What's he doing?"

"Painting pictures."

"He has not been near The Manor?"

"No. And what is more, he told me to-day that he did not intend to go near the house. I don't think you need be afraid, Pine. Lambert is a man of honor, and I hope to get him to be my husband."

"He shall never be my wife's husband," said the millionaire between his teeth and scowling heavily. "I know that I shan't live to anything like three score and ten. Your infernal hot-house civilization has killed me. But if Lambert thinks to marry my widow he shall do so in the face of Garvington's opposition, and will find Agnes a pauper."

"What do you mean exactly?" Miss Greeby flung away the stump of her cigarette and rose to her feet.

Pine wiped his brow and breathed heavily. "I mean that I have left Agnes my money, only on condition that she does not marry Lambert. She can marry any one else she has a mind to. I except her cousin."

"Because she loves him?"

"Yes, and because he loves her, d—n him."

"He doesn't," cried Miss Greeby, lying fluently, and heartily wishing that her lie could be a truth. "He loves me, and I intend to marry him. Now you can understand what I meant when I declared that I had honor enough to keep your secret. Lambert is my honor."

"Oh, then I believe in your honor," sneered Pine cynically. "It is a selfish quality in this case, which can only be gratified by preserving silence. If Agnes knew that I was a true Romany tramp, she might run away with Lambert, and as you want him to be your husband, it is to your interest to hold your tongue. Thank you for nothing, Miss Greeby."

"I tell you Lambert loves me," cried the woman doggedly, trying to persuade her heart that she spoke truly. "And whether you leave your money to your wife, or to any one else, makes no manner of difference."

"I think otherwise," he retorted. "And it is just as well to be on the safe side. If my widow marries Lambert, she loses my millions, and they go to—" He checked himself abruptly. "Never mind who gets them. It is a person in whom you can take no manner of interest."

Miss Greeby pushed the point of her bludgeon into the spongy ground, and looked thoughtful. "If Lambert loves Agnes still, which I don't believe," she observed, after a pause, "he would marry her even if she hadn't a shilling. Your will excluding him as her second husband is merely the twisting of a rope of sand, Pine."

"You forget," said the man quickly, "that I declared also, he would have to marry her in the face of Garvington's opposition."

"In what way?"

"Can't you guess? Garvington only allowed me to marry his sister because I am a wealthy man. I absolutely bought my wife by helping him, and she gave herself to me without love to save the family name from disgrace. She is a good woman, is Agnes, and always places duty before inclination. Marriage with her pauper cousin meant practically the social extinction of the Lambert family, and nothing would have remained but the title. Therefore she married me, and I felt mean at the time in accepting the sacrifice. But I was so deeply in love with her that I did so. I love her still, and I am mean enough still to be jealous of this cousin. She shall never marry him, and I know that Garvington will appeal to his sister's strong desire to save the family once more; so that she may not be foolish enough to lose the money. And two millions, more or less," ended Pine cynically, "is too large a sum to pay for a second husband."

"Does Agnes know these conditions?"

"No. Nor do I intend that she should know. You hold your tongue."

Miss Greeby pulled on her heavy gloves and nodded. "I told you that I had some notion of honor. Will you let Lambert know that you are in this neighborhood?"

"No. There is no need. I am stopping here only for a time to see a certain person. Silver will look after Agnes, and is coming to the camp to report upon what he has observed."

"Silver then knows that you are Ishmael Hearne?"

"Yes. He knows all my secrets, and I can trust him thoroughly, since he owes everything to me."

Miss Greeby laughed scornfully. "That a man of your age and experience should believe in gratitude. Well, it's no business of mine. You may be certain that for my own purpose I shall hold my tongue and shall keep Lambert from seeking your wife. Not that he loves her," she added hastily, as Pine's brows again drew together. "But she loves him, and may use her arts—"

"Don't you dare to speak of arts in connection with my wife," broke in the man roughly. "She is no coquette, and I trust her—"

"So long as Silver looks after her," finished Miss Greeby contemptuously. "What chivalrous confidence. Well, I must be going. Any message to your—"

"No! No! No!" broke in Pine once more. "She is not to know that I am here, or anything about my true position and name. You promised, and you will keep your promise. But there, I know that you will, as self-interest will make you."

"Ah, now you talk common sense. It is a pity you don't bring it to bear in the case of Silver, whom you trust because you have benefited him. Good-day, you very unsophisticated person. I shall see you again—"

"In London as Hubert Pine," said the millionaire abruptly, and Miss Greeby, with a good-humored shrug, marched away, swinging her stick and whistling gayly. She was very well satisfied with the knowledge she had obtained, as the chances were that it would prove useful should Lambert still hanker after the unattainable woman. Miss Greeby had lulled Pine's suspicions regarding the young man's love for Agnes, but she knew in her heart that she had only done so by telling a pack of miserable lies. Now, as she walked back to The Manor, she reflected that by using her secret information dexterously, she might improve such falsehood into tolerable truth.

Pine flung himself down again when she departed, and coughed in his usual violent manner. His throat and lungs ached, and his brow was wet with perspiration. With his elbows on his knees and his face between his hands, he sat miserably thinking over his troubles. There was no chance of his living more than a few years, as the best doctors in Europe and England had given him up, and when he was placed below ground, the chances were that Agnes would marry his rival. He had made things as safe as was possible against such a contingency, but who knew if her love for Lambert might not make her willing to surrender the millions. "Unless Garvington can manage to arouse her family pride," groaned Pine drearily. "She sacrificed herself before for that, and perhaps she will do so again. But who knows?" And he could find no answer to this question, since it is impossible for any man to say what a woman will do where her deepest emotions are concerned.

A touch on Pine's shoulder made him leap to his feet with the alertness of a wild animal on the lookout for danger. By his side stood Chaldea, and her eyes glittered, as she came to the point of explanation without any preamble. The girl was painfully direct. "I have heard every word," she said triumphantly. "And I know what you are, brother."

"Why did you come here?" demanded Pine sharply, and frowning.

"I wanted to hear what a Romany had to do with a Gorgio lady, brother. And what do I hear. Why, that you dwell in the Gentile houses, and take a Gentile name, and cheat in a Gentile manner, and have wed with a Gentile romi. Speaking Romanly, brother, it is not well."

"It is as I choose, sister," replied Pine quietly, for since Chaldea had got the better of him, it was useless to quarrel with her. "And from what I do good will come to our people."

Chaldea laughed, and blew from her fingers a feather, carelessly picked up while in the thicket which had concealed her eavesdropping. "For that, I care that," said she, pointing to the floating feather slowly settling. "I looks to myself and to my love, brother."

"Hey?" Pine raised his eyebrows.

"It's a Gorgio my heart is set on," pursued Chaldea steadfastly. "A regular Romany Rye, brother. Do you think Lambert is a good name?"

"It's the name of the devil, sister," cried Pine hastily.

"The very devil I love. To me sweet, as to you sour. And speaking Romanly, brother, I want him to be my rom in the Gentile fashion, as you have a romi in your Gorgious lady."

"What will Kara say?" said Pine, and his eyes flashed, for the idea of getting rid of Lambert in this way appealed to him. The girl was beautiful, and with her added cleverness she might be able to gain her ends, and these accomplished, would certainly place a barrier between Agnes and her cousin, since the woman would never forgive the man for preferring the girl.

"Kara plays on the fiddle, but not on my heart-strings," said Chaldea in a cool manner, and watched Pine wickedly. "You'd better help me, brother, if you don't want that Gorgious romi of yours to pad the hoof with the rye."

The blood rushed to Pine's dark cheeks. "What's that?"

"No harm to my rye and I tell you, brother. Don't use the knife."

"That I will not do, if a wedding-ring from him to you will do as well."

"It will do, brother," said Chaldea calmly. "My rye doesn't love me yet, but he will, when I get him away from the Gentile lady's spells. They draw him, brother, they draw him."

"Where do they draw him to?" demanded Pine, his voice thick with passion.

"To the Gorgious house of the baro rai, the brother of your romi. Like an owl does he go after dusk to watch the nest."

"Owl," muttered Pine savagely. "Cuckoo, rather. Prove this, my sister, and I help you to gain the love you desire."

"It's a bargain, brother"—she held out her hand inquiringly—"but no knife."

Pine shook hands. "It's a bargain, sister. Your wedding-ring will part them as surely as any knife. Tell me more!" And Chaldea in whispers told him all.

CHAPTER V

THE WOMAN AND THE MAN

Quite unaware that Destiny, that tireless spinner, was weaving sinister red threads of hate and love into the web of his life, Lambert continued to live quietly in his woodland retreat. In a somewhat misanthropic frame of mind he had retired to this hermitage, after the failure of his love affair, since, lacking the society of Agnes, there was nothing left for him to desire. From a garden of roses, the world became a sandy desert, and denied the sole gift of fortune, which would have made him completely happy, the disconsolate lover foreswore society for solitude. As some seek religion, so Lambert hoped by seeking Nature's breast to assuage the pains of his sore heart. But although the great Mother could do so much, she could not do all, and the young man still felt restless and weary. Hard work helped him more than a little, but he had his dark hours during those intervals when hand and brain were too weary to create pictures.

In one way he blamed Agnes, because she had married for money; in another way he did not blame her, because that same money had been necessary to support the falling fortunes of the noble family to which Lambert belonged. An ordinary person would not have understood this, and would have seen in the mercenary marriage simply a greedy grasping after the loaves and fishes. But Lambert, coming at the end of a long line of lordly ancestors, considered that both he and his cousin owed something to those of the past who had built up the family. Thus his pride told him that Agnes had acted rightly in taking Pine as her husband, while his love cried aloud that the sacrifice was too hard upon their individual selves. He was a Lambert, but he was also a human being, and the two emotions of love and pride strove mightily against one another. Although quite three years had elapsed since the victim had been offered at the altar—and a willing victim to the family fetish—the struggle was still going on. And because of its stress and strain, Lambert withdrew from society, so that he might see as little as possible of the woman he loved. They had met, they had talked, they had looked, in a conventionally light-hearted way, but both were relieved when circumstances parted them. The strain was too great.

Pine arranged the circumstances, for hearing here, there, and everywhere, that his wife had been practically engaged to her cousin before he became her husband, he looked with jealous eyes upon their chance meetings. Neither to Agnes nor Lambert did he say a single word, since he had no reason to utter it, so scrupulously correct was their behavior, but his eyes were sufficiently eloquent to reveal his jealousy. He took his wife for an American tour, and when he brought her back to London, Lambert, knowing only too truly the reason for that tour, had gone away in his turn to shoot big game in Africa. An attack of malaria contracted in the Congo marshes had driven him back to England, and it was then that he had begged Garvington to give him The Abbot's Wood Cottage. For six months he had been shut up here, occasionally going to London, or for a week's walking tour, and during that time he had done his best to banish the image of Agnes from his heart. Doubtless she was attempting the same conquest, for she never even wrote to him. And now these two sorely-tried people were within speaking distance of one another, and strange results might be looked for unless honor held them sufficiently true. Seeing that the cottage was near the family seat, and that Agnes sooner or later would arrive to stay with her brother and sister-in-law, Lambert might have expected that such a situation would come about in the natural course of things. Perhaps he did, and perhaps—as some busybodies said—he took the cottage for that purpose; but so far, he had refrained from seeking the society of Pine's wife. He would not even dine at The Manor, nor would he join the shooting-party, although Garvington, with a singular blindness, urged him to do so. While daylight lasted, the artist painted desperately hard, and after dark wandered round the lanes and roads and across the fields, haunting almost unconsciously the Manor Park, if only to see in moonlight and twilight the casket which held the rich jewel he had lost. This was foolish, and Lambert acknowledged that it was foolish, but at the same time he added inwardly that he was a man and not an angel, a sinner and not a saint, so that there were limits, etc., etc., etc., using impossible arguments to quieten a lively conscience that did not approve of this dangerous philandering.

The visit of Miss Greeby awoke him positively to a sense of danger, for if she talked—and talk she did—other people would talk also. Lambert asked himself if it would be better to visit The Manor and behave like a man who has got over his passion, or to leave the cottage and betake himself to London. While turning over this problem in his mind, he painted feverishly, and for three days after Miss Greeby had come to stir up muddy water, he remained as much as possible in his studio. Chaldea visited him, as usual, to be painted, and brought Kara with his green coat and beloved violin and hairy looks. The girl chatted, Kara played, and Lambert painted, and all three pretended to be very happy and careless. This was merely on the surface, however, for the artist was desperately wretched, because the other half of himself was married to another man, while Chaldea, getting neither love-look nor caress, felt savagely discontented. As for Kara, he had long since loved Chaldea, who treated him like a dog, and he could not help seeing that she adored the Gentile artist—a knowledge which almost broke his heart. But it was some satisfaction for him to note that Lambert would have nothing to do with the siren, and that she could not charm him to her feet, sang she ever so tenderly. It was an unhappy trio at the best.

The gypsies usually came in the morning, since the light was then better for artistic purposes, but they always departed at one o'clock, so that Lambert had the afternoon to himself. Chaldea would fain have lingered in order to charm the man she loved into subjection; but he never gave her the least encouragement, so she was obliged to stay away. All the same, she often haunted the woods near the cottage, and when Lambert came out for a stroll, which he usually did when it became too dark to paint, he was bound to run across her. Since he had not the slightest desire to make love to her, and did not fathom the depth of her passion, he never suspected that she purposely contrived the meetings which he looked upon as accidental.

Since Chaldea hung round the house, like a moth round a candle, she saw every one who came and went from the woodland cottage. On the afternoon of the third day since Pine's arrival at the camp in the character of Ishmael Hearne, the gypsy saw Lady Agnes coming through the wood. Chaldea knew her at once, having often seen her when she had come to visit Mother Cockleshell a few months previously. With characteristic cunning, the girl dived into the undergrowth, and there remained concealed for the purpose of spying on the Gentile lady whom she regarded as a rival. Immediately, Chaldea guessed that Lady Agnes was on her way to the cottage, and, as Lambert was alone as usual for the afternoon, the two would probably have a private conversation. The girl swiftly determined to listen, so that she might learn exactly how matters stood between them. It might be that she would discover something which Pine—Chaldea now thought of him as Pine—might like to know. So having arranged this in her own unscrupulous mind, the girl behind a juniper bush jealously watched the unsuspecting lady. What she saw did not please her overmuch, as Lady Agnes was rather too beautiful for her unknown rival's peace of mind.

Sir Hubert's wife was not really the exquisitely lovely creature Chaldea took her to be, but her fair skin and brown hair were such a contrast to the gypsy's swarthy face and raven locks, that she really looked like an angel of light compared with the dark child of Nature. Agnes was tall and slender, and moved with a great air of dignity and calm self-possession, and this to the uncontrolled Chaldea was also a matter of offence. She inwardly tried to belittle her rival by thinking what a milk-and-water useless person she was, but the steady and resolute look in the lady's brown eyes gave the lie to this mental assertion. Lady Agnes had an air of breeding and command, which, with all her beauty, Chaldea lacked, and as she passed along like a cold, stately goddess, the gypsy rolled on the grass in an ecstasy of rage. She could never be what her rival was, and what her rival was, as she suspected, formed Lambert's ideal of womanhood. When she again peered through the bush, Lady Agnes had disappeared. But there was no need for Chaldea to ask her jealous heart where she had gone. With the stealth and cunning of a Red Indian, the gypsy took up the trail, and saw the woman she followed enter the cottage. For a single moment she had it in her mind to run to the camp and bring Pine, but reflecting that in a moment of rage the man might kill Lambert, Chaldea checked her first impulse, and bent all her energies towards getting sufficiently near to listen to a conversation which was not meant for her ears.

Meanwhile, Agnes had been admitted by Mrs. Tribb, a dried-up little woman with the rosy face of a winter apple, and a continual smile of satisfaction with herself and with her limited world. This consisted of the cottage, in the wood, and of the near villages, where she repaired on occasions to buy food. Sometimes, indeed, she went to The Manor, for, born and bred on the Garvington estates, Mrs. Tribb knew all the servants at the big house. She had married a gamekeeper, who had died, and unwilling to leave the country she knew best, had gladly accepted the offer of Lord Garvington to look after the woodland cottage. In this way Lambert became possessed of an exceedingly clean housekeeper, and a wonderfully good cook. In fact so excellent a cook was Mrs. Tribb, that Garvington had frequently suggested she should come to The Manor. But, so far, Lambert had managed to keep the little woman to himself. Mrs. Tribb adored him, since she had known him from babyhood, and declined to leave him under any circumstances. She thought Lambert the best man in the world, and challenged the universe to find another so handsome and clever, and so considerate.

"Dear me, my lady, is it yourself?" said Mrs. Tribb, throwing up her dry little hands and dropping a dignified curtsey. "Well, I do call it good of you to come and see Master Noel. He don't go out enough, and don't take enough interest in his stomach, if your ladyship will pardon my mentioning that part of him. But you don't know, my lady, what it is to be a cook, and to see the dishes get cold, while he as should eat them goes on painting, not but what Master Noel don't paint like an angel, as I've said dozens of times."

While Mrs. Tribb ran on in this manner her lively black eyes twinkled anxiously. She knew that her master and Lady Agnes had been, as she said herself, "next door to engaged," and knew also that Lambert was fretting over the match which had been brought about for the glorification of the family. The housekeeper, therefore, wondered why Lady Agnes had come, and asked herself whether it would not be wise to say that Master Noel—from old associations, she always called Lambert by this juvenile title—was not at home. But she banished the thought as unworthy, the moment it entered her active brain, and with another curtsey in response to the visitor's greeting, she conducted her to the studio. "Them two angels will never do no wrong, anyhow," was Mrs. Tribb's reflection, as she closed the door and left the pair together. "But I do hope as that black-faced husband won't ever learn. He's as jealous as Cain, and I don't want Master Noel to be no Abel!"

If Mrs. Tribb, instead of going to the kitchen, which she did, had gone out of the front door, she would have found Chaldea lying full length amongst the flowers under the large window of the studio. This was slightly open, and the girl could hear every word that was spoken, while so swiftly and cleverly had she gained her point of vantage, that those within never for one moment suspected her presence. If they had, they would assuredly have kept better guard over their tongues, for the conversation was of the most private nature, and did not tend to soothe the eavesdropper's jealousy.

Lambert was so absorbed in his painting—he was working at the Esmeralda-Quasimodo picture—that he scarcely heard the studio door open, and it was only when Mrs. Tribb's shrill voice announced the name of his visitor, that he woke to the surprising fact that the woman he loved was within a few feet of him. The blood rushed to his face, and then retired to leave him deadly pale, but Agnes was more composed, and did not let her heart's tides mount to high-water mark. On seeing her self-possession, the man became ashamed that he had lost his own, and strove to conceal his momentary lapse into a natural emotion, by pushing forward an arm-chair.

"This is a surprise, Agnes," he said in a voice which he strove vainly to render steady. "Won't you sit down?"

"Thank you," and she took her seat like a queen on her throne, looking fair and gracious as any white lily. What with her white dress, white gloves and shoes, and straw hat tied under her chin with a broad white ribbon in old Georgian fashion, she looked wonderfully cool, and pure, and—as Lambert inwardly observed—holy. Her face was as faintly tinted with color as is a tea-rose, and her calm, brown eyes, under her smooth brown hair, added to the suggestive stillness of her looks. She seemed in her placidity to be far removed from any earthly emotion, and resembled a picture of the Madonna, serene, peaceful, and somewhat sad. Yet who could tell what anguished feelings were masked by her womanly pride?

"I hope you do not find the weather too warm for walking," said Lambert, reining in his emotions with an iron hand, and speaking conventionally.

"Not at all. I enjoyed the walk. I am staying at The Manor."

"So I understand."

"And you are staying here?"

"There can be no doubt on that point."

"Do you think you are acting wisely?" she asked with great calmness.

"I might put the same question to you, Agnes, seeing that you have come to live within three miles of my hermitage."

"It is because you are living in what you call your hermitage that I have come," rejoined Agnes, with a slight color deepening her cheeks. "Is it fair to me that you should shut yourself up and play the part of the disappointed lover?"

Lambert, who had been touching up his picture here and there, laid down his palette and brushes with ostentatious care, and faced her doggedly. "I don't understand what you mean," he declared.

"Oh, I think you do; and in the hope that I may induce you, in justice to me, to change your conduct, I have come over."

"I don't think you should have come," he observed in a low voice, and threw himself on the couch with averted eyes.

Lady Agnes colored again. "You are talking nonsense," she said with some sharpness. "There is no harm in my coming to see my cousin."

"We were more than cousins once."

"Exactly, and unfortunately people know that. But you needn't make matters worse by so pointedly keeping away from me."

Lambert looked up quickly. "Do you wish me to see you often?" he asked, and there was a new note in his voice which irritated her.

"Personally I don't, but—"

"But what?" He rose and stood up, very tall and very straight, looking down on her with a hungry look in his blue eyes.

"People are talking," murmured the lady, and stared at the floor, because she could not face that same look.

"Let them talk. What does it matter?"

"Nothing to you, perhaps, but to me a great deal. I have a husband."

"As I know to my cost," he interpolated.

"Then don't let me know it to my cost," she said pointedly. "Sit down and let us talk common sense."

Lambert did not obey at once. "I am only a human being, Agnes—"

"Quite so, and a man at that. Act like a man, then, and don't place the burden on a woman's shoulders."

"What burden?"

"Oh, Noel, can't you understand?"

"I daresay I can if you will explain. I wish you hadn't come here to-day. I have enough to bear without that."

"And have I nothing to bear?" she demanded, a flash of passion ruffling her enforced calm. "Do you think that anything but the direst need brought me here?"

"I don't know what brought you here. I am waiting for an explanation."

"What is the use of explaining what you already know?"

"I know nothing," he repeated doggedly. "Explain."

"Well," said Lady Agnes with some bitterness, "it seems to me that an explanation is really necessary, as apparently I am talking to a child instead of a man. Sit down and listen."

This time Lambert obeyed, and laughed as he did so. "Your taunts don't hurt me in the least," he observed. "I love you too much."

"And I love in return. No! Don't rise again. I did not come here to revive the embers of our dead passion."

"Embers!" cried Lambert with bitter scorn. "Embers, indeed! And a dead passion; how well you put it. So far as I am concerned, Agnes, the passion is not dead and never will be."

"I am aware of that, and so I have come to appeal to that passion. Love means sacrifice. I want you to understand that."

"I do, by experience. Did I not surrender you for the sake of the family name? Understand! I should think I did understand."

"I—think—not," said Lady Agnes slowly and gently. "It is necessary to revive your recollections. We loved one another since we were boy and girl, and we intended, as you know, to marry. There was no regular engagement between us, but it was an understood family arrangement. My father always approved of it; my brother did not."

"No. Because he saw in you an article of sale out of which he hoped to make money," sneered Lambert, nursing his ankle.

Lady Agnes winced. "Don't make it too hard for me," she said plaintively. "My life is uncomfortable enough as it is. Remember that when my father died we were nearly ruined. Only by the greatest cleverness did Garvington manage to keep interest on the mortgages paid up, hoping that he would marry a rich wife—an American for choice—and so could put things straight. But he married Jane, as you know—"

"Because he is a glutton, and she knows all about cooking."

"Well, gluttony may be as powerful a vice as drinking and gambling, and all the rest of it. It is with Garvington, although I daresay that seeing the position he was in, people would laugh to think he should marry a poor woman, when he needed a rich wife. But at that time Hubert wanted to marry me, and Garvington got his cook-wife, while I was sacrificed."

"Seeing that I loved you and you loved me, I wonder—"

"Yes, I know you wondered, but you finally accepted my explanation that I did it to save the family name."

"I did, and, much as I hated your sacrifice, it was necessary."

"More necessary than you think," said Lady Agnes, sinking her voice to a whisper and glancing round, "In a moment of madness Garvington altered a check which Hubert gave him, and was in danger of arrest. Hubert declared that he would give up the check if I married him. I did so, to save my brother and the family name."

"Oh, Agnes!" Lambert jumped up. "I never knew this."

"It was not necessary to tell you. I made the excuse of saving the family name and property generally. You thought it was merely the bankruptcy court, but I knew that it meant the criminal court. However, I married Hubert, and he put the check in the fire in my presence and in Garvington's. He has also fulfilled his share of the bargain which he made when he bought me, and has paid off a great many of the mortgages. However, Garvington became too outrageous in his demands, and lately Hubert has refused to help him any more. I don't blame him; he has paid enough for me."

"You are worth it," said Lambert emphatically.

"Well, you may think so, and perhaps he does also. But does it not strike you, Noel, what a poor figure I and Garvington, and the whole family, yourself included, cut in the eyes of the world? We were poor, and I was sold to get money to save the land."

"Yes, but this changing of the check also—"

"The world doesn't know of that," said Agnes hurriedly. "Hubert has been very loyal to me. I must be loyal to him."

"You are. Who dares to say that you are not?"

"No one—as yet," she replied pointedly.

"What do you mean by that?" he demanded, flushing through his fair skin.

"I mean that if you met me in the ordinary way, and behaved to me as an ordinary man, people would not talk. But you shun my society, and even when I am at The Manor, you do not come near because of my presence."

"It is so hard to be near you and yet, owing to your marriage, so far from you," muttered the man savagely.

"If it is hard for you, think how hard it must be for me," said the woman vehemently, her passion coming to the surface. "People talk of the way in which you avoid me, and hint that we love one another still."

"It is true! Agnes, you know it is true!"

"Need the whole world know that it is true?" cried Agnes, rising, with a gust of anger passing over her face. "If you would only come to The Manor, and meet me in London, and accept Hubert's invitations to dinner, people would think that our attachment was only a boy and girl engagement, that we had outgrown. They would even give me credit for loving Hubert—"

"But you don't?" cried Lambert with a jealous pang.

"Yes, I do. He is my chosen husband, and has carried out his part of the bargain by freeing many of Garvington's estates. Surely the man ought to have something for his money. I don't love him as a wife should love her husband, not with heart-whole devotion, that is. But I give him loyalty, and I respect him, and I try to make him happy in every way. I do my part, Noel, as you do yours. Since I have been compelled to sacrifice love for money, at least let us be true to the sacrifice."

"You didn't sacrifice yourself wholly for money."

"No, I did not. It was because of Garvington's crime. But no one knows of that, and no one ever shall know. In fact, so happy am I and Hubert—"

"Happy?" said Lambert wincing.

"Yes," she declared firmly. "He thinks so, and whatever unhappiness I may feel, I conceal from him. But you must come to The Manor, and meet me here, there, and everywhere, so that people shall not say, as they are doing, that you are dying of love, and that, because I am a greedy fortune-hunter, I ruined your life."

"They do not dare. I have not heard any—"

"What can you hear in this jungle?" interrupted Lady Agnes with scorn. "You stop your ears with cotton wool, but I am in the world, hearing everything. And the more unpleasant the thing is, the more readily do I hear it. You can end this trouble by coming out of your lovesick retirement, and by showing that you no longer care for me."

"That would be acting a lie."

"And do I not act a lie?" she cried fiercely. "Is not my whole marriage a lie? I despise myself for my weakness in yielding, and yet, God help me, what else could I do when Garvington's fair fame was in question? Think of the disgrace, had he been prosecuted by Hubert. And Hubert knows that you and I loved; that I could not give him the love he desired. He was content to accept me on those terms. I don't say he was right; but am I right, are you right, is Garvington right? Is any one of us right? Not one, not one. The whole thing is horrible, but I make the best of it, since I did what I did do, openly and for a serious purpose of which the world knows nothing. Do your part, Noel, and come to The Manor, if only to show that you no longer care for me. You understand"—she clasped her hands in agony. "You surely understand."

"Yes," said Lambert in a low voice, and suddenly looked years older. "I understand at last, Agnes. You shall no longer bear the burden alone. I shall be a loyal friend to you, my dear," and he took her hand.

"Will you be a loyal friend to my husband?" she asked, withdrawing it.

"Yes," said Lambert, and he bit his lip. "God helping me, I will."

CHAPTER VI

THE MAN AND THE WOMAN

The interview between Lady Agnes and Lambert could scarcely be called a love-scene, since it was dominated by a stern sense of duty. Chaldea, lying at length amongst the crushed and fragrant flowers, herself in her parti-colored attire scarcely distinguishable from the rainbow blossoms, was puzzled by the way in which the two reined in their obvious passions. To her simple, barbaric nature, the situation appeared impossible. If he loved her and she loved him, why did they not run away to enjoy life together? The husband who had paid money for the wife did not count, nor did the brother, who had sold his sister to hide his criminal folly. That Lady Agnes should have traded herself to save Garvington from a well-deserved punishment, seemed inexcusable to the gypsy. If he had been the man she loved, then indeed might she have acted rightly. But having thrown over that very man in this silly fashion, for the sake of what did not appear to be worth the sacrifice, Chaldea felt that Agnes did not deserve Lambert, and she then and there determined that the Gentile lady should never possess him.

Of course, on the face of it, there was no question of possession. The man being weaker than the woman would have been only too glad to elope, and thus cut the Gordian knot of the unhappy situation. But the woman, having acted from a high sense of duty, which Chaldea could not rise to, evidently was determined to continue to be a martyr. The question was, could she keep up that pose in the face of the undeniable fact that she loved her cousin? The listening girl thought not. Sooner or later the artificial barrier would be broken through by the held-back flood of passion, and then Lady Agnes would run away from the man who had bought her. And quite right, too, thought Chaldea, although she had no notion of permitting such an elopement to take place. That Agnes would hold to her bargain all her life, because Hubert had fulfilled his part, never occurred to the girl. She was not civilized enough to understand this problem of a highly refined nature.

Since the situation was so difficult, Lambert was glad to see the back of his cousin. He escorted her to the door, but did not attend her through the wood. In fact, they parted rather abruptly, which was wise. All had been said that could be said, and Lambert had given his promise to share the burden with Agnes by acting the part of a lover who had never really been serious. But it did not do to discuss details, as these were too painful, so the woman hurried away without a backward glance, and Lambert, holding his heart between his teeth, returned to the studio. Neither one of the two noticed Chaldea crouching amongst the flowers. Had they been less pre-occupied, they might have done so; as it was she escaped observation.

As soon as the coast was clear, Chaldea stole like a snake along the ground, through the high herbage of the garden, and beyond the circle of the mysterious monoliths. Even across the lawns of the glade did she crawl, so as not to be seen, although she need not have taken all this trouble, since Lambert, with a set face and a trembling hand, was working furiously at a minor picture he utilized to get rid of such moods. But the gypsy did not know this, and so writhed into the woods like the snake of Eden—and of that same she was a very fair sample—until, hidden by the boles of ancient trees, she could stand upright. When she did so, she drew a long breath, and wondered what was best to be done.

The most obvious course was to seek Ishmael and make a lying report of the conversation. That his wife should have been with Lambert would be quite enough to awaken the civilized gypsy's jealousy, for after all his civilization was but skin deep. Still, if she did this, Chaldea was clever enough to see that she would precipitate a catastrophe, and either throw Agnes into Lambert's arms, or make the man run the risk of getting Pine's knife tickling his fifth rib. Either result did not appeal to her. She wished to get Lambert to herself, and his safety was of vital importance to her. After some consideration, she determined that she would boldly face the lover, and confess that she had overheard everything. Then she would have him in her power, since to save the wife from the vengeance of the husband, although there was no reason for such vengeance, he would do anything to keep the matter of the visit quiet. Of course the interview had been innocent, and Chaldea knew that such was the case. Nevertheless, by a little dexterous lying, and some vivid word-painting, she could make things extremely unpleasant for the couple. This being so, Lambert would have to subscribe to her terms. And these were, that he should leave Agnes and marry her. That there was such a difference in their rank mattered nothing to the girl. Love levelled all ranks, in her opinion.

But while arranging what she should do, if Lambert proved obstinate, Chaldea also arranged to fascinate him, if possible, into loving her. She did not wish to use her power of knowledge until her power of fascination failed. And this for two reasons. In the first place, it was not her desire to drive the man into a corner lest he should defy her and fight, which would mean—to her limited comprehension—that everything being known to Pine, the couple would confess all and elope. In the second place, Chaldea was piqued to think that Lambert should prove to be so indifferent to her undeniable beauty, as to love this pale shadow of a Gentile lady. She would make certain, she told herself, if he really preferred the lily to the full-blown rose, and on his choice depended her next step. Gliding back to the camp, she decided to attend to one thing at a time, and the immediate necessity was to charm the man into submission. For this reason Chaldea sought out the Servian gypsy, who was her slave.

Her slave Kara certainly was, but not her rom. If he had been her husband she would not have dared to propose to him what she did propose. He was amiable enough as a slave, because he had no hold over her, but if she married him according to the gypsy law, he would then be her master, and should she indulge her fancy for a Gentile, he would assuredly use a very nasty-looking knife, which he wore under the green coat. Even as it was, Kara would not be pleased to fiddle to her dancing, since he already was jealous of Lambert. But Chaldea knew how to manage this part of the business, risky though it was. The hairy little ape with the musician's soul had no claim on her, unless she chose to give him that of a husband. Then, indeed, things would be different, but the time had not come for marital slavery.

The schemer found Kara at the hour of sunset sitting at the door of the tent he occupied, drawing sweet tones from his violin. This was the little man's way of conversing, for he rarely talked to human beings. He spoke to the fiddle and the fiddle spoke to him, probably about Chaldea, since the girl was almost incessantly in his thoughts. She occupied them now, and when he raised his shaggy head at the touch on his hump-back, he murmured with joy at the sight of her flushed beauty. Had he known that the flush came from jealousy of a rival, Kara might not have been so pleased. The two conversed in Romany, since the Servian did not speak English.

"Brother?" questioned Chaldea, standing in the glory of the rosy sunset which slanted through the trees. "What of Ishmael?"

"He is with Gentilla in her tent, sister. Do you wish to see him?"

Chaldea shook her proud head. "What have I to do with the half Romany? Truly, brother, his heart is Gentile, though his skin be of Egypt."

"Why should that be, sister, when his name signifies that he is of the gentle breed?" asked Kara, laying down his violin.

"Gentile but not gentle," said Chaldea punning, then checked herself lest she should say too much. She had sworn to keep Pine's secret, and intended to do so, until she could make capital out of it. At present she could not, so behaved honorably. "But he's Romany enough to split words with the old witch by the hour, so let him stay where he is. Brother, would you make money?" Kara nodded and looked up with diamond eyes, which glittered and gloated on the beauty of her dark face. "Then, brother," continued the girl, "the Gorgio who paints gives me gold to dance for him."

The Servian's face—what could be seen of it for hair—grew sombre, and he spat excessively. "Curses on the Gentile!" he growled low in his throat.

"On him, but not on the money, brother," coaxed the girl, stooping to pat his face. "It's fine work, cheating the rye. But jealous you must not be, if the gold is to chink in our pockets."

Kara still frowned. "Were you my romi, sister—"

"Aye, if I were. Then indeed. But your romi I am not yet."

"Some day you will be. It would be a good fortune, sister. I am as ugly as you are lovely, and we two together, you dancing to my playing, would make pockets of red gold. White shows best when placed on black."

"What a mine of wisdom you are," jeered Chaldea, nodding. "Yes. It is so, and my rom you may be, if you obey."

"But if you let the Gorgio make love to you—"

"Hey! Am I not a free Roman, brother? You have not yet caught the bird. It still sings on the bough. If I kiss him I suck gold from his lips. If I put fond arms around his neck I but gather wealth for us both. Can you snare a mouse without cheese, brother?"

Kara looked at her steadily, and then lifted his green coat to show the gleam of a butcher knife. "Should you go too far," he said significantly; and touched the blade.

Chaldea bent swiftly, and snatching the weapon from his belt, flung it into the coarse grass under the trees. "So I fling you away," said she, and stamped with rage. "Truly, brother, speaking Romanly, you are a fool of fools, and take cheating for honesty. I lure the Gorgio at my will, and says you whimpering-like, 'She's my romi,' the which is a lie. Bless your wisdom for a hairy toad, and good-bye, for I go to my own people near Lundra, and never will he who doubted my honesty see me more."

She turned away, and Kara limped after her to implore forgiveness. He assured her that he trusted her fully, and that whatever tricks she played the Gentile would not be taken seriously by himself. "Poison him I would," grumbled the little gnome in his beard. "For his golden talk makes you smile sweetly upon him. But for the gold—"

"Yes, for the gold we must play the fox. Well, brother, now that you talk so, wait until the moon is up, then hide in the woods round the cottage dell with your violin to your chin. I lure the rabbit from its hole, and then you play the dance that delights the Gorgios. But what I do, with kisses or arm-loving, my brother," she added shaking her finger, "is but the play of the wind to shake the leaves. Believe me honest and my rom you shall be—some day!" and she went away laughing, to eat and drink, for the long watching had tired her. As for Kara he crawled again into the underwood to search for his knife. Apparently he did not trust Chaldea as much as she wanted him to.

Thus it came about that when the moon rolled through a starry sky like a golden wheel, Lambert, sighing at his studio window, saw a slim and graceful figure glide into the clear space of lawn beyond the monoliths. So searching was the thin moonlight that he recognized Chaldea at once, as she wandered here and there restless as a butterfly, and apparently as aimless. But, had he known it, she had her eyes on the cottage all the time, and had he failed to come forth she would have come to inquire if he was at home. But the artist did come forth, thinking to wile away an hour with the fascinating gypsy girl. Always dressing for dinner, even in solitude, for the habit of years was too strong to lay aside—and, moreover, he was fastidious in his dress to preserve his self-respect—he appeared at the door looking slender and well-set up in his dark clothes. Although it was August the night was warm, and Lambert did not trouble to put on cap or overcoat. With his hands in his pockets and a cigar between his lips he strolled over to the girl, where she swayed and swung in the fairy light.

"Hullo, Chaldea," he said leisurely, and leaning against one of the moss-grown monoliths, "what are you doing here?"

"The rye," exclaimed Chaldea, with a well-feigned start of surprise. "Avali the rye. Sarishan, my Gorgious gentleman, you, too, are a nightbird. Have you come out mousing like an owl? Ha! ha! and you hear the nightingale singing, speaking in the Gentile manner," and clapping her hands she lifted up a full rich voice.

"Dyal o pani repedishis,
M'ro pirano hegedishis."

"What does that mean, Chaldea?"

"It is an Hungarian song, and means that while the stream flows I hear the violin of my love. Kara taught me the ditty."

"And Kara is your love?"

"No. Oh, no; oh, no," sang Chaldea, whirling round and round in quite a magical manner. "No rom have I, but a mateless bird I wander. Still I hear the violin of my true love, my new love, who knows my droms, and that means my habits, rye," she ended, suddenly speaking in a natural manner.

"I don't hear the violin, however," said Lambert lazily, and thinking what a picturesque girl she was in her many-hued rag-tag garments, and with the golden coins glittering in her black hair.

"You will, rye, you will," she said confidentially. "Come, my darling gentleman, cross my hand with silver and I dance. I swear it. No hokkeny baro will you behold when the wind pipes for me."

"Hokkeny baro."

"A great swindle, my wise sir. Hai, what a pity you cannot patter the gentle Romany tongue. Kek! Kek! What does it matter, when you speak Gentile gibberish like an angel. Sit, rye, and I dance for you."

"Quite like Carmen and Don José in the opera," murmured Lambert, sliding down to the foot of the rude stone.

"What of her and of him? Were they Romans?"

"Carmen was and José wasn't. She danced herself into his heart."

Chaldea's eyes flashed, and she made a hasty sign to attract the happy omen of his saying to herself. "Kushto bak," cried Chaldea, using the gypsy for good luck. "And to me, to me," she clapped her hand. "Hark, my golden rye, and watch me dance your love into my life."

The wind was rising and sighed through the wood, shaking myriad leaves from the trees. Blending with its faint cry came a long, sweet, sustained note of music. Lambert started, so weird and unexpected was the sound. "Kara, isn't it?" he asked, looking inquiringly at Chaldea.

"He talks to the night—he speaks with the wind. Oh-ah-ah-ah. Ah-oha-oha-oha-ho," sang the gypsy, clapping her hands softly, then, as the music came breathing from the hidden violin in dreamy sensuous tones, she raised her bare arms and began to dance. The place, the dancer, the hour, the mysterious music, and the pale enchantments of the moon—it was like fairyland.

Lambert soon let his cigar go out, so absorbed did he become in watching the dance. It was a wonderful performance, sensuous and weirdly unusual. He had never seen a dance exactly like it before. The violin notes sounded like actual words, and the dancer answered them with responsive movements of her limbs, so that without speech the onlooker saw a love-drama enacted before his eyes. Chaldea—so he interpreted the dance—swayed gracefully from the hips, without moving her feet, in the style of a Nautch girl. She was waiting for some one, since to right and left she swung with a delicate hand curved behind her ear. Suddenly she started, as if she heard an approaching footstep, and in maidenly confusion glided to a distance, where she stood with her hands across her bosom, the very picture of a surprised nymph. Mentally, the dance translated itself to Lambert somewhat after this fashion:

"She waits for her lover. That little run forward means that she sees him coming. She falls at his feet; she kisses them. He raises her—I suppose that panther spring from the ground means that he raises her. She caresses him with much fondling and many kisses. By Jove, what pantomime! Now she dances to please him. She stops and trembles; the dance does not satisfy. She tries another. No! No! Not that! It is too dreamy—the lover is in a martial mood. This time she strikes his fancy. Kara is playing a wild Hungarian polonaise. Wonderful! Wonderful!"

He might well say so, and he struggled to his feet, leaning against the pillar of stone to see the dancer better. From the wood came the fierce and stirring Slav music, and Chaldea's whole expressive body answered to every note as a needle does to a magnet. She leaped, clicking her heels together, advanced, as if on the foe, with a bound—was flung back—so it seemed—and again sprang to the assault. She stiffened to stubborn resistance—she unexpectedly became pliant and yielding and graceful, and voluptuous, while the music took on the dreamy tones of love. And Lambert translated the change after his own idea:

"The music does not please the dancer—it is too martial. She fears lest her lover should rush off to the wars, and seeks to detain him by the dance of Venus. But he will go. He rises; he speeds away; she breaks off the dance. Ah! what a cry of despair the violin gave just now. She follows, stretching out her empty arms. But it is useless—he is gone. Bah! She snaps her fingers. What does she care! She will dance to please herself, and to show that her heart is yet whole. What a Bacchanalian strain. She whirls and springs and swoops and leaps. She comes near to me, whirling like a Dervish; she recedes, and then comes spinning round again, like a mad creature. And then—oh, hang it! What do you mean? Chaldea, what are you doing?"

Lambert had some excuse for suddenly bursting into speech, when he cried out vigorously: "Oh, hang it!" for Chaldea whirled right up to him and had laid her arms round his neck, and her lips against his cheek. The music stopped abruptly, with a kind of angry snarl, as if Kara, furious at the sight, had put his wrath into the last broken note. Then all was silent, and the artist found himself imprisoned in the arms of the woman, which were locked round his neck. With an oath he unlinked her fingers and flung her away from him fiercely.

"You fool—you utter fool!" cried Lambert, striving to calm down the beating of his heart, and restrain the racing of his blood, for he was a man, and the sudden action of the gypsy had nearly swept away his self-restraint.

"I love you—I love you," panted Chaldea from the grass, where he had thrown her. "Oh, my beautiful one, I love you."

"You are crazy," retorted Lambert, quivering with many emotions to which he could scarcely put a name, so shaken was he by the experience. "What the devil do you mean by behaving in this way?" and his voice rose in such a gust of anger that Kara, hidden in the wood, rejoiced. He could not understand what was being said, but the tone of the voice was enough for him. He did not know whether Chaldea was cheating the Gentile, or cheating him; but he gathered that in either case, she had been repulsed. The girl knew that also, when her ardent eyes swept across Lambert's white face, and she burst into tears of anger and disappointment.

"Oh, rye, I give you all, and you take nothing," she wailed tearfully.

"I don't want anything. You silly girl, do you think that for one moment I was ever in love with you?"

"I—I—want you—to—to—love me," sobbed Chaldea, grovelling on the grass.

"Then you want an impossibility," and to Lambert's mind's eye there appeared the vision of a calm and beautiful face, far removed in its pure looks from the flushed beauty of the fiery gypsy. To gain control of himself, he took out a cigar and lighted it. But his hand trembled. "You little fool," he muttered, and sauntered, purposely, slowly toward the cottage.

Chaldea gathered herself up with the spring of a tigress, and in a moment was at his elbow with her face black with rage. Her tears had vanished and with them went her softer mood. "You—you reject me," she said in grating tones, and shaking from head to foot as she gripped his shoulder.

"Take away your hand," commanded Lambert sharply, and when she recoiled a pace he faced her squarely. "You must have been drinking," he declared, hoping to insult her into common sense. "What would Kara say if—"

"I don't want Kara. I want you," interrupted Chaldea, her breast heaving, and looking sullenly wrathful.

"Then you can't have me. Why should you think of me in this silly way? We were very good friends, and now you have spoiled everything. I can never have you to sit for me again."

Chaldea's lip drooped. "Never again? Never again?"

"No. It is impossible, since you have chosen to act in this way. Come, you silly girl, be sensible, and—"

"Silly girl! Oh, yes, silly girl," flashed out Chaldea. "And what is she?"

"She?" Lambert stiffened himself. "What do you mean?"

"I mean the Gentile lady. I was under the window this afternoon. I heard all you were talking about."

The man stepped back a pace and clenched his hands. "You—listened?" he asked slowly, and with a very white face.

Chaldea nodded with a triumphant smile.

"Avali! And why not? You have no right to love another man's romi."

"I do not love her," began Lambert, and then checked himself, as he really could not discuss so delicate a matter with this wildcat. "Why did you listen, may I ask?" he demanded, passing his tongue over his dry lips.

"Because I love you, and love is jealous."

Lambert restrained himself by a violent effort from shaking her. "You are talking nonsense," he declared with enforced calmness. "And it is ridiculous for you to love a man who does not care in the least for you."

"It will come—I can wait," insisted Chaldea sullenly.

"If you wait until Doomsday it will make no difference. I don't love you, and I have never given you any reason to think so."

"Chee-chee!" bantered the girl. "Is that because I am not a raclan?"

"A raclan?"

"A married Gentile lady, that is. You love her?"

"I—I—see, here, Chaldea, I am not going to talk over such things with you, as my affairs are not your business."

"They are the business of the Gorgious female's rom."

"Rom? Her husband, you mean. What do you know of—"

"I know that the Gentle Pine is really one of us," interrupted the girl quickly. "Ishmael Hearne is his name."

"Sir Hubert Pine?"

"Ishmael Hearne," insisted Chaldea pertly. "He comes to the fire of the Gentle Romany when he wearies of your Gorgious flesh-pots."

"Pine a gypsy," muttered Lambert, and the memory of that dark, lean, Eastern face impressed him with the belief that what the girl said was true.

"Avali. A true son of the road. He is here."

"Here?" Lambert started violently. "What do you mean?"

"I say what I mean, rye. He you call Pine is in our camp enjoying the old life. Shall I bring him to you?" she inquired demurely.

In a flash Lambert saw his danger, and the danger of Agnes, seeing that the millionaire was as jealous as Othello. However, it seemed to him that honesty was the best policy at the moment. "I shall see him myself later," he declared after a pause. "If you listened, you must know that there is no reason why I should not see him. His wife is my cousin, and paid me a friendly visit—that is all."

"Yes; that is all," mocked the girl contemptuously. "But if I tell him—"

"Tell him what?"

"That you love his romi!"

"He knows that," said Lambert quietly. "And knows also that I am an honorable man. See here, Chaldea, you are dangerous, because this silly love of yours has warped your common sense. You can make a lot of mischief if you so choose, I know well."

"And I shall choose, my golden rye, if you love me not."

"Then set about it at once," said Lambert boldly. "It is best to be honest, my girl. I have done nothing wrong, and I don't intend to do anything wrong, so you can say what you like. To-night I shall go to London, and if Pine, or Hearne, or whatever you call him, wants me, he knows my town address."

"You defy me?" panted Chaldea, her breast rising and falling quickly.

"Yes; truth must prevail in the end. I make no bargain with a spy," and he gave her a contemptuous look, as he strode into the cottage and shut the door with an emphatic bang.

"Hai!" muttered the gypsy between her teeth. "Hatch till the dood wells apré," which means: "Wait until the moon rises!" an ominous saying for Lambert.

CHAPTER VII

THE SECRETARY

"Was ever a man in so uncomfortable a position?"

Lambert asked himself this question as soon as he was safe in his studio, and he found it a difficult one to answer. It was true that what he had said to Agnes, and what Agnes had said to him, was perfectly honest and extremely honorable, considering the state of their feelings. But the conversation had been overheard by an unscrupulous woman, whose jealousy would probably twist innocence into guilt. It was certain that she would go to Pine and give him a garbled version of what had taken place, in which case the danger was great, both to himself and to Agnes. Lambert had spoken bravely enough to the marplot, knowing that he had done no wrong, but now he was by no means sure that he had acted rightly. Perhaps it would have been better to temporize but that would have meant a surrender young to Chaldea's unmaidenly wooing. And, as the man had not a spark of love for her in a heart given entirely to another woman, he was unwilling even to feign playing the part of a lover.

On reflection he still held to his resolution to go to London, thinking that it would be best for him to be out of reach of Agnes while Pine was in the neighborhood. The news that the millionaire was a gypsy had astonished him at first; but now that he considered the man's dark coloring and un-English looks, he quite believed that what Chaldea said was true. And he could understand also that Pine—or Hearne, since that was his true name—would occasionally wish to breathe the free air of heath and road since he had been cradled under a tent, and must at times feel strongly the longing for the old lawless life. But why should he revert to his beginnings so near to his brother-in-law's house, where his wife was staying? "Unless he came to keep an eye on her," murmured Lambert, and unconsciously hit on the very reason of the pseudo-gypsy's presence at Garvington.

After all, it would be best to go to London for a time to wait until he saw what Chaldea would do. Then he could meet Pine and have an understanding with him. The very fact that Pine was a Romany, and was on his native heath, appealed to Lambert as a reason why he should not seek out the man immediately, as he almost felt inclined to do, in order to forestall Chaldea's story. As

Hearne, the millionaire's wild instincts would be uppermost, and he would probably not listen to reason, whereas if the meeting took place in London, Pine would resume to a certain extent his veneer of civilization and would be more willing to do justice.

"Yes," decided Lambert, rising and stretching himself. "I shall go to London and wait to turn over matters in my own mind. I shall say nothing to Agnes until I know what is best to be done about Chaldea. Meanwhile, I shall see the girl and get her to hold her tongue for a time—Damn!" He frowned. "It's making the best of a dangerous situation, but I don't see my way to a proper adjustment yet. The most necessary thing is to gain time."

With this in his mind he hastily packed a gladstone bag, changed into tweeds, and told Mrs. Tribb that he was going to London for a day or so. "I shall get a trap at the inn and drive to the station," he said, as he halted at the door. "You will receive a wire saying when I shall return," and leaving the dry little woman, open-mouthed at this sudden departure, the young man hastened away.

Instead of going straight to the village, he took a roundabout road to the camp on the verge of Abbot's Wood. Here he found the vagrants in a state of great excitement, as Lord Garvington had that afternoon sent notice by a gamekeeper that they were to leave his land the next day. Taken up with his own private troubles, Lambert did not pay much attention to those of the tribe, and looked about for Chaldea. He finally saw her sitting by one of the fires, in a dejected attitude, and touched her on the shoulder. At once, like a disturbed animal, she leaped to her feet.

"The rye!" said Chaldea, with a gasp, and a hopeful look on her face.

"Give me three days before you say anything to Pine," said Lambert in a low voice, and a furtive look round. "You understand."

"No," said the girl boldly. "Unless you mean—"

"Never mind what I mean," interrupted the man hastily, for he was determined not to commit himself. "Will you hold your tongue for three days?"

Chaldea looked hard at his face, upon which the red firelight played brightly, but could not read what was in his mind. However, she thought that the request showed a sign of yielding, and was a mute confession that he knew he was in her power. "I give you three days," she murmured. "But—"

"I have your promise then, so good-bye," interrupted Lambert abruptly, and walked away hastily in the direction of Garvington village. His mind was more or less of a chaos, but at all events he had gained time to reduce the chaos to some sort of order. Still as yet he could not see the outcome of the situation and departed swiftly in order to think it over.

Chaldea made a step or two, as if to follow, but a reflection that she could do no good by talking at the moment, and a certainty that she held him in the hollow of her hand, made her pause. With a hitch of her shapely shoulders she resumed her seat by the fire, brooding sombrely on the way in which this Gentile had rejected her love. Bending her black brows and showing her white teeth like an irritated dog, she inwardly cursed herself for cherishing so foolish a love. Nevertheless, she did not try to overcome it, but resolved to force the Gorgio to her feet. Then she could spurn him if she had a mind to, as he had spurned her. But she well knew, and confessed it to herself with a sigh, that there would be no spurning on her part, since her wayward love was stronger than her pride.

"Did the Gentile bring the gold, my sister?" asked a harsh voice, and she raised her head to see Kara's hairy face bent to her ear.

"No, brother. He goes to Lundra to get the gold. Did I not play my fish in fine style?"

"I took it for truth, sister!" said Kara, looking at her searchingly.

Chaldea nodded wearily. "I am a great witch, as you can see."

"You will be my romi when the gold chinks in our pockets?"

"Yes, for certain, brother. It's a true fortune!"

"Before our camp is changed, sister?" persisted the man greedily.

"No; for to-morrow we may take the road, since the great lord orders us off his land. And yet—" Chaldea stood up, suddenly recollecting what had been said by Pine's wife. "Why should we leave?"

"The rabbit can't kick dust in the fox's face, sister," said Kara, meaning that Garvington was too strong for the gypsies.

"There are rabbits and rabbits," said Chaldea sententiously. "Where is Hearne, brother?"

"In Gentilla's tent with a Gorgious gentleman. He's trading a horse with the swell rye, and wants no meddling with his time, sister."

"I meddle now," snapped Chaldea, and walked away in her usual free and graceful manner. Kara shrugged his shoulders and then took refuge in talking to his violin, to which he related his doubts of the girl's truth. And he smiled grimly, as he thought of the recovered knife which was again snugly hidden under his weather-worn green coat.

Chaldea, who did not stand on ceremony, walked to the end of the camp without paying any attention to the excited gypsies, and flung back the flap of the old woman's tent. Mother Cockleshell was not within, as she had given the use of her abode to Pine and his visitor. This latter was a small, neat man with a smooth, boyish face and reddish hair. He had the innocent expression of a fox-terrier, and rather resembled one. He was neatly and inoffensively dressed in blue serge, and although he did not look exactly like a gentleman, he would have passed for one in a crowd. When Chaldea made her abrupt entrance he was talking volubly to Pine, and the millionaire addressed him—when he answered—as Silver. Chaldea, remembering the conversation she had overheard between Pine and Miss Greeby, speedily reached the conclusion that the neat little man was the secretary referred to therein. Probably he had come to report about Lady Agnes.

"What is it, sister?" demanded Pine sharply, and making a sign that Silver should stop talking.

"Does the camp travel to-morrow, brother?"

"Perhaps, yes," retorted Pine abruptly.

"And perhaps no, brother, if you use your power."

Silver raised his faint eyebrows and looked questioningly at his employer, as if to ask what this cryptic sentence meant. Pine knew only too well, since Chaldea had impressed him thoroughly with the fact that she had overheard many of his secrets. Therefore he did not waste time in argument, but nodded quietly. "Sleep in peace, sister. The camp shall stay, if you wish it."

"I do wish it!" She glanced at Silver and changed her speech to Romany. "The ring will be here," tapping her finger, "in one week if we stay."

"So be it, sister," replied Pine, also in Romany, and with a gleam of satisfaction in his dark eyes. "Go now and return when this Gentile goes. What of the golden Gorgious one?"

"He seeks Lundra this night."

"For the ring, sister?"

Chaldea looked hard at him. "For the ring" she said abruptly, then dropping the tent-flap which she had held all the time, she disappeared.

Silver looked at his master inquiringly, and noted that he seemed very satisfied. "What did she say in Romany?" he asked eagerly.

"True news and new news, and news you never heard of," mocked Pine. "Don't ask questions, Mark."

"But since I am your secretary—"

"You are secretary to Hubert Pine, not to Ishmael Hearne," broke in the other man. "And when Romany is spoken it concerns the last."

Silver's pale-colored, red-rimmed eyes twinkled in an evil manner. "You are afraid that I may learn too much about you."

"You know all that is to be known," retorted Pine sharply. "But I won't have you meddle with my Romany business. A Gentile such as you are cannot understand the chals."

"Try me."

"There is no need. You are my secretary—my trusted secretary—that is quite enough. I pay you well to keep my secrets."

"I don't keep them because you pay me," said Silver quickly, and with a look of meekness belied by the sinister gleam in his pale bluish eyes. "It is devotion that makes me honest. I owe everything to you."

"I think you do," observed Pine quietly. "When I found you in Whitechapel you were only a pauper toymaker."

"An inventor of toys, remember. You made your fortune out of my inventions."

"The three clever toys you invented laid the foundations of my wealth," corrected the millionaire calmly. "But I made my money in the South African share business. And if I hadn't taken up your toys, you would have been now struggling in Whitechapel, since there was no one but me to exploit your brains in the toy-making way. I have rescued you from starvation; I have made you my secretary, and pay you a good salary, and I have introduced you to good society. Yes, you do indeed owe everything to me. Yet—" he paused.

"Yet what?"

"Miss Greeby observed that those who have most cause to be grateful are generally the least thankful to those who befriend them. I am not sure but what she is right."

Silver pushed up his lower lip contemptuously, and a derisive expression came over his clean-shaven face. "Does a clever man like you go to that emancipated woman for experience?"

"Emancipated women are usually very clever," said Pine dryly, "as they combine the logic of the male with the intuition of the female. And I have observed myself, in many cases, that kindness brings out ingratitude."

Silver looked sullen and uneasy. "I don't know why you should talk to me in this strain," he said irritably. "I appreciate what you have done for me, and have no reason to treat you badly. If I did—"

"I would break you," flamed out his employer, angered by the mere thought. "So long as you serve me well, Silver, I am your friend, and I shall treat you as I have always done, with every consideration. But you play any tricks on me, and—" he paused expressively.

"Oh, I won't betray you, if that's what you mean."

"I am quite sure you won't," said the millionaire with emphasis. "For if you do, you return to your original poverty. And remember, Mark, that there is nothing in my life which has any need of concealment."

Silver cast a look round the tent and at the rough clothes of the speaker. "No need of any concealment?" he asked significantly.

"Certainly not," rejoined Pine violently. "I don't wish my gypsy origin to be known in the Gentile world. But if the truth did come to light, there is nothing to be ashamed of. I commit no crime in calling myself by a Gorgio name and in accumulating a fortune. You have no hold over me." The man's look was so threatening that Silver winced.

"I don't hint at any hold over you," he observed mildly. "I am bound to you both by gratitude and self-interest."

"Aha. That last is better. It is just as well that we have come to this understanding. If you—" Pine's speech was ended by a sharp fit of coughing, and Silver looked at his contortions with a thin-lipped smile.

"You'll kill yourself if you live this damp colonial sort of tent-life," was his observation. "Here, take a drink of water."

Pine did so, and wiped his mouth with the sleeve of his rough coat. "You're a Gorgio," he said, weakly, for the fit had shaken him, "and can't understand how a bred and born Romany longs for the smell of the smoke, the space of the open country, and the sound of the kalo jib. However, I did not ask you here to discuss these things, but to take my instructions."

"About Lady Agnes?" asked the secretary, his eyes scintillating.

"You have had those long ago, although, trusting my wife as I do, there was really no need for me to ask you to watch her."

"That is very true. Lady Agnes is exceedingly circumspect."

"Is she happy?"

Silver lifted his shoulders. "As happy as a woman can be who is married to one man while she loves another."

He expected an outburst of anger from his employer, but none came. On the contrary, Pine sighed, restlessly. "Poor soul. I did her a wrong in making her my wife. She would have been happier with Lambert in his poverty."

"Probably! Her tastes don't lie like those of other women in the direction of squandering money. By the way, I suppose, since you are here, that you know Lambert is staying in the Abbot's Wood Cottage?"

"Yes, I know that. And what of it?" demanded the millionaire sharply.

"Nothing; only I thought you would like to know. I fancied you had come here to see if—"

"I did not. I can trust you to see that my wife and Lambert do not meet without spying myself."

"If you love and trust your wife so entirely, I wonder you ask me to spy on her at all," said Silver with a faint sneer.

"She is a woman, and we gypsies have sufficient of the Oriental in us to mistrust even the most honest women. Lambert has not been to The Manor?"

"No. That's a bad sign. He can't trust himself in her presence."

"I'll choke the life out of you, rat that you are, if you talk in such a way about my wife. What you think doesn't matter. Hold your tongue, and come to business. I asked you here to take my instructions."

Silver was rather cowed by this outburst, as he was cunning enough to know precisely how far he could venture with safety. "I am waiting," he observed in sullen tones.

"Garvington—as I knew he would—has ordered us off the land. As the wood is really mine, since I hold it as security, having paid off the mortgage, I don't choose that he should deal with it as though it were his own. Here"—he passed along a letter—"I have written that on my office paper, and you will see that it says, I have heard how gypsies are camping here, and that it is my wish they should remain. Garvington is not to order them off on any pretext whatsoever. You understand?"

"Yes." Silver nodded, and slipped the paper into his breast pocket after a hasty glance at the contents, which were those the writer had stated. "But if Garvington wishes to know why you take such an interest in the gypsies, what am I to say?"

"Say nothing. Simply do what I have told you."

"Garvington may suspect that you are a Romany."

"He won't. He thinks that I'm in Paris, and will never connect me with Ishmael Hearne. If he asks questions when we meet I can tell him my own tale. By the way, why is he so anxious to get rid of the tribe?"

"There have been many burglaries lately in various parts of Hengishire," explained the secretary. "And Garvington is afraid lest the gypsies should be mixed up with them. He thinks, this camp being near, some of the men may break into the house."

"What nonsense! Gypsies steal, I don't deny, but in an open way. They are not burglars, however, and never will be. Garvington has never seen any near The Manor that he should take fright in this way."

"I am not so sure of that. Once or twice I have seen that girl who came to you hanging about the house."

"Chaldea?" Pine started and looked earnestly at his companion.

"Yes. She told Mrs. Belgrove's fortune one day when she met her in the park, and also tried to make Lady Agnes cross her hand with silver for the same purpose. Nothing came of that, however, as your wife refused to have her fortune told."

Pine frowned and looked uneasy, remembering that Chaldea knew of his Gentile masquerading. However, as he could see no reason to suspect that the girl had betrayed him, since she had nothing to gain by taking such a course, he passed the particular incident over. "I must tell Chaldea not to go near The Manor," he muttered.

"You will be wise; and tell the men also. Garvington has threatened to shoot any one who tries to enter his house."

"Garvington's a little fool," said Pine violently. "There is no chance that the Romany will enter his house. He can set his silly mind at rest."

"Well, you're warned," said Silver with an elaborate pretence of indifference.

Pine looked up, growling. "What the devil do you mean, Mark? Do you think that I intend to break in. Fool! A Romany isn't a thief of that sort."

"I fancied from tradition that they were thieves of all sorts," retorted the secretary coolly. "And suppose you took a fancy to come quietly and see your wife?"

"I should never do that in this dress," interrupted the millionaire in a sharp tone. "My wife would then know my true name and birth. I wish to keep that from her, although there is nothing disgraceful in the secret. I wonder why you say that?" he said, looking searchingly at the little man.

"Only because Lambert is in the—"

"Lambert! Lambert! You are always harping on Lambert."

"I have your interest at heart."

Pine laughed doubtfully. "I am not so sure of that. Self-interest rather. I trust my wife—"

"You do, since you make me spy on her," said Silver caustically.

"I trust my wife so far," pursued the other man, "if you will permit me to finish my sentence. There is no need for her to see her cousin, and—as they have kept apart for so long—I don't think there is any chance of their seeking one another's company."

"Absence makes the heart grow fonder," remarked the secretary sententiously. "And you may be living in a fool's paradise. Lambert is within running-away distance of her, remember."

Pine laughed in a raucous manner. "An elopement would have taken place long ago had it been intended," he snapped tartly.

"Don't imagine impossibilities, Mark. Agnes married me for my money, so that I might save the credit of the Lambert family. But for me, Garvington would have passed through the Bankruptcy Court long ago. I have paid off certain mortgages, but I hold them as security for my wife's good behavior. She knows that an elopement with her cousin would mean the ruin of her brother."

"You do, indeed, trust her," observed Silver sarcastically.

"I trust her so far and no further," repeated Pine with an angry snarl. "A Gentile she is, and Gentiles are tricky." He stretched out a slim, brown hand significantly and opened it. "I hold her and Garvington there," and he tapped the palm lightly.

"You don't hold Lambert, and he is the dangerous one."

"Only dangerous if Agnes consents to run away with him, and she won't do that," replied Pine coolly.

"Well, she certainly doesn't care for money."

"She cares for the credit of her family, and gave herself to me, so that the same might be saved."

Silver shrugged his narrow shoulders. "What fools these aristocrats are," he observed pleasantly. "Even if Garvington were sold up he would still have his title and enough to live on in a quiet way."

"Probably. But it was not entirely to save his estates that he agreed to my marriage with his sister," said Pine pointedly and quietly.

"Eh! What?" The little man's foxy face became alive with eager inquiry.

"Nothing," said Pine roughly, and rose heavily to his feet. "Mind your own infernal business, and mine also. Go back and show that letter to Garvington. I want my tribe to stay here."

"My tribe," laughed Silver, scrambling to his feet; and when he took his departure he was still laughing. He wondered what Garvington would say did he know that his sister was married to a full-blooded Romany.

Pine, in the character of a horse-coper, saw him out of the camp, and was staring after him when Chaldea, on the watch, touched his shoulder.

"I come to your tent, brother," she said with very bright eyes.

"Eh? Yes!" Pine aroused himself out of a brown study. "Avali, miri pen. You have things to say to me?"

"Golden things, which have to do with your happiness and mine, brother."

"Hai? A wedding-ring, sister."

"Truly, brother, if you be a true Romany and not the Gentile you call yourself."

CHAPTER VIII

AT MIDNIGHT

Silver's delivery of his employer's orders to Lord Garvington were apparently carried out, for no further intimation was given to the gypsies that they were to vacate Abbot's Wood. The master of The Manor grumbled a good deal at the high tone taken by his brother-in-law, as, having the instincts of a landlord, he strongly objected to the presence of such riff-raff on his estates. However, as Pine had the whip-hand of him, he was obliged to yield, although he could not understand why the man should favor the Romany in this way.

"Some of his infernal philanthropy, I suppose," said Garvington, in a tone of disgust, to the secretary. "Pine's always doing this sort of thing, and people ain't a bit grateful."

"Well," said Silver dryly, "I suppose that's his look-out."

"If it is, let him keep to his own side of the road," retorted the other. "Since I don't interfere with his business, let him not meddle with mine."

"As he holds the mortgage and can foreclose at any moment, it is his business," insisted Silver tartly. "And, after all, the gypsies are doing no very great harm."

"They will if they get the chance. I'd string up the whole lot if I had my way, Silver. Poachers and blackguards every one of them. I know that Pine is always helping rotters in London, but I didn't know that he had any cause to interfere with this lot. How did he come to know about them?"

"Well, Mr. Lambert might have told him," answered the secretary, not unwilling to draw that young man into the trouble. "He is at Abbot's Wood."

"Yes, I lent him the cottage, and this is my reward. He meddles with my business along with Pine. Why can't he shut his mouth?"

"I don't say that Mr. Lambert did tell him, but he might have done so."

"I am quite sure that he did," said Garvington emphatically, and growing red all over his chubby face. "Otherwise Pine would never have heard, since he is in Paris. I shall speak to Lambert."

"You won't find him at home. I looked in at his cottage to pass the time, and his housekeeper said that he had gone to London all of a sudden, this very evening."

"Oh, he'll turn up again," said Garvington carelessly. "He's sick of town, Silver, since—" The little man hesitated.

"Since when?" asked the secretary curiously.

"Never mind," retorted the other gruffly, for he did not wish to mention the enforced marriage of his sister, to Silver. Of course, there was no need to, as Garvington, aware that the neat, foxy-faced man was his brother-in-law's confidential adviser, felt sure that everything was known to him. "I'll leave those blamed gypsies alone meanwhile," finished Garvington, changing and finishing the conversation. "But I'll speak to Pine when I see him."

"He returns from Paris in three weeks," remarked Silver, at which information the gross little lord simply hunched his fat shoulders. Much as Pine had done for him, Garvington hated the man with all the power of his mean and narrow mind, and as the millionaire returned this dislike with a feeling of profound contempt, the two met as seldom as possible. Only Lady Agnes was the link between them, the visible object of sale and barter, which had been sold by one to the other.

It was about this time that the house-party at The Manor began to break up; since it was now the first week in September, and many of the shooters wished to go north for better sport. Many of the men departed, and some of the women, who were due at other country houses; but Mrs. Belgrove and Miss Greeby still remained. The first because she found herself extremely comfortable, and appreciated Garvington's cook; and the second on account of Lambert being in the vicinity. Miss Greeby had been very disappointed to learn that the young man had gone to London, but heard from Mrs. Tribb that he was expected back in three days. She therefore lingered so as to have another conversation with him, and meanwhile haunted the gypsy camp for the purpose of keeping an eye on Chaldea, who was much too beautiful for her peace of mind. Sometimes Silver accompanied her, as the lady had given him to understand that she knew Pine's real rank and name, so the two were made free of the Bohemians and frequently chatted with Ishmael Hearne. But they kept his secret, as did Chaldea; and Garvington had no idea that the man he dreaded and hated—who flung money to him as if he were tossing a bone to a dog—was within speaking distance. If he had known, he would assuredly have guessed the reason why Sir Hubert Pine had interested himself in the doings of a wandering tribe of undesirable creatures.

A week passed away and still, although Miss Greeby made daily inquiries, Lambert did not put in an appearance at the forest cottage. Thinking that he had departed to escape her, she made up her impatient mind to repair to London, and to hunt him up at his club. With this idea she intimated to Lady Garvington that she was leaving The Manor early next morning. The ladies had just left the dinner-table, and were having coffee in the drawing-room when Miss Greeby made this abrupt announcement.

"Oh, my dear," said Lady Garvington, in dismay. "I wish you would change your mind. Nearly everyone has gone, and the house is getting quite dull."

"Thanks ever so much," remarked Mrs. Belgrove lightly. She sat near the fire, for the evening was chilly, and what with paint and powder, and hair-dye, to say nothing of her artistic and carefully chosen dress, looked barely thirty-five in the rosy lights cast by the shaded lamps.

"I don't mean you, dear," murmured the hostess, who was even more untidy and helpless than usual. "You are quite a host in yourself. And that recipe you gave me for Patagonian soup kept Garvington in quite a good humor for ever so long. But the house will be dull for you without Clara."

"Agnes is here, Jane."

"I fear Agnes is not much of an entertainer," said that lady, smiling in a weary manner, for this society chatter bored her greatly.

"That's not to be wondered at," struck in Miss Greeby abruptly. "For of course you are thinking of your husband."

Lady Agnes colored slightly under Miss Greeby's very direct gaze, but replied equably enough, to save appearances, "He is still in Paris."

"When did you last hear from him, dear?" questioned Lady Garvington, more to manufacture conversation than because she really cared.

"Only to-day I had a letter. He is carrying out some special business and will return in two or three weeks."

"You will be glad to see him, no doubt," sneered Miss Greeby.

"I am always glad to see my husband and to be with him," answered Lady Agnes in a dignified manner. She knew perfectly well that Miss Greeby hated her, and guessed the reason, but she was not going to give her any satisfaction by revealing the true feelings of her heart.

"Well, I intend to stay here, Jane, if it's all the same to you," cried Mrs. Belgrove in her liveliest manner and with a side glance, taking in both Miss Greeby and Lady Agnes. "Only this morning I received a chit-chat letter from Mr. Lambert—we are great friends you know—saying that he intended to come here for a few days. Such a delightful man he is."

"Oh, dear me, yes," cried Lady Garvington, starting. "I remember. He wrote yesterday from London, asking if he might come. I told him yes, although I mentioned that we had hardly anyone with us just now."

Miss Greeby looked greatly annoyed, as Mrs. Belgrove maliciously saw, for she knew well that the heiress would now regret having so hastily intimated her approaching departure. What was the expression on Lady Agnes's face, the old lady could not see, for the millionaire's wife shielded it—presumably from the fire—with a large fan of white feathers. Had Mrs. Belgrove been able to read that countenance she would have seen satisfaction written thereon, and would probably have set down the expression to a wrong cause. In reality, Agnes was glad to think that Lambert's promise was being kept, and that he no longer intended to avoid her company so openly.

But if she was pleased, Miss Greeby was not, and still continued to look annoyed, since she had burnt her boats by announcing her departure. And what annoyed her still more than her hasty decision was, that she would leave Lambert in the house along with the rival she most dreaded. Though what the young man could see in this pale, washed-out creature Miss Greeby could not imagine. She glanced at a near mirror and saw her own opulent, full-blown looks clothed in a pale-blue dinner-gown, which went so well—as she inartistically decided, with her ruddy locks, Mrs. Belgrove considered that Miss Greeby looked like a paint-box, or a sunset, or one of Turner's most vivid pictures, but the heiress was very well pleased with herself. Lady Agnes, in her favorite white, with her pale face and serious looks, was but a dull person of the nun persuasion. And Miss Greeby did not think that Lambert cared for nuns, when he had an Amazonian intelligent pal—so she put it—at hand. But, of course, he might prefer dark beauties like Chaldea. Poor Miss Greeby; she was pursuing her wooing under very great difficulties, and became silent in order to think out some way of revoking in some natural manner the information of her departure.

There were other women in the room, who joined in the conversation, and all were glad to hear that Mr. Lambert intended to pay a visit to his cousin, for, indeed, the young man was a general favorite. And then as two or three decided—Mrs. Belgrove amongst the number—there really could be nothing in the report that he loved Lady Agnes still, else he would scarcely come and stay where she was. As for Pine's wife, she was a washed-out creature, who had never really loved her cousin as people had thought. And after all, why should she, since he was so poor, especially when she was married to a millionaire with the looks of an Eastern prince, and manners of quite an original nature, although these were not quite conventional. Oh, yes, there was nothing in the scandal that said

Garvington had sold his sister to bolster up the family property. Lady Agnes was quite happy, and her husband was a dear man, who left her a great deal to her own devices—which he wouldn't have done had he suspected the cousin; and who gave her pots of money to spend. And what more could a sensible woman want?

In this way those in the drawing-room babbled, while Agnes stared into the fire, bracing herself to encounter Lambert, who would surely arrive within the next two or three days, and while Miss Greeby savagely rebuked herself for having so foolishly intimated her departure. Then the men straggled in from their wine, and bridge became the order of the night with some, while others begged for music. After a song or so and the execution of a Beethoven sonata, to which no one paid any attention, a young lady gave a dance after the manner of Maud Allan, to which everyone attended. Then came feats of strength, in which Miss Greeby proved herself to be a female Sandow, and later a number of the guests sojourned to the billiard-room to play. When they grew weary of that, tobogganing down the broad staircase on trays was suggested and indulged in amidst shrieks of laughter. Afterwards, those heated by this horse-play strayed on to the terrace to breathe the fresh air, and flirt in the moonlight. In fact, every conceivable way of passing the time was taken advantage of by these very bored people, who scarcely knew how to get through the long evening.

"They seem to be enjoying themselves, Freddy," said Lady Garvington to her husband, when she drifted against him in the course of attending to her guests. "I really think they find this jolly."

"I don't care a red copper what they find," retorted the little man, who was looking worried, and not quite his usual self. "I wish the whole lot would get out of the house. I'm sick of them."

"Ain't you well, Freddy? I knew that Patagonian soup was too rich for you."

"Oh, the soup was all right—ripping soup," snorted Freddy, smacking his lips over the recollection. "But I'm bothered over Pine."

"He isn't ill, is he?" questioned Lady Garvington anxiously. She liked her brother-in-law, who was always kind to her.

"No, hang him; nothing worse than his usual lung trouble, I suppose. But he is in Paris, and won't answer my letters."

"Letters, Freddy dear."

"Yes, Jane dear," he mocked. "Hang it, I want money, and he won't stump up. I can't even get an answer."

"Speak to Mr. Silver."

"Damn Mr. Silver!"

"Well, I'm sure, Frederick, you needn't swear at me," said poor, wan Lady Garvington, drawing herself up. "Mr. Silver is very kind. He went to that gypsy camp and found out how they cook hedgehog. That will be a new dish for you, dear. You haven't eaten hedgehog."

"No. And what's more, I don't intend to eat it. But you may as well tell me how these gypsies cook it," and Freddy listened with both his red ears to the description, on hearing which he decided that his wife might instruct the cook how to prepare the animal. "But no one will eat it but me."

Lady Garvington shuddered. "I shan't touch it myself. Those horrid snails you insisted on being cooked a week ago made me quite ill. You are always trying new experiments, Freddy."

"Because I get so tired of every-day dishes," growled Lord Garvington. "These cooks have no invention. I wish I'd lived in Rome when they had those banquets you read of in Gibbon."

"Did he write a book on cookery?" asked Lady Garvington very naturally.

"No. He turned out a lot of dull stuff about wars and migrations of tribes: you are silly, Jane."

"What's that about migration of tribes?" asked Mrs. Belgrove, who was in a good humor, as she had won largely at bridge. "You don't mean those dear gypsies at Abbot's Wood do you, Lord Garvington? I met one of them the other day—quite a girl and very pretty in a dark way. She told my fortune, and said that I would come in for a lot of money. I'm sure I hope so," sighed Mrs. Belgrove. "Celestine is so expensive, but no one can fit me like she can. And she knows it, and takes advantage, the horrid creature."

"I wish the tribe of gypsies would clear out," snapped Freddy, standing before the fire and glaring at the company generally. "I know they'll break in here and rob."

"Well," drawled Silver, who was hovering near, dressed so carefully that he looked more of a foxy, neat bounder than ever. "I have noticed that some of the brutes have been sneaking round the place."

Mrs. Belgrove shrieked. "Oh, how lucky I occupy a bedroom on the third floor. Just like a little bird in its tiny-weeny nest. They can't get at me there, can they, Lord Garvington?"

"They don't want you," observed Miss Greeby in her deep voice. "It's your diamonds they'd like to get."

"Oh!" Mrs. Belgrove shrieked again. "Lock my diamonds up in your strong room, Lord Garvington. Do! do! do! To please poor little me," and she effusively clasped her lean hands, upon which many of the said diamonds glittered.

"I don't think there is likely to be any trouble with these poor gypsies, Mrs. Belgrove," remarked Lady Agnes negligently. "Hubert has told me a great deal about them, and they are really not so bad as people make out."

"Your husband can't know anything of such ragtags," said Miss Greeby, looking at the beautiful, pale face, and wondering if she really had any suspicion that Pine was one of the crew she mentioned.

"Oh, but Hubert does," answered Lady Agnes innocently. "He has met many of them when he has been out helping people. You have no idea, any of you, how good Hubert is," she added, addressing the company generally. "He walks on the Embankment sometimes on winter nights and gives the poor creatures money. And in the country I have often seen him stop to hand a shilling to some tramp in the lanes."

"A gypsy for choice," growled Miss Greeby, marvelling that Lady Agnes could not see the resemblance between the tramps' faces and that of her own husband. "However, I hope Pine's darlings won't come here to rob. I'll fight for my jewels, I can promise you."

One of the men laughed. "I shouldn't like to get a blow from your fist."

Miss Greeby smiled grimly, and looked at his puny stature. "Women have to protect themselves from men like you," she said, amidst great laughter, for the physical difference between her and the man was quite amusing.

"It's all very well talking," said Garvington crossly. "But I don't trust these gypsies."

"Why don't you clear them off your land then?" asked Silver daringly.

Garvington glared until his gooseberry eyes nearly fell out of his red face. "I'll clear everyone to bed, that's what I'll do," he retorted, crossing the room to the middle French window of the drawing-room. "I wish you fellows would stop your larking out there," he cried. "It's close upon midnight, and all decent people should be in bed."

"Since when have you joined the Methodists, Garvington?" asked an officer who had come over from some twelve-mile distant barracks to pass the night, and a girl behind him began to sing a hymn.

Lady Agnes frowned. "I wish you wouldn't do that, Miss Ardale," she said in sharp rebuke, and the girl had the sense to be silent, while Garvington fussed over the closing of the window shutters.

"Going to stand a siege?" asked Miss Greeby, laughing. "Or do you expect burglars, particularly on this night."

"I don't expect them at all," retorted the little man. "But I tell you I hate the idea of these lawless gypsies about the place. Still, if anyone comes," he added grimly, "I shall shoot."

"Then the attacking person or party needn't bother," cried the officer. "I shouldn't mind standing up to your fire, myself, Garvington."

With laughter and chatter and much merriment at the host's expense, the guests went their several ways, the women to chat in one another's dressing-rooms and the men to have a final smoke and a final drink. Garvington, with two footmen, and his butler, went round the house, carefully closing all the shutters, and seeing that all was safe. His sister rather marvelled at this excessive precaution, and said as much to her hostess.

"It wouldn't matter if the gypsies did break in," she said when alone with Lady Garvington in her own bedroom. "It would be some excitement, for all these people must find it very dull here."

"I'm sure I do my best, Agnes," said the sister-in-law plaintively.

"Of course, you do, you poor dear," said the other, kissing her. "But Garvington always asks people here who haven't two ideas. A horrid, rowdy lot they are. I wonder you stand it."

"Garvington asks those he likes, Agnes."

"I see. He hasn't any brains, and his guests suit him for the same reason."

"They eat a great deal," wailed Lady Garvington. "I'm sure I might as well be a cook. All my time is taken up with feeding them."

"Well, Freddy married you, Jane, because you had a genius for looking after food. Your mother was much the same; she always kept a good table." Lady Agnes laughed. "Yours was a most original wooing, Jane."

"I'd like to live on bread and water for my part, Agnes."

"Put Freddy on it, dear. He's getting too stout. I never thought that gluttony was a crime. But when I look at Freddy"—checking her speech, she spread out her hands with an ineffable look—"I'm glad that Noel is coming," she ended, rather daringly. "At least he will be more interesting than any of these frivolous people you have collected."

Lady Garvington looked at her anxiously. "You don't mind Noel coming?"

"No, dear. Why should I?"

"Well you see, Agnes, I fancied—"

"Don't fancy anything. Noel and I entirely understand one another."

"I hope," blurted out the other woman, "that it is a right understanding?"

Agnes winced, and looked at her with enforced composure. "I am devoted to my husband," she said, with emphasis. "And I have every reason to be. He has kept his part of the bargain, so I keep mine. But," she added with a pale smile, "when I think how I sold myself to keep up the credit of the family, and now see Freddy entertaining this riff-raff, I am sorry that I did not marry Noel, whom I loved so dearly."

"That would have meant our ruin," bleated Lady Garvington, sadly.

"Your ruin is only delayed, Jane. Freddy is a weak, self-indulgent fool, and is eating his way into the next world. It will be a happy day for you when an apoplectic fit makes you a widow."

"My dear," the wife was shocked, "he is your brother."

"More's the pity. I have no illusions about Freddy, Jane, and I don't think you have either. Now, go away and sleep. It's no use lying awake thinking over to-morrow's dinner. Give Freddy the bread and water you talked about."

Lady Garvington laughed in a weak, aimless way, and then kissed her sister-in-law with a sigh, after which she drifted out of the room in her usual vague manner. Very shortly the clock over the stables struck midnight, and by that time Garvington the virtuous had induced all his men guests to go to bed. The women chatted a little longer, and then, in their turn, sought repose. By half-past twelve the great house was in complete darkness, and bulked a mighty mass of darkness in the pale September moonlight.

Lady Agnes got to bed quickly, and tired out by the boredom of the evening, quickly fell asleep. Suddenly she awoke with all her senses on the alert, and with a sense of vague danger hovering round. There were sounds of running feet and indistinct oaths and distant cries, and she could have sworn that a pistol-shot had startled her from slumber. In a moment she was out of bed and ran to open her window. On looking out she saw that the moonlight was very brilliant, and in it beheld a tall man running swiftly from the house. He sped down the broad path, and just when he was abreast of a miniature shrubbery, she heard a second shot, which seemed to be fired there-from. The man staggered, and stumbled and fell. Immediately afterwards, her brother—she recognized his voice raised in anger—ran out of the house, followed by some of the male guests. Terrified by the sight and the sound of the shots, Lady Agnes huddled on her dressing-gown hastily, and thrust her bare feet into slippers. The next moment she was out of her bedroom and down the stairs. A wild idea had entered her mind that perhaps Lambert had come secretly to The Manor, and had been shot by Garvington in mistake for a burglar. The corridors and the hall were filled with guests more or less lightly attired, mostly women, white-faced and startled. Agnes paid no attention to their shrieks, but hurried into the side passage which terminated at the door out of which her brother had left the house. She went outside also and made for the group round the fallen man.

"What is it? who is it?" she asked, gasping with the hurry and the fright.

"Go back, Agnes, go back," cried Garvington, looking up with a distorted face, strangely pale in the moonlight.

"But who is it? who has been killed?" She caught sight of the fallen man's countenance and shrieked. "Great heavens! it is Hubert; is he dead?"

"Yes," said Silver, who stood at her elbow. "Shot through the heart."

CHAPTER IX

AFTERWARDS

With amazing and sinister rapidity the news spread that a burglar had been shot dead while trying to raid The Manor. First, the Garvington villagers learned it; then it became the common property of the neighborhood, until it finally reached the nearest county town, and thus brought the police on the scene. Lord Garvington was not pleased when the local inspector arrived, and intimated as much in a somewhat unpleasant fashion. He was never a man who spared those in an inferior social position.

"It is no use your coming over, Darby," he said bluntly to the red-haired police officer, who was of Irish extraction. "I have sent to Scotland Yard."

"All in good time, my lord," replied the inspector coolly. "As the murder has taken place in my district I have to look into the matter, and report to the London authorities, if it should be necessary."

"What right have you to class the affair as a murder?" inquired Garvington.

"I only go by the rumors I have heard, my lord. Some say that you winged the man and broke his right arm. Others tell me that a second shot was fired in the garden, and it was that which killed Ishmael Hearne."

"It is true, Darby. I only fired the first shot, as those who were with me will tell you. I don't know who shot in the garden, and apparently no one else does. It was this unknown individual in the garden that killed Hearne. By the way, how did you come to hear the name?"

"Half a dozen people have told me, my lord, along with the information I have just given you. Nothing else is talked of far and wide."

"And it is just twelve o'clock," muttered the stout little lord, wiping his scarlet face pettishly. "Ill news travels fast. However, as you are here, you may as well take charge of things until the London men arrive."

"The London men aren't going to usurp my privileges, my lord," said Darby, firmly. "There's no sense in taking matters out of my hands. And if you will pardon my saying so, I should have been sent for in the first instance."

"I daresay," snapped Garvington, coolly. "But the matter is too important to be left in the hands of a local policeman."

Darby was nettled, and his hard eyes grew angry. "I am quite competent to deal with any murder, even if it is that of the highest in England, much less with the death of a common gypsy."

"That's just where it is, Darby. The common gypsy who has been shot happens to be my brother-in-law."

"Sir Hubert Pine?" questioned the inspector, thoroughly taken aback.

"Yes! Of course I didn't know him when I fired, or I should not have done so, Darby. I understood, and his wife, my sister, understood, that Sir Hubert was in Paris. It passes my comprehension to guess why he should have come in the dead of night, dressed as a gypsy, to raid my house."

"Perhaps it was a bet," said Darby, desperately puzzled.

"Bet, be hanged! Pine could come openly to this place whenever he liked. I never was so astonished in my life as when I saw him lying dead near the shrubbery. And the worst of it is, that my sister ran out and saw him also. She fainted and has been in bed ever since, attended by Lady Garvington."

"You had no idea that the man you shot was Sir Hubert, my lord?"

"Hang it, no! Would I have shot him had I guessed who he was?"

"No, no, my lord! of course not," said the officer hastily. "But as I have come to take charge of the case, you will give me a detailed account of what has taken place."

"I would rather wait until the Scotland Yard fellows come," grumbled Garvington, "as I don't wish to repeat my story twice. Still, as you are on the spot, I may as well ask your advice. You may be able to throw some light on the subject. I'm hanged if I can."

Darby pulled out his notebook. "I am all attention, my lord."

Garvington plunged abruptly into his account, first having looked to see if the library door was firmly closed. "As there have been many burglaries lately in this part of the world," he said, speaking with deliberation, "I got an idea into my head that this house might be broken into."

"Natural enough, my lord," interposed Darby, glancing round the splendid room. "A historic house such as this is, would tempt any burglar."

"So I thought," remarked the other, pleased that Darby should agree with him so promptly. "And I declared several times, within the hearing of many people, that if a raid was made, I should shoot the first man who tried to enter. Hang it, an Englishman's house is his castle, and no man has a right to come in without permission."

"Quite so, my lord. But the punishment of the burglar should be left to the law," said the inspector softly.

"Oh, the deuce take the law! I prefer to execute my own punishments. However, to make a long story short, I grew more afraid of a raid when these gypsies came to camp at Abbot's Wood, as they are just the sort of scoundrels who would break in and steal."

"Why didn't you order them off your land?" asked the policeman, alertly.

"I did, and then my brother-in-law sent a message through his secretary, who is staying here, asking me to allow them to remain. I did."

"Why did Sir Hubert send that message, my lord?"

"Hang it, man, that's just what I am trying to learn, and I am the more puzzled because he came last night dressed as a gypsy."

"He must be one," said Darby, who had seen Pine and now recalled his dark complexion and jetty eyes. "It seems, from what I have been told, that he stopped at the Abbot's Wood camp under the name of Ishmael Hearne."

"So Silver informed me."

"Who is he?"

"Pine's secretary, who knows all his confidential affairs. Silver declared, when the secret could be kept no longer, that Pine was really a gypsy, called Ishmael Hearne. Occasionally longing for the old life, he stepped down from his millionaire pedestal and mixed with his own people. When he was supposed to be in Paris, he was really with the gypsies, so you can now understand why he sent the message asking me to let these vagrants stay."

"You told me a few moments ago, that you could not understand that message, my lord," said Darby quickly, and looking searchingly at the other man. Garvington grew a trifle confused. "Did I? Well, to tell you the truth, Darby, I'm so mixed up over the business that I can't say what I do know, or what I don't know. You'd better take all I tell you with a grain of salt until I am quite myself again."

"Natural enough, my lord," remarked the inspector again, and quite believed what he said. "And the details of the murder?"

"I went to bed as usual," said Garvington, wearily, for the events of the night had tired him out, "and everyone else retired some time about midnight. I went round with the footmen and the butler to see that everything was safe, for I was too anxious to let them look after things without me. Then I heard a noise of footsteps on the gravel outside, just as I was dropping off to sleep—"

"About what time was that, my lord?"

"Half-past one o'clock; I can't be certain as to a minute. I jumped up and laid hold of my revolver, which was handy. I always kept it beside me in case of a burglary. Then I stole downstairs in slippers and pajamas to the passage,—oh, here." Garvington rose quickly. "Come with me and see the place for yourself!"

Inspector Darby put on his cap, and with his notebook still in his hand, followed the stout figure of his guide. Garvington led him through the entrance hall and into a side-passage, which terminated in a narrow door. There was no one to spy on them, as the master of the house had sent all the servants to their own quarters, and the guests were collected in the drawing-room and smoking-room, although a few of the ladies remained in their bedrooms, trying to recover from the night's experience.

"I came down here," said Garvington, opening the door, "and heard the burglar, as I thought he was, prowling about on the other side. I threw open the door in this way and the man plunged forward to enter. I fired, and got him in the right arm, for I saw it swinging uselessly by his side as he departed."

"Was he in a hurry?" asked Darby, rather needlessly.

"He went off like greased lightning. I didn't follow, as I thought that others of his gang might be about, but closing the door again I shouted blue murder. In a few minutes everyone came down, and while I was waiting—it all passed in a flash, remember, Darby—I heard a second shot. Then the servants and my friends came and we ran out, to find the man lying by that shrubbery quite dead. I turned him over and had just grasped the fact that he was my brother-in-law, when Lady Agnes ran out. When she learned the news she naturally fainted. The women carried her back to her room, and we took the body of Pine into the house. A doctor came along this morning—for I sent for a doctor as soon as it was dawn—and said that Pine had been shot through the heart."

"And who shot him?" asked Darby sagely.

Garvington pointed to the shrubbery. "Someone was concealed there," he declared.

"How do you know, that, my lord?"

"My sister, attracted by my shot, jumped out of bed and threw up her window. She saw the man—of course she never guessed that he was Pine—running down the path and saw him fall by the shrubbery when the second shot was fired."

"Her bedroom is then on this side of the house, my lord?"

"Up there," said Garvington, pointing directly over the narrow door, which was painted a rich blue color, and looked rather bizarre, set in the puritanic greyness of the walls. "My own bedroom is further along towards the right. That is why I heard the footsteps so plainly on this gravel." And he stamped hard, while with a wave of his hand he invited the inspector to examine the surroundings.

Darby did so with keen eyes and an alert brain. The two stood on the west side of the mansion, where it fronted the three-miles distant Abbot's Wood. The Manor was a heterogeneous-looking sort of place, suggesting the whims and fancies of many generations, for something was taken away here, and something was taken away there, and this had been altered, while that had been left in its original state, until the house seemed to be made up of all possible architectural styles. It was a tall building of three stories, although the flattish red-tiled roofs took away somewhat from its height, and spread over an amazing quantity of land. As Darby thought, it could have housed a regiment, and must have cost something to keep up. As wind and weather and time had mellowed its incongruous parts into one neutral tint, it looked odd and attractive. Moss and lichen, ivy and Virginia creeper—this last flaring in crimson glory—clothed the massive stone walls with a gracious mantle of natural beauty. Narrow stone steps, rather chipped, led down from the blue door to the broad, yellow path, which came round the rear of the house and swept down hill in a wide curve, past the miniature shrubbery, right into the bosom of the park.

"This path," explained Garvington, stamping again, "runs right through the park to a small wicket gate set in the brick wall, which borders the high road, Darby."

"And that runs straightly past Abbot's Wood," mused the inspector. "Of course, Sir Hubert would know of the path and the wicket gate?"

"Certainly; don't be an ass, Darby," cried Garvington petulantly. "He has been in this house dozens of times and knows it as well as I do myself. Why do you ask so obvious a question?"

"I was only wondering if Sir Hubert came by the high road to the wicket gate you speak of, Lord Garvington."

"That also is obvious," retorted the other, irritably. "Since he wished to come here, he naturally would take the easiest way."

"Then why did he not enter by the main avenue gates?"

"Because at that hour they would be shut, and—since it is evident that his visit was a secret one—he would have had to knock up the lodge-keeper."

"Why was his visit a secret one?" questioned Darby pointedly.

"That is the thing that puzzles me. Anything more?"

"Yes? Why should Sir Hubert come to the blue door?"

"I can't answer that question, either. The whole reason of his being here, instead of in Paris, is a mystery to me."

"Oh, as to that last, the reply is easy," remarked the inspector. "Sir Hubert wished to revert to his free gypsy life, and pretended to be in Paris, so that he would follow his fancy without the truth becoming known. But why he should come on this particular night, and by this particular path to this particular door, is the problem I have to solve!"

"Quite so, and I only hope that you will solve it, for the sake of my sister."

Darby reflected for a moment or so. "Did Lady Agnes ask her husband to come here to see her privately?"

"Hang it, no man!" cried Garvington, aghast. "She believed, as we all did, that her husband was in Paris, and certainly never dreamed that he was masquerading as a gypsy three miles away."

"There was no masquerading about the matter, my lord," said Darby, dryly; "since Sir Hubert really was a gypsy called Ishmael Hearne. That fact will come out at the inquest."

"It has come out now: everyone knows the truth. And a nice thing it is for me and Lady Agnes."

"I don't think you need worry about that, Lord Garvington. The honorable way in which the late Sir Hubert attained rank and gained wealth will reflect credit on his humble origin. When the papers learn the story—"

"Confound the papers!" interrupted Garvington fretfully. "I sincerely hope that they won't make too great a fuss over the business."

The little man's hope was vain, as he might have guessed that it would be, for when the news became known in Fleet Street, the newspapers were only too glad to discover an original sensation for the dead season. Every day journalists and special correspondents were sent down in such numbers that the platform of Wanbury Railway Station was crowded with them. As the town—it was the chief town of Hengishire—was five miles away from the village of Garvington, every possible kind of vehicle was used to reach the scene of the crime, and The Manor became a rendezvous for all the morbid people, both in the neighborhood and out of it. The reporters in particular poked and pried all over the place, passing from the great house to the village, and thence to the gypsy camp on the borders of Abbot's Wood. From one person and another they learned facts, which were published with such fanciful additions that they read like fiction. On the authority of Mother Cockleshell—who was not averse to earning a few shillings—a kind of Gil Blas tale was put into print, and the wanderings of Ishmael Hearne were set forth in the picturesque style of a picarooning romance. But of the time when the adventurous gypsy assumed his Gentile name, the Romany could tell nothing, for obvious reasons. Until the truth became known, because of the man's tragic and unforeseen death, those in the camp were not aware that he was a Gorgio millionaire. But where the story of Mother Cockleshell left off, that of Mark Silver began, for the secretary had been connected with his employer almost from the days of Hearne's first exploits as Pine in London. And Silver—who also charged for the blended fact and fiction which he supplied—freely related all he knew.

"Hearne came to London and called himself Hubert Pine," he stated frankly, and not hesitating to confess his own lowly origin. "We met when I was starving as a toymaker in Whitechapel. I invented some penny toys, which Pine put on the market for me. They were successful and he made money. I am bound to confess that he paid me tolerably well, although he certainly took the lion's share. With the money he made in this way, he speculated in South African shares, and, as the boom was then on, he simply coined gold. Everything he touched turned into cash, and however deeply he plunged into the money market, he always came out top in the end. By turning over his money and re-investing it, and by fresh speculations, he became a millionaire in a wonderfully short space of time. Then he made me his secretary and afterwards took up politics. The Government gave him a knighthood for services rendered to his party, and he became a well-known figure in the world of finance. He married Lady Agnes Lambert, and—and—that's all."

"You were aware that he was a gypsy, Mr. Silver?" asked the reporter.

"Oh, yes. I knew all about his origin from the first days of our acquaintanceship. He asked me to keep his true name and rank secret. As it was none of my business, I did so. At times Hearne—or rather Pine, as I know him best by that name—grew weary of civilization, and then would return to his own life of the tent and road. No one suspected amongst the Romany that he was anything else but a horse-coper. He always pretended to be in Paris, or Berlin, on financial affairs, when he went back to his people, and I transacted all business during his absence."

"You knew that he was at the Abbot's Wood camp?"

"Certainly. I saw him there once or twice to receive instructions about business. I expostulated with him for being so near the house where his brother-in-law and wife were living, as I pointed out that the truth might easily become known. But Pine merely said that his safety in keeping his secret lay in his daring to run the risk."

"Have you any idea that Sir Hubert intended to come by night to Lord Garvington's house?"

"Not the slightest. In fact, I told him that Lord Garvington was afraid of burglars, and had threatened to shoot any man who tried to enter the house."

All this Silver said in a perfectly frank, free-and-easy manner, and also related how the dead man had instructed him to ask Garvington to allow the gypsies to remain in the wood. The reporter published the interview with sundry comments of his own, and it was read with great avidity by the public at large and by the many friends of the millionaire, who were surprised to learn of the double life led by the man. Of course, there was nothing disgraceful in Pine's past as Ishmael Hearne, and all attempts to discover something shady about his antecedents were vain. Yet—as was pointed out—there must have been something wrong, else the adventurer, as he plainly was, would not have met so terrible a death. But in spite of every one's desire to find fire to account for the smoke, nothing to Pine's disadvantage could be learned. Even at the inquest, and when the matter was thoroughly threshed out, the dead man's character proved to be honorable, and—save in the innocent concealment of his real name and origin—his public and private life was all that could be desired. The whole story was not criminal, but truly romantic, and the final tragedy gave a grim touch to what was regarded, even by the most censorious, as a picturesque narrative.

In spite of all his efforts, Inspector Darby, of Wanbury, could produce no evidence likely to show who had shot the deceased. Lord Garvington, under the natural impression that Pine was a burglar, had certainly wounded him in the right arm, but it was the second shot, fired by some one outside the house, which had pierced the heart. This was positively proved by the distinct evidence of Lady Agnes herself. She rose from her sick-bed to depose how she had opened her window, and had seen the actual death of the unfortunate man, whom she little guessed was her husband. The burglar—as she reasonably took him to be—was running down the path when she first caught sight of him, and after the first shot had been fired. It was the second shot, which came from the shrubbery—marked on the plan placed before the Coroner and jury—which had laid the fugitive low. Also various guests and servants stated that they had arrived in the passage in answer to Lord Garvington's outcries, to find that he had closed the door pending their coming. Some had even heard the second shot while descending the stairs. It was proved, therefore, in a very positive manner, that the master of the house had not murdered the supposed robber.

"I never intended to kill him," declared Garvington when his evidence was taken. "All I intended to do, and all I did do, was to wing him, so that he might be captured on the spot, or traced later. I closed the door after firing the shot, as I fancied that he might have had some accomplices with him, and I wished to make myself safe until assistance arrived."

"You had no idea that the man was Sir Hubert Pine?" asked a juryman.

"Certainly not. I should not have fired had I recognized him. The moment I opened the door he flung himself upon me. I fired and he ran away. It was not until we all went out and found him dead by the shrubbery that I recognized my brother-in-law. I thought he was in Paris."

Inspector Darby deposed that he had examined the shrubbery, and had noted broken twigs here and there, which showed that some one must have been concealed behind the screen of laurels. The grass—somewhat long in the thicket—had been trampled. But nothing had been discovered likely to lead to the discovery of the assassin who had been ambushed in this manner.

"Are there no footmarks?" questioned the Coroner.

"There has been no rain for weeks to soften the ground," explained the witness, "therefore it is impossible to discover any footmarks. The broken twigs and trampled grass show that some one was hidden in the shrubbery, but when this person left the screen of laurels, there is nothing to show in which direction the escape was made."

And indeed all the evidence was useless to trace the criminal. The Manor had been bolted and barred by Lord Garvington himself, along with some footmen and his butler, so no one within could have fired the second shot. The evidence of Mother Cockleshell, of Chaldea, and of various other gypsies, went to show that no one had left the camp on that night with the exception of Hearne, and even his absence had not been made known until the fact of the death was made public next morning. Hearne, as several of the gypsies stated, had retired about eleven to his tent and had said nothing about going to The Manor, much less about leaving the camp. Silver's statements revealed nothing, since, far from seeking his brother-in-law's house, Pine had pointedly declared that in order to keep his secret he would be careful not to go near the place.

"And Pine had no enemies to my knowledge who desired his death," declared the secretary. "We were so intimate that had his life been in danger he certainly would have spoken about it to me."

"You can throw no light on the darkness?" asked the Coroner hopelessly.

"None," said the witness. "Nor, so far as I can see, is any one else able to throw any light on the subject. Pine's secret was not a dishonorable one, as he was such an upright man that no one could have desired to kill him."

Apparently there was no solution to the mystery, as every one concluded, when the evidence was fully threshed out. An open verdict was brought in, and the proceedings ended in this unsatisfactory manner.

"Wilful murder against some person or persons unknown," said Lambert, when he read the report of the inquest in his St. James's Street rooms. "Strange. I wonder who cut the Gordian knot of the rope which bound Agnes to Pine?"

He could find no reply to this question, nor could any one else.

CHAPTER X

A DIFFICULT POSITION

Lord Garvington was not a creditable member of the aristocracy, since his vices greatly exceeded his virtues. With a weak nature, and the tastes of a sybarite, he required a great deal of money to render him happy. Like the immortal Becky Sharp, he could have been fairly honest if possessed of a large income; but not having it he stopped short of nothing save actual criminality in order to indulge his luxurious tastes to the full. Candidly speaking, he had already overstepped the mark when he altered the figures of a check his brother-in-law had given him, and, had not Pine been so generous, he would have undoubtedly occupied an extremely unpleasant position. However, thanks to Agnes, the affair had been hushed up, and with characteristic promptitude, Garvington had conveniently forgotten how nearly he had escaped the iron grip of Justice. In fact, so entirely did it slip his memory that—on the plea of Pine's newly discovered origin—he did not desire the body to be placed in the family vault. But the widow wished to pay this honor to her husband's remains, and finally got her own way in the matter, for the simple reason that now she was the owner of Pine's millions Garvington did not wish to offend her. But, as such a mean creature would, he made capital out of the concession.

"Since I do this for you, Agnes," he said bluntly, when the question was being decided, "you must do something for me."

"What do you wish me to do?"

"Ah—hum—hey—ho!" gurgled Garvington, thinking cunningly that it was too early yet to exploit her. "We can talk about it when the will has been read, and we know exactly how we stand. Besides your grief is sacred to me, my dear. Shut yourself up and cry."

Agnes had a sense of humor, and the blatant hypocrisy of the speech made her laugh outright in spite of the genuine regret she felt for her husband's tragic death. Garvington was quite shocked. "Do you forget that the body is yet in the house?" he asked with heavy solemnity.

"I don't forget anything," retorted Agnes, becoming scornfully serious. "Not even that you count on me to settle your wretched financial difficulties out of poor Hubert's money."

"Of course you will, my dear. You are a Lambert."

"Undoubtedly; but I am not necessarily a fool."

"Oh, I can't stop and hear you call yourself such a name," said Garvington, ostentatiously dense to her true meaning. "It is hysteria that speaks, and not my dear sister. Very natural when you are so grieved. We are all mortal."

"You are certainly silly in addition," replied the widow, who knew how useless it was to argue with the man. "Go away and don't worry me. When poor Hubert is buried, and the will is read, I shall announce my intentions."

"Intentions! Intentions!" muttered the corpulent little lord, taking a hasty departure out of diplomacy. "Surely, Agnes won't be such a fool as to let the family estates go."

It never struck him that Pine might have so worded the will that the inheritance he counted upon might not come to the widow, unless she chose to fulfil a certain condition. But then he never guessed the jealousy with which the hot-blooded gypsy had regarded the early engagement of Agnes and Lambert. If he had done so, he assuredly would not have invited the young man down to the funeral. But he did so, and talked about doing so, with a frequent mention that the body was to rest in the sacred vault of the Lamberts so that every one should applaud his generous humility.

"Poor Pine was only a gypsy," said Garvington, on all and every occasion. "But I esteemed him as a good and honest man. He shall have every honor shown to his memory. Noel and I, as representatives of his wife, my dear sister, shall follow him to the Lambert vault, and there, with my ancestors, the body of this honorable, though humble, man shall rest until the Day of Judgment."

A cynic in London laughed when the speech was reported to him. "If Garvington is buried in the same vault," he said contemptuously, "he will ask Pine for money, as soon as they rise to attend the Great Assizes!" which bitter remark showed that the little man could not induce people to believe him so disinterested as he should have liked them to consider him.

However, in pursuance of this artful policy, he certainly gave the dead man, what the landlady of the village inn called, "a dressy funeral." All that could be done in the way of pomp and ceremony was done, and the procession which followed Ishmael Hearne to the grave was an extraordinarily long one. The villagers came because, like all the lower orders, they loved the excitement of an interment; the gypsies from the camp followed, since the deceased was of their blood; and many people in financial and social circles came down from London for the obvious reason that Pine was a well-known figure in the City and the West End, and also a member of Parliament. As for Lambert, he put in an appearance, in response to his cousin's invitation, unwillingly enough, but in order to convince Agnes that he had every desire to obey her commands. People could scarcely think that Pine had been jealous of the early engagement to Agnes, when her former lover attended the funeral of a successful rival.

Of course, the house party at The Manor had broken up immediately after the inquest. It would have disintegrated before only that Inspector Darby insisted that every one should remain for examination in connection with the late tragical occurrence. But in spite of questioning and cross-questioning, nothing had been learned likely to show who had murdered the millionaire. There was a great deal of talk after the body had been placed in the Lambert vault, and there was more talk in the newspapers when an account was given of the funeral. But neither by word of mouth, nor in print, was any suggestion made likely to afford the slightest clue to the name or the whereabouts of the assassin. Having regard to Pine's romantic career, it was thought by some that the act was one of revenge by a gypsy jealous that the man should attain to such affluence, while others hinted that the motive for the crime was to be found in connection with the millionaire's career as a Gentile. Gradually, as all conjecture proved futile, the gossip died away, and other events usurped the interest of the public. Pine, who was really Hearne, had been murdered and buried; his assassin would never be discovered, since the trail was too well hidden; and Lady Agnes inherited at least two millions on which she would probably marry her cousin and so restore the tarnished splendors of the Lambert family. In this way the situation was summed up by the gossips, and then they began to talk of something else. The tragedy was only a nine minutes' wonder after all.

The gossips both in town and country were certainly right in assuming that the widow inherited the vast property of her deceased husband. But what they did not know was that a condition attached to such inheritance irritated Agnes and caused Garvington unfeigned alarm. Pine's solicitor—he was called Jarwin and came from a stuffy little office in Chancery Lane—called Garvington aside, when the mourners returned from the funeral, and asked that the reading of the will might be confined to a few people whom he named.

"There is a condition laid down by the testator which need not be made public," said Mr. Jarwin blandly. "A proposition which, if possible, must be kept out of print."

Garvington, with a sudden recollection of his iniquity in connection with the falsified check, did not dare to ask questions, but hastily summoned the people named by the lawyer. As these were the widow, Lady Garvington, himself, and his cousin Noel, the little man had no fear of what might be forthcoming, since with relatives there could be no risk of betrayal. All the same, he waited for the reading of the will with some perturbation, for the suggested secrecy hinted at some posthumous revenge on the part of the dead man. And, hardened as he was, Garvington did not wish his wife and Lambert to become acquainted with his delinquency. He was, of course, unaware that the latter knew about it through Agnes, and knew also how it had been used to coerce her—for the pressure amounted to coercion—into a loveless marriage.

The quintette assembled in a small room near the library, and when the door and window were closed there was no chance that any one would overhear the conference. Lambert was rather puzzled to know why he had been requested to be present, as he had no idea that Pine would mention him in the will. However, he had not long to wait before he learned the reason, for the document produced by Mr. Jarwin was singularly short and concise. Pine had never been a great speaker, and carried his reticence into his testamentary disposition. Five minutes was sufficient for the reading of the will, and those present learned that all real and personal property had been left unreservedly to Agnes Pine, the widow of the testator, on condition that she did not marry Noel Tamsworth Leighton Lambert. If she did so, the money was to pass to a certain person, whose name was mentioned in a sealed envelope held by Mr. Jarwin. This was only to be opened when Agnes Pine formally relinquished her claim to the estate by marrying Noel Lambert. Seeing that the will disposed of two millions sterling, it was a remarkably abrupt document, and the reading of it took the hearers' breath away.

Garvington, relieved from the fears of his guilty conscience, was the first to recover his power of speech. He looked at the lean, dry lawyer, and demanded fiercely if no legacy had been left to him. "Surely Pine did not forget me?" he lamented, with more temper than sorrow.

"You have heard the will," said Mr. Jarwin, folding up the single sheet of legal paper on which the testament was inscribed.

"There are no legacies."

"None at all."

"Hasn't Pine remembered Silver?"

"He has remembered nothing and no one save Lady Agnes." Jarwin bowed to the silent widow, who could not trust herself to speak, so angered was she by the cruel way in which her husband had shown his jealousy.

"It's all very dreadful and very disagreeable," said Lady

Garvington in her weak and inconsequent way. "I'm sure I was always nice to Hubert and he might have left me a few shillings to get clothes. Everything goes in cooks and food and—"

"Hold your tongue, Jane," struck in her husband crossly. "You're always thinking of frocks and frills. But I agree with you this will is dreadful. I am not going to sit under such a beastly sell you know," he added, turning to Jarwin. "I shall contest the will."

The lawyer coughed dryly and smiled. "As you are not mentioned in the testament, Lord Garvington, I fail to see what you can do."

"Hum! hum! hum!" Garvington was rather disconcerted. "But Agnes can fight it."

"Why should I?" questioned the widow, who was very pale and very quiet.

"Why should you?" blustered her brother. "It prevents your marrying again."

"Pardon me, it does not," corrected Mr. Jarwin, with another dry cough. "Lady Agnes can marry any one she chooses to, save—" His eyes rested on the calm and watchful face of Lambert.

The young man colored, and glancing at Agnes, was about to speak. But on second thoughts he checked himself, as he did not wish to add to the embarrassment of the scene. It was the widow who replied. "Did Sir Hubert tell you why he made such a provision?" she asked, striving to preserve her calmness, which was difficult under the circumstances.

"Why, no," said Jarwin, nursing his chin reflectively. "Sir Hubert was always of a reticent disposition. He simply instructed me to draw up the will you have heard, and gave me no explanation. Everything is in order, and I am at your service, madam, whenever you choose to send for me."

"But suppose I marry Mr. Lambert—"

"Agnes, you won't be such a fool!" shouted her brother, growing so scarlet that he seemed to be on the point of an apoplectic fit.

She turned on him with a look, which reduced him to silence, but carefully avoided the eyes of the cousin. "Suppose I marry Mr. Lambert?" she asked again.

"In that case you will lose the money," replied Jarwin, slightly weary of so obvious an answer having to be made. "You have heard the will."

"Who gets the money then?"

This was another ridiculous question, as Jarwin, and not without reason, considered.

"Would you like me to read the will again?" he asked sarcastically.

"No. I am aware of what it contains."

"In that case, you must know, madam, that the money goes to a certain person whose name is mentioned in a sealed envelope, now in my office safe."

"Who is the person?" demanded Garvington, with a gleam of hope that Pine might have made him the legatee.

"I do not know, my lord. Sir Hubert Pine wrote down the name and address, sealed the envelope, and gave it into my charge. It can only be opened when the ceremony of marriage takes place between—" he bowed again to Lady Agnes and this time also to Lambert.

"Pine must have been insane," said Garvington, fuming. "He disguises himself as a gypsy, and comes to burgle my house, and makes a silly will which ought to be upset."

"Sir Hubert never struck me as insane," retorted Jarwin, putting the disputed will into his black leather bag. "A man who can make two million pounds in so short a space of time can scarcely be called crazy."

"But this masquerading as a gypsy and a burglar," urged Garvington irritably.

"He was actually a gypsy, remember, my lord, and it was natural that he should wish occasionally to get back to the life he loved. As to his being a burglar, I venture to disagree with you. He had some reason to visit this house at the hour and in the manner he did, and doubtless if he had lived he would have explained. But whatever might have been his motive, Lord Garvington, I am certain it was not connected with robbery."

"Well," snapped the fat little man candidly, "if I had known that Pine was such a blighter as to leave me nothing, I'm hanged if I'd have allowed him to be buried in such decent company."

"Freddy, Freddy, the poor man is dead. Let him rest," said Lady Garvington, who looked more limp and untidy than ever.

"I wish he was resting somewhere else than in my vault. A damned gypsy!"

"And my husband," said Lady Agnes sharply. "Don't forget that, Garvington."

"I wish I could forget it. Much use he has been to us."

"You have no cause to complain," said his sister with a meaning glance, and Garvington suddenly subsided.

"Won't you say something, Noel?" asked Lady Garvington dismally.

"I don't see what there is to say," he rejoined, not lifting his eyes from the ground.

"There you are wrong," remarked Agnes with a sudden flush.

"There is a very great deal to say, but this is not the place to say it. Mr. Jarwin," she rose to her feet, looking a queenly figure in her long black robes, "you can return to town and later will receive my instructions."

The lawyer looked hard at her marble face, wondering whether she would choose the lover or the money. It was a hard choice, and a very difficult position. He could not read in her eyes what she intended to do, so mutely bowed and took a ceremonious departure, paying a silent tribute to the widow's strength of mind. "Poor thing; poor thing," thought the solicitor, "I believe she loves her cousin. It is hard that she can only marry him at the cost of becoming a pauper. A difficult position for her, indeed. H'm! she'll hold on to the money, of course; no woman would be such a fool as to pay two millions sterling for a husband."

In relation to nine women out of ten, this view would have been a reasonable one to take, but Agnes happened to be the tenth, who had the singular taste—madness some would have called it—to prefer love to hard cash. Still, she made no hasty decision, seeing that the issues involved in her renunciation were so great. Garvington, showing a characteristic want of tact, began to argue the question almost the moment Jarwin drove away from The Manor, but his sister promptly declined to enter into any discussion.

"You and Jane can go away," said she, cutting him short. "I wish to have a private conversation with Noel."

"For heaven's sake don't give up the money," whispered Garvington in an agonized tone when at the door.

"I sold myself once to help the family," she replied in the same low voice; "but I am not so sure that I am ready to do so twice."

"Quite right, dear," said Lady Garvington, patting the widow's hand. "It is better to have love than money. Besides, it only means that Freddy will have to give up eating rich dinners which don't agree with him."

"Come away, you fool!" cried Freddy, exasperated, and, seizing her arm, he drew her out of the room, growling like a sick bear.

Agnes closed the door, and returned to look at Lambert, who still continued to stare at the carpet with folded arms. "Well?" she demanded sharply.

"Well?" he replied in the same tone, and without raising his eyes.

"Is that all you have to say, Noel?"

"I don't see what else I can say. Pine evidently guessed that we loved one another, although heaven knows that our affection has been innocent enough, and has taken this way to part us forever."

"Will it part us forever?"

"I think so. As an honorable man, and one who loves you dearly, I can't expect you to give up two millions for the sake of love in a cottage with me. It is asking too much."

"Not when a woman loves a man as I love you."

This time Lambert did look up, and his eyes flashed with surprise and delight. "Agnes, you don't mean to say that you would—"

She cut him short by sitting down beside him and taking his hand. "I would rather live on a crust with you in the Abbot's Wood Cottage than in Park Lane a lonely woman with ample wealth."

"You needn't remain lonely long," said Lambert moodily. "Pine's will does not forbid you to marry any one else."

"Do I deserve that answer, Noel, after what I have just said?"

"No, dear, no." He pressed her hand warmly. "But you must make some allowance for my feelings. It is right that a man should sacrifice all for a woman, but that a woman should give up everything for a man seems wrong."

"Many women do, if they love truly as I do."

"But, Agnes, think what people will say about me."

"That will be your share of the sacrifice," she replied promptly. "If I do this, you must do that. There is no difficulty when the matter is looked on in that light. But there is a graver question to be answered."

Lambert looked at her in a questioning manner and read the answer in her eyes. "You mean about the property of the family?"

"Yes." Agnes heaved a sigh and shook her head. "I wish I had been born a village girl rather than the daughter of a great house. Rank has its obligations, Noel. I recognized that before, and therefore married Hubert. He was a good, kind man, and, save that I lost you, I had no reason to regret becoming his wife. But I did not think that he would have put such an insult on me."

"Insult, dear?" Lambert flushed hotly.

"What else can you call this forbidding me to marry you? The will is certain to be filed at Somerset House, and the contents will be made known to the public in the usual way, through the newspapers. Then what will people say, Noel? Why, that I became Hubert's wife in order to get his money, since, knowing that he was consumptive, I hoped he would soon die, and that as a rich widow I could console myself with you. They will chuckle to see how my scheme has been overturned by the will."

"But you made no such scheme."

"Of course not. Still, everyone will credit me with having done so. As a woman, who has been insulted, and by a man who has no reason to mistrust me, I feel inclined to renounce the money and marry you, if only to show how I despise the millions. But as a Lambert I must think again of the family as I thought before. The only question is, whether it is wise to place duty above love for the second time, considering the misery we have endured, and the small thanks we have received for our self-denial?"

"Surely Garvington's estates are free by now?"

"No; they are not. Hubert, as I told you when we spoke in the cottage, paid off many mortgages, but retained possession of them. He did not charge Garvington any interest, and let him have the income of the mortgaged land. No one could have behaved better than Hubert did, until my brother's demands became so outrageous that it was impossible to go on lending and giving him money. Hubert did not trust him so far as to give back the mortgages, so these will form a portion of his estate. As that belongs to me, I can settle everything with ease, and place Garvington in an entirely satisfactory condition. But I do that at the cost of losing you, dear. Should the estates pass to this unknown person, the mortgages would be foreclosed, and our family would be ruined."

"Are things as bad as that?"

"Every bit as bad. Hubert told me plainly how matters stood. For generations the heads of the family have been squandering money. Freddy is just as bad as the rest, and, moreover, has no head for figures. He does not know the value of money, never having been in want of it. But if everything was sold up—and it must be if I marry you and lose the millions—he will be left without an acre of land and only three hundred a year."

"Oh, the devil!" Lambert jumped up and began to walk up and down the room with a startled air. "That would finish the Lambert family with a vengeance, Agnes. What do you wish me to do?" he asked, after a pause.

"Wait," she said quietly.

"Wait? For what—the Deluge?"

"It won't come while I hold the money. I have a good business head, and Hubert taught me how to deal with financial matters. I could not give him love, but I did give him every attention, and I believe that I was able to help him in some ways. I shall utilize my experience to see the family lawyer and go into matters thoroughly. Then we shall know for certain if things are as bad as Hubert made out. If they are, I must sacrifice you and myself for the sake of our name; if they are not—"

"Well?" asked Lambert, seeing how she hesitated. Agnes crossed the room and placed her arms round his neck with a lovely color tinting her wan cheeks. "Dear," she whispered, "I shall marry you. In doing so I am not disloyal to Hubert's memory, since I have always loved you, and he accepted me as his wife on the understanding that I could not give him my heart. And now that he has insulted me," she drew back, and her eyes flashed, "I feel free to become your wife."

"I see," Lambert nodded. "We must wait?"

"We must wait. Duty comes before love. But I trust that the sacrifice will not be necessary. Good-bye, dear," and she kissed him.

"Good-bye," repeated Lambert, returning the kiss. Then they parted.

CHAPTER XI

BLACKMAIL

Having come to the only possible arrangement, consistent with the difficult position in which they stood, Lambert and Lady Agnes took their almost immediate departure from The Manor. The young man had merely come to stay there in response to his cousin's request, so that his avoidance of her should not be too marked, and the suspicions of Pine excited. Now that the man was dead, there was no need to behave in this judicious way, and having no great love for Garvington, whom he thoroughly despised, Lambert returned to his forest cottage. There he busied himself once more with his art, and waited patiently to see what the final decision of Agnes would be. He did not expect to hear for some weeks, or even months, as the affairs of Garvington, being very much involved, could not be understood in a moment. But the lovers, parted by a strict sense of duty, eased their minds by writing weekly letters to one another.

Needless to say, Garvington did not at all approve of the decision of his sister, which she duly communicated to him. He disliked Lambert, both as the next heir to the estates, and because he was a more popular man than himself. Even had Pine not prohibited the marriage in his will, Garvington would have objected to Agnes becoming the young man's wife; as it was, he stormed tempests, but without changing the widow's determination. Being a remarkably selfish creature, all he desired was that Agnes should live a solitary life as a kind of banker, to supply him with money whenever he chose to ask for the same. Pine he had not been able to manage, but he felt quite sure that he could bully his sister into doing what he wanted. It both enraged and surprised him to find that she had a will of her own and was not content to obey his egotistical orders. Agnes would not even remain under his roof—as he wanted her to, lest some other person should get hold of her and the desirable millions—but returned to her London house. The only comfort he had was that Lambert was not with her, and therefore—as he devoutly hoped—she would meet some man who would cause her to forget the Abbot's Wood recluse. So long as Agnes retained the money, Garvington did not particularly object to her marrying, as he always hoped to cajole and bully ready cash out of her, but he would have preferred had she remained single, as then she could be more easily plundered.

"And yet I don't know," he said to his long-suffering wife. "While she's a widow there's always the chance that she may take the bit between her teeth and marry Noel, in which case she loses everything. It will be as well to get her married."

"You will have no selection of the husband this time," said Lady Garvington, whose sympathies were entirely for Agnes. "She will choose for herself."

"Let her," retorted Garvington, with feigned generosity. "So long as she does not choose Noel; hang him!"

"He's the very man she will choose;" replied his wife, and Garvington, uneasily conscious that she was probably right, cursed freely all women in general and his sister in particular. Meanwhile he went to Paris to look after a famous chef, of whom he had heard great things, and left his wife in London with strict injunctions to keep a watch on Agnes.

The widow was speedily made aware of these instructions, for when Lady Garvington came to stay with her sister-in-law at the sumptuous Mayfair mansion, she told her hostess about the conversation. More than that, she even pressed her to marry Noel, and be happy.

"Money doesn't do so much, after all, when you come to think of it," lamented Lady Garvington. "And I know you'd be happier with Noel, than living here with all this horrid wealth."

"What would Freddy say if he heard you talk so, Jane?"

"I don't know what else he can say," rejoined the other reflectively. "He's never kept his temper or held his tongue with me. His liver is nearly always out of order with over-eating. However," she added cheering up, "he is sure to die of apoplexy before long, and then I shall live on tea and buns for the rest of my life. I simply hate the sight of a dinner table."

"Freddy isn't a pretty sight during a meal," admitted his sister with a shrug. "All the same you shouldn't wish him dead, Jane. You might have a worse husband."

"I'd rather have a profligate than a glutton, Agnes. But Freddy won't die, my dear. He'll go to Wiesbaden, or Vichy, or Schwalbach, and take the waters to get thin; then he'll return to eat himself to the size of a prize pig again. But thank goodness," said Lady Garvington, cheering up once more, "he's away for a few weeks, and we can enjoy ourselves. But do let us have plain joints and no sauces, Agnes."

"Oh, you can live on bread and water if you choose," said the widow good-humoredly. "It's a pity I am in mourning, as I can't take you out much. But the motor is always at your disposal, and I can give you all the money you want. Get a few dresses—"

"And hats, and boots, and shoes, and—and—oh, I don't know what else. You're a dear, Agnes, and although I don't want to ruin you, I do want heaps of things. I'm in rags, as Freddy eats up our entire income."

"You can't ruin a woman with two millions, Jane. Get what you require and I'll pay. I am only too glad to give you some pleasure, since I can't attend to you as I ought to. But you see, nearly three times a week I have to consult the lawyers about settling Freddy's affairs."

On these conditions four or five weeks passed away very happily for the two women. Lady Garvington certainly had the time of her life, and regained a portion of her lost youth. She revelled in shopping, went in a quiet way to theatres, patronized skating rinks, and even attended one or two small winter dances. And to her joy, she met with a nice young man, who was earnestly in pursuit of a new religion, which involved much fasting and occasional vegetarian meals. He taught her to eat nuts, and eschew meats, talking meanwhile of the psychic powers which such abstemiousness would develop in her. Of course Lady Garvington did not overdo this asceticism, but she was thankful to meet a man who had not read Beeton's Cookery Book. Besides, he flirted quite nicely.

Agnes, pleased to see her sister-in-law enjoying life, gave her attention to Garvington's affairs, and found them in a woeful mess. It really did appear as if she would have to save the Lambert family from ever-lasting disgrace, and from being entirely submerged, by keeping hold of her millions. But she did not lose heart, and worked on bravely in the hope that an adjustment would save a few thousand a year for Freddy, without touching any of Pine's money. If she could manage to secure him a sufficient income to keep up the title, and to prevent the sale of The Manor in Hengishire, she then intended to surrender her husband's wealth and retire to a country life with Noel as her husband.

"He can paint and I can look after the cottage along with Mrs. Tribb," she told Mrs. Belgrove, who called to see her one day, more painted and dyed and padded and tastefully dressed than ever. "We can keep fowls and things, you know," she added vaguely.

"Quite an idyl," tittered the visitor, and then went away to tell her friends that Lady Agnes must have been in love with her cousin all the time. And as the contents of the will were now generally known, every one agreed that the woman was a fool to give up wealth for a dull existence in the woods. "All the same it's very sweet," sighed Mrs. Belgrove, having made as much mischief as she possibly could. "I should like it myself if I could only dress as a Watteau shepherdess, you know, and carry a lamb with a blue ribbon round its dear neck."

Of course, Lady Agnes heard nothing of this ill-natured chatter, since she did not go into society during her period of mourning, and received only a few of her most intimate friends. Moreover, besides attending to Garvington's affairs, it was necessary that she should have frequent consultations with Mr. Jarwin in his stuffy Chancery Lane office, relative to the large fortune left by her late husband. There, on three occasions she met Silver, the ex-secretary, when he came to explain various matters to the solicitor. With the consent of Lady Agnes, the man had been discharged, when Jarvin took over the management of the millions, but having a thorough knowledge of Pine's financial dealings, it was necessary that he should be questioned every now and then.

Silver was rather sulky over his abrupt dismissal, but cunningly concealed his real feelings when in the presence of the widow, since she was too opulent a person to offend. It was Silver who suggested that a reward should be offered for the detection of Pine's assassin. Lady Agnes approved of the idea, and indeed was somewhat shocked that she had not thought of taking this course herself. Therefore, within seven days every police office in the United Kingdom was placarded with bills, stating that the sum of one thousand pounds would be given to the person or persons who should denounce the culprit. The amount offered caused quite a flutter of excitement, and public interest in the case was revived for nearly a fortnight. At the conclusion of that period, as nothing fresh was discovered, people ceased to discuss the matter. It seemed as though the reward, large as it was, would never be claimed.

But having regard to the fact that Silver was interesting himself in the endeavor to avenge his patron's death, Lady Agnes was not at all surprised to receive a visit from him one foggy November afternoon. She certainly did not care much for the little man, but feeling dull and somewhat lonely, she quite welcomed his visit. Lady Garvington had gone with her ascetic admirer to a lecture on "Souls and Sorrows!" therefore Agnes had a spare hour for the ex-secretary. He was shown into her own particular private sitting-room, and she welcomed him with studied politeness, for try as she might it was impossible for her to overcome her mistrust.

"Good-day, Mr. Silver," she said, when he bowed before her. "This is an unexpected visit. Won't you be seated?"

Silver accepted her offer of a chair with an air of demure shyness, and sitting on its edge stared at her rather hard. He looked neat and dapper in his Bond Street kit, and for a man who had started life as a Whitechapel toymaker, his manners were inoffensive. While Pine's secretary he had contrived to pick up hints in the way of social behavior, and undoubtedly he was clever, since he so readily adapted himself to his surroundings. He was not a gentleman, but he looked like a gentleman, and therein lay a subtle difference as Lady Agnes decided. She unconsciously in her manner, affable as it was, suggested the gulf between them, and Silver, quickly contacting the atmosphere, did not love her any the more for the hint.

Nevertheless, he admired her statuesque beauty, the fairness of which was accentuated by her sombre dress. Blinking like a well-fed cat, Silver stared at his hostess, and she looked questioningly at him. With his foxy face, his reddish hair, and suave manners, too careful to be natural, he more than ever impressed her with the idea that he was a dangerous man. Yet she could not see in what way he could reveal his malignant disposition.

"What do you wish to see me about, Mr. Silver?" she asked kindly, but did not—as he swiftly noticed—offer him a cup of tea, although it was close upon five o'clock.

"I have come to place my services at your disposal," he said in a low voice.

"Really, I am not aware that I need them," replied Lady Agnes coldly, and not at all anxious to accept the offer.

"I think," said Silver dryly, and clearing his throat, "that when you hear what I have to say you will be glad that I have come."

"Indeed! Will you be good enough to speak plainer?"

She colored hotly when she asked the question, as it struck her suddenly that perhaps this plotter knew of Garvington's slip regarding the check. But as that had been burnt by Pine at the time of her marriage, she reflected that even if Silver knew about it, he could do nothing. Unless, and it was this thought that made her turn red, Garvington had again risked contact with the criminal courts. The idea was not a pleasant one, but being a brave woman, she faced the possibility boldly.

"Well?" she asked calmly, as he did not reply immediately. "What have you to say?"

"It's about Pine's death," said Silver bluntly.

"Sir Hubert, if you please."

"And why, Lady Agnes?" Silver raised his faint eyebrows. "We were more like brothers than master and servant. And remember that it was by the penny toys that I invented your husband first made money."

"In talking to me, I prefer that you should call my late husband

Sir Hubert," insisted the widow haughtily. "What have you discovered relative to his death?"

Silver did not answer the question directly. "Sir Hubert, since you will have it so, Lady Agnes, was a gypsy," he remarked carelessly.

"That was made plain at the inquest, Mr. Silver."

"Quite so, Lady Agnes, but there were other things not made plain on that occasion. It was not discovered who shot him."

"You tell me nothing new. I presume you have come to explain that you have discovered a clew to the truth?"

Silver raised his pale face steadily. "Would you be glad if I had?"

"Certainly! Can you doubt it?"

The man shirked a reply to this question also. "Sir Hubert did not treat me over well," he observed irrelevantly.

"I fear that has nothing to do with me, Mr. Silver."

"And I was dimissed from my post," he went on imperturbably.

"On Mr. Jarwin's advice," she informed him quickly. "There was no need for you to be retained. But I believe that you were given a year's salary in lieu of notice."

"That is so," he admitted. "I am obliged to you and to Mr. Jarwin for the money, although it is not a very large sum. Considering what I did for Sir Hubert, and how he built up his fortune out of my brains, I think that I have been treated shabbily."

Lady Agnes rose, and moved towards the fireplace to touch the ivory button of the electric bell. "On that point I refer you to Mr. Jarwin," she said coldly. "This interview has lasted long enough and can lead to nothing."

"It may lead to something unpleasant unless you listen to me," said Silver acidly. "I advise you not to have me turned out, Lady Agnes."

"What do you mean?" She dropped the hand she had extended to ring the bell, and faced the smooth-faced creature suddenly. "I don't know what you are talking about."

"If you will sit down, Lady Agnes, I can explain."

"I can receive your explanation standing," said the widow, frowning. "Be brief, please."

"Very well. To put the matter in a nutshell, I want five thousand pounds."

"Five thousand pounds!" she echoed, aghast.

"On account," said Silver blandly. "On account, Lady Agnes."

"And for what reason?"

"Sir Hubert was a gypsy," he said again, and with a significant look.

"Well?"

"He stopped at the camp near Abbot's Wood."

"Well?"

"There is a gypsy girl there called Chaldea."

"Chaldea! Chaldea!" muttered the widow, passing her hand across her brow. "I have heard that name. Oh, yes. Miss Greeby mentioned it to me as the name of a girl who was sitting as Mr. Lambert's model."

"Yes," assented Silver, grinning. "She is a very beautiful girl."

The color rushed again to the woman's cheeks, but she controlled her emotions with an effort. "So Miss Greeby told me!" She knew that the man was hinting that Lambert admired the girl in question, but her pride prevented her admitting the knowledge. "Chaldea is being painted as Esmeralda to the Quasimodo of her lover, a Servian gypsy called Kara, as I have been informed, Mr. Silver. But what has all this to do with me?"

"Don't be in a hurry, Lady Agnes. It will take time to explain."

"How dare you take this tone with me?" demanded the widow, clenching her hands. "Leave the room, sir, or I shall have you turned out."

"Oh, I shall leave since you wish it," replied Silver, rising slowly and smoothing his silk hat with his sleeve. "But of course I shall try and earn the reward you offered, by taking the letter to the police."

Agnes was so surprised that she closed again the door she had opened for her visitor's exit. "What letter?"

"That one which was written to inveigle Sir Hubert to The Manor on the night he was murdered," replied Silver slowly, and suddenly raising his eyes he looked at her straightly.

"I don't understand," she said in a puzzled way. "I have never heard that such a letter was in existence. Where is it?"

"Chaldea has it, and will not give it up unless she receives five thousand pounds," answered the man glibly. "Give it to me and it passes into your possession, Lady Agnes."

"Give you what?"

"Five thousand pounds—on account."

"On account of blackmail. How dare you make such a proposition to me?"

"You know," said Silver pointedly.

"I know nothing. It is the first time I have heard of any letter. Who wrote it, may I ask?"

"You know," said Silver again.

Lady Agnes was so insulted by his triumphant look that she could have struck his grinning face. However, she had too strong a nature to lower herself in this way, and pointed to a chair. "Let me ask you a few questions, Mr. Silver," she said imperiously.

"Oh, I am quite ready to answer whatever you choose to ask," he retorted, taking his seat again and secretly surprised at her self-control.

"You say that Chaldea holds a letter which inveigled my husband to his death?" demanded Lady Agnes coolly.

"Yes. And she wants five thousand pounds for it."

"Why doesn't she give it to the police?"

"One thousand pounds is not enough for the letter. It is worth more—to some people," and Silver raised his pale eyes again.

"To me, I presume you mean;" then when he bowed, she continued her examination. "The five thousand pounds you intimate is on account, yet you say that Chaldea will deliver the letter for that sum."

"To me," rejoined the ex-secretary impudently. "And when it is in my possession, I can give it to you for twenty thousand pounds."

Lady Agnes laughed in his face. "I am too good a business woman to make such a bargain," she said with a shrug.

"Well, you know best," replied Silver, imitating her shrug.

"I know nothing; I am quite in the dark as to the reason for your blackmailing, Mr. Silver."

"That is a nasty word, Lady Agnes."

"It is the only word which seems to suit the situation. Why should I give twenty-five thousand pounds for this letter?"

"Its production will place the police on the track of the assassin."

"And is not that what I desire? Why did I offer a reward of one thousand pounds if I did not hope that the wretch who murdered my husband should be brought to justice?"

Silver exhibited unfeigned surprise. "You wish that?"

"Certainly I do. Where was this letter discovered?"

"Chaldea went to the tent of your husband in the camp and found it in the pocket of his coat. He apparently left it behind by mistake when he went to watch."

"Watch?"

"Yes! The letter stated that you intended to elope that night with Mr. Lambert, and would leave the house by the blue door. Sir Hubert went to watch and prevent the elopement. In that way he came by his death, since Lord Garvington threatened to shoot a possible burglar. Of course, Sir Hubert, when the blue door was opened by Lord Garvington, who had heard the footsteps of the supposed burglar, threw himself forward, thinking you were coming out to meet Mr. Lambert. Sir Hubert was first shot in the arm by

Lord Garvington, who really believed for the moment that he had to do with a robber. But the second shot," ended Silver with emphasis, "was fired by a person concealed in the shrubbery, who knew that Sir Hubert would walk into the trap laid by the letter."

During this amazing recital, Lady Agnes, with her eyes on the man's face, and her hands clasped in sheer surprise, had sat down on a near couch. She could scarcely believe her ears. "Is this true?" she asked in a faltering voice.

Silver shrugged his shoulders again. "The letter held by Chaldea certainly set the snare in which Sir Hubert was caught. Unless the person in the shrubbery knew about the letter, the person would scarcely have been concealed there with a revolver. I know about the letter for certain, since Chaldea showed it to me, when I went to ask questions about the murder in the hope of gaining the reward. The rest of my story is theoretical."

"Who was the person who fired the shot?" asked Lady Agnes abruptly.

"I don't know."

"Who wrote the letter which set the snare?"

Silver shuffled. "Chaldea loves Mr. Lambert," he said hesitating.

"Go on," ordered the widow coldly and retaining her self-control.

"She is jealous of you, Lady Agnes, because—"

"There is no reason to explain," interrupted the listener between her teeth.

"Well, then, Chaldea hating you, says that you wrote the letter."

"Oh, indeed." Lady Agnes replied calmly enough, although her conflicting emotions almost suffocated her. "Then I take it that this gypsy declares me to be a murderess."

"Oh, I shouldn't say that exactly."

"I do say it," cried Lady Agnes, rising fiercely. "If I wrote the letter, and set the snare, I must necessarily know that some one was hiding in the shrubbery to shoot my husband. It is an abominable lie from start to finish."

"I am glad to hear you say so. But the letter?"

"The police will deal with that."

"The police? You will let Chaldea give the letter to the police?"

"I am innocent and have no fear of the police. Your attempt to blackmail me has failed, Mr. Silver."

"Be wise and take time for reflection," he urged, walking towards the door, "for I have seen this letter, and it is in your handwriting."

"I never wrote such a letter."

"Then who did—in your handwriting?"

"Perhaps you did yourself, Mr. Silver, since you are trying to blackmail me in this bareface way."

Silver snarled and gave her an ugly look. "I did no such thing," he retorted vehemently, and, as it seemed, honestly enough. "I had every reason to wish that Sir Hubert should live, since my income and my position depended upon his existence. But you—"

"What about me?" demanded Lady Agnes, taking so sudden a step forward that the little man retreated nearer the door.

"People say—"

"I know what people say and what you are about to repeat," she said in a stifled voice. "You can tell the girl to take that forged letter to the police. I am quite able to face any inquiry."

"Is Mr. Lambert also able?"

"Mr. Lambert?" Agnes felt as though she would choke.

"He was at his cottage on that night."

"I deny that; he went to London."

"Chaldea can prove that he was at his cottage, and—"

"You had better go," said Lady Agnes, turning white and looking dangerous. "Go, before you say what you may be sorry for. I shall tell Mr. Lambert the story you have told me, and let him deal with the matter."

Silver threw off the mask, as he was enraged she should so boldly withstand his demands. "I give you one week," he said harshly. "And, if you do not pay me twenty-five thousand pounds, that letter goes to the inspector at Wanbury."

"It can go now," she declared dauntlessly.

"In that case you and Mr. Lambert will be arrested at once."

Agnes gripped the man's arm as he was about to step through the door. "I take your week of grace," she said with a sudden impulse of wisdom.

"I thought you would," retorted Silver insultingly. "But remember I must get the money at the end of seven days. It's twenty-five thousand pounds for me, or disgrace to you," and with an abrupt nod he disappeared sneering.

"Twenty-five thousand pounds or disgrace," whispered Agnes to herself.

CHAPTER XII

THE CONSPIRACY

It was lucky that Lambert did not know of the ordeal to which Agnes had to submit, unaided, since he was having a most unhappy time himself. In a sketching expedition he had caught a chill, which had developed once more a malarial fever, contracted in the Congo marshes some years previously. Whenever his constitution weakened, this ague fit would reappear, and for days, sometimes weeks, he would shiver with cold, and alternately burn with fever. As the autumn mists were hanging round the leafless Abbot's Wood, it was injudicious of him to sit in the open, however warmly clothed, seeing that he was predisposed to disease. But his desire for the society of the woman he loved, and the hopelessness of the outlook, rendered him reckless, and he was more often out of doors than in. The result was that when Agnes came down to relate the interview with Silver, she found him in his sitting-room swathed in blankets, and reclining in an arm-chair placed as closely to a large wood fire as was possible. He was very ill indeed, poor man, and she uttered an exclamation when she saw his wan cheeks and hollow eyes. Lambert was now as weak as he had been strong, and with the mothering instinct of a woman, she rushed forward to kneel beside his chair.

"My dear, my dear, why did you not send for me?" she wailed, keeping back her tears with an effort.

"Oh, I'm all right, Agnes," he answered cheerfully, and fondly clasping her hand. "Mrs. Tribb is nursing me capitally."

"I'm doing my best," said the rosy-faced little housekeeper, who stood at the door with her podgy hands primly folded over her apron. "Plenty of bed and food is what I give Master Noel; but bless you, my lady, he won't stay between the blankets, being always a worrit from a boy."

"It seems to me that I am very much between the blankets now," murmured Lambert in a tired voice, and with a glance at his swathed limbs. "Go away, Mrs. Tribb, and get Lady Agnes something to eat."

"I only want a cup of tea," said Agnes, looking anxiously into her lover's bluish-tinted face. "I'm not hungry."

Mrs. Tribb took a long look at the visitor and pursed up her lips, as she shook her head. "Hungry you mayn't be, my lady, but food you must have, and that of the most nourishing and delicate. You look almost as much a corpse as Master Noel there."

"Yes, Agnes, you do seem to be ill," said Lambert with a startled glance at her deadly white face, and at the dark circles under her eyes. "What is the matter, dear?"

"Nothing! Nothing! Don't worry."

Mrs. Tribb still continued to shake her head, and, to vary the movement, nodded like a Chinese mandarin. "You ain't looked after proper, my lady, for all your fine London servants, who ain't to be trusted, nohow, having neither hands to do nor hearts to feel for them as wants comforts and attentions. I remember you, my lady, a blooming young rose of a gal, and now sheets ain't nothing to your complexion. But rose you shall be again, my lady, if wine and food can do what they're meant to do. Tea you shan't have, nohow, but a glass or two of burgundy, and a plate of patty-foo-grass sandwiches, and later a bowl of strong beef tea with port wine to strengthen the same," and Mrs. Tribb, with a determined look on her face, went away to prepare these delicacies.

"My dear! my dear!" murmured Agnes again when the door closed. "You should have sent for me."

"Nonsense," answered Lambert, smoothing her hair. "I'm not a child to cry out at the least scratch. It's only an attack of my old malarial fever, and I shall be all right in a few days."

"Not a few of these days," said Agnes, looking out of the window at the gaunt, dripping trees and gray sky and melancholy monoliths. "You ought to come to London and see the doctor."

"Had I come, I should have had to pay you a visit, and I thought that you did not wish me to, until things were adjusted."

Agnes drew back, and, kneeling before the fire, spread out her hands to the blaze. "Will they ever be adjusted?" she asked herself despairingly, but did not say so aloud, as she was unwilling to worry the sick man. "Well, I only came down to The Manor for a few days," she said aloud, and in a most cheerful manner. "Jane wants to get the house in order for Garvington, who returns from Paris in a week."

"Agnes! Agnes!" Lambert shook his head. "You are not telling me the truth. I know you too well, my dear."

"I really am staying with Jane at The Manor," she persisted.

"Oh, I believe that; but you are in trouble and came down to consult me."

"Yes," she admitted faintly. "I am in great trouble. But I don't wish to worry you while you are in this state."

"You will worry me a great deal more by keeping silence," said Lambert, sitting up in his chair and drawing the blankets more closely round him. "Do not trouble about me. I'm all right. But you—" he looked at her keenly and with a dismayed expression. "The trouble must be very great," he remarked.

"It may become so, Noel. It has to do with—oh, here is Mrs. Tribb!" and she broke off hurriedly, as the housekeeper appeared with a tray.

"Now, my lady, just you sit in that arm-chair opposite to Master Noel, and I'll put the tray on this small stool beside you. Sandwiches and burgundy wine, my lady, and see that you eat and drink all you can. Walking over on this dripping day," cried Mrs. Tribb, bustling about. "Giving yourself your death of cold, and you with carriages and horses, and them spitting cats of motive things. You're as bad as Master Noel, my lady. As for him, God bless him evermore, he's—" Mrs. Tribb raised her hands to show that words failed her, and once more vanished through the door to get ready the beef tea.

Agnes did not want to eat, but Lambert, who quite agreed with the kind-hearted practical housekeeper, insisted that she should do so. To please him she took two sandwiches, and a glass of the strong red wine, which brought color back to her cheeks in some degree. When she finished, and had drawn her chair closer to the blaze, he smiled.

"We are just like Darby and Joan," said Lambert, who looked much better for her presence. "I am so glad you are here, Agnes. You are the very best medicine I can have to make me well."

"The idea of comparing me to anything so nasty as medicine," laughed Agnes with an attempt at gayety. "But indeed, Noel, I wish my visit was a pleasant one. But it is not, whatever you may say; I am in great trouble."

"From what—with what—in what?" stuttered Lambert, so confusedly and anxiously that she hesitated to tell him.

"Are you well enough to hear?"

"Of course I am," he answered fretfully, for the suspense began to tell on his nerves. "I would rather know the worst and face the worst than be left to worry over these hints. Has the trouble to do with the murder?"

"Yes. And with Mr. Silver."

"Pine's secretary? I thought you had got rid of him?"

"Oh, yes. Mr. Jarwin said that he was not needed, so I paid him a year's wages instead of giving him notice, and let him go. But I have met him once or twice at the lawyers, as he has been telling Mr. Jarwin about poor Hubert's investments. And yesterday afternoon he came to see me."

"What about?"

Agnes came to the point at once, seeing that it would be better to do so, and put an end to Lambert's suspense. "About a letter supposed to have been written by me, as a means of luring Hubert to The Manor to be murdered."

Lambert's sallow and pinched face grew a deep red. "Is the man mad?"

"He's sane enough to ask twenty-five thousand pounds for the letter," she said in a dry tone. "There's not much madness about that request."

"Twenty-five thousand pounds!" gasped Lambert, gripping the arms of his chair and attempting to rise.

"Yes. Don't get up, Noel, you are too weak." Agnes pressed him back into the seat. "Twenty thousand for himself and five thousand for Chaldea."

"Chaldea! Chaldea! What has she got to do with the matter?"

"She holds the letter," said Agnes with a side-glance. "And being jealous of me, she intends to make me suffer, unless I buy her silence and the letter. Otherwise, according to Mr. Silver, she will show it to the police. I have seven days, more or less, in which to make up my mind. Either I must be blackmailed, or I must face the accusation."

Lambert heard only one word that struck him in this speech. "Why is Chaldea jealous of you?" he demanded angrily.

"I think you can best answer that question, Noel."

"I certainly can, and answer it honestly, too. Who told you about Chaldea?"

"Mr. Silver, for one, as I have just confessed. Clara Greeby for another. She said that the girl was sitting to you for some picture."

"Esmeralda and Quasimodo," replied the artist quickly. "You will find what I have done of the picture in the next room. But this confounded girl chose to fall in love with me, and since then I have declined to see her. I need hardly tell you, Agnes, that I gave her no encouragement."

"No, dear. I never for one moment supposed that you would."

"All the same, and in spite of my very plain speaking, she continues to haunt me, Agnes. I have avoided her on every occasion, but she comes daily to see Mrs. Tribb, and ask questions about my illness."

"Then, if she comes this afternoon, you must get that letter from her," was the reply. "I wish to see it."

"Silver declares that you wrote it?"

"He does. Chaldea showed it to him."

"It is in your handwriting?"

"So Mr. Silver declares."

Lambert rubbed the bristles of his three days' beard, and

wriggled uncomfortably in his seat. "I can't gather much from these hints," he said with the fretful impatience of an invalid. "Give me a detailed account of this scoundrel's interview with you, and report his exact words if you can remember them, Agnes."

"I remember them very well. A woman does not forget such insults easily."

"Damn the beast!" muttered Lambert savagely. "Go on, dear."

Agnes patted his hand to soothe him, and forthwith related all that had passed between her and the ex-secretary. Lambert frowned once or twice during the recital, and bit his lip with anger. Weak as he was, he longed for Silver to be within kicking distance, and it would have fared badly with the foxy little man had he been in the room at the moment. When Agnes ended, her lover reflected for a few minutes.

"It's a conspiracy," he declared.

"A conspiracy, Noel?"

"Yes. Chaldea hates you because the fool has chosen to fall in love with me. The discovery of this letter has placed a weapon in her hand to do you an injury, and for the sake of money Silver is assisting her. I will do Chaldea the justice to say that I don't believe she asks a single penny for the letter. To spite you she would go at once to the police. But Silver, seeing that there is money in the business, has prevented her doing so. As to this letter—" He stopped and rubbed his chin again vexedly.

"It must be a forgery."

"Without doubt, but not of your handwriting, I fancy, in spite of what this daring blackguard says. He informed you that the letter stated how you intended to elope with me on that night, and would leave The Manor by the blue door. Also, on the face of it, it would appear that you had written the letter to your husband, since otherwise it would not have been in his possession. You would not have given him such a hint had an elopement really been arranged."

Agnes frowned. "There was no chance of an elopement being arranged," she observed rather coldly.

"Of course not. You and I know as much, but I am looking at the matter from the point of view of the person who wrote the letter. It can't be your forged handwriting, for Pine would never have believed that you would put him on the track as it were. No, Agnes. Depend upon it, the letter was a warning sent by some sympathetic friend, and is probably an anonymous one."

Agnes nodded meditatively. "You may be right, Noel. But who wrote to Hubert?"

"We must see the letter and find out."

"But if it is my forged handwriting?"

"I don't believe it is," said Lambert decisively. "No conspirator would be so foolish as to conduct his plot in such a way. However, Chaldea has the letter, according to Silver, and we must make her give it up. She is sure to be here soon, as she always comes bothering Mrs. Tribb in the afternoon about my health. Just ring that hand-bell, Agnes."

"Do you think Chaldea wrote the letter?" she asked, having obeyed him.

"No. She has not the education to forge, or even to write decently."

"Perhaps Mr. Silver—but no. I taxed him with setting the trap, and he declared that Hubert was more benefit to him alive than dead, which is perfectly true. Here is Mrs. Tribb, Noel."

Lambert turned his head. "Has that gypsy been here to-day?" he asked sharply.

"Not yet, Master Noel, but there's no saying when she may come, for she's always hanging round the house. I'd tar and feather her and slap and pinch her if I had my way, say what you like, my lady. I've no patience with gals of that free-and-easy, light-headed, butter-won't-melt-in-your-mouth kind."

"If she comes to-day, show her in here," said Lambert, paying little attention to Mrs. Tribb's somewhat German speech of mouth-filling words.

The housekeeper's black eyes twinkled, and she opened her lips, then she shut them again, and looking at Lady Agnes in a questioning way, trotted out of the room. It was plain that Mrs. Tribb knew of Chaldea's admiration for her master, and could not understand why he wished her to enter the house when Lady Agnes was present. She did not think it a wise thing to apply fire to gunpowder, which, in her opinion, was what Lambert was doing.

There ensued silence for a few moments. Then Agnes, staring into the fire, remarked in a musing manner, "I wonder who did shoot Hubert. Mr. Silver would not have done so, as it was to his interest to keep him alive. Do you think that to hurt me, Noel, Chaldea might have—"

"No! No! No! It was to her interest also that Pine should live, since she knew that I could not marry you while he was alive."

Agnes nodded, understanding him so well that she did not need to ask for a detailed explanation. "It could not have been any of those staying at The Manor," she said doubtfully, "since every one was indoors and in bed. Garvington, of course, only broke poor Hubert's arm under a misapprehension. Who could have been the person in the shrubbery?"

"Silver hints that I am the individual," said Lambert grimly.

"Yes, he does," assented Lady Agnes quickly. "I declared that you were in London, but he said that you returned on that night to this place."

"I did, worse luck. I went to town, thinking it best to be away while Pine was in the neighborhood, and—"

"You knew that Hubert was a gypsy and at the camp?" interrupted Agnes in a nervous manner, for the information startled her.

"Yes! Chaldea told me so, when she was trying to make me fall in love with her. I did not tell you, as I thought that you might be vexed, although I dare say I should have done so later. However, I went to town in order to prevent trouble, and only returned for that single night. I went back to town next morning very early, and did not hear about the murder until I saw a paragraph in the evening papers. Afterwards I came down to the funeral because Garvington asked me to, and I thought that you would like it."

"Why did you come back on that particular night?"

"My dear Agnes, I had no idea that Hubert would be murdered on that especial night, so did not choose it particularly. I returned because I had left behind a parcel of your letters to me when we were engaged. I fancied that Chaldea might put Hubert up to searching the cottage while I was away, and if he had found those letters he would have been more jealous than ever, as you can easily understand."

"No, I can't understand," flashed out Agnes sharply. "Hubert knew that we loved one another, and that I broke the engagement to save the family. I told him that I could not give him the affection he desired, and he was content to marry me on those terms. The discovery of letters written before I became his wife would not have caused trouble, since I was always loyal to him. There was no need for you to return, and your presence here on that night lends color to Mr. Silver's accusation."

"But you don't believe—"

"Certainly I don't. All the same it is awkward for both of us."

"I think it was made purposely awkward, Agnes. Whosoever murdered Hubert must have known of my return, and laid the trap on that night, so that I might be implicated."

"But who set the trap?"

"The person who wrote that letter."

"And who wrote the letter?"

"That is what we have to find out from Chaldea!"

At that moment; as if he had summoned her, the gypsy suddenly flung open the door and walked in with a sulky expression on her dark face. At first she had been delighted to hear that

Lambert wanted to see her, but when informed by Mrs. Tribb that Lady Agnes was with the young man, she had lost her temper. However, the chance of seeing Lambert was too tempting to forego, so she marched in defiantly, ready to fight with her rival if there was an opportunity of doing so. But the Gentile lady declined the combat, and took no more notice of the jealous gypsy than was absolutely necessary. On her side Chaldea ostentatiously addressed her conversation to Lambert.

"How are you, rye?" she asked, stopping with effort in the middle of the room, for her impulse was to rush forward and gather him to her heaving bosom. "Have you taken drows, my precious lord?"

"What do you mean by drows, Chaldea?"

"Poison, no less. You look drabbed, for sure."

"Drabbed?"

"Poisoned. But I waste the kalo jib on you, my Gorgious. God bless you for a sick one, say I, and that's a bad dukkerin, the which in gentle Romany means fortune, my Gentile swell."

"Drop talking such nonsense," said Lambert sharply, and annoyed to see how the girl ignored the presence of Lady Agnes. "I have a few questions to ask you about a certain letter."

"Kushto bak to the rye, who showed it to the lady," said Chaldea, tossing her head so that the golden coins jingled.

"He did not show it to me, girl," remarked Lady Agnes coldly.

"Hai! It seems that the rumy of Hearne can lie."

"I shall put you out of the house if you speak in that way," said Lambert sternly. "Silver went to Lady Agnes and tried to blackmail her."

"He's a boro pappin, and that's Romany for a large goose, my Gorgious rye, for I asked no gold."

"You told him to ask five thousand pounds."

"May I die in a ditch if I did!" cried Chaldea vehemently. "Touch the gold of the raclan I would not, though I wanted bread. The tiny rye took the letter to give to the prastramengro, and that's a policeman, my gentleman, so that there might be trouble. But I wished no gold from her. Romany speaking, I should like to poison her. I love you, and—"

"Have done with this nonsense, Chaldea. Talk like that and out you go. I can see from what you admit, that you have been making mischief."

"That's as true as my father," laughed the gypsy viciously. "And glad am I to say the word, my boro rye. And why should the raclan go free-footed when she drew her rom to be slaughtered like a pig?"

"I did nothing of the sort," cried Agnes, with an angry look.

"Duvel, it is true." Chaldea still addressed Lambert, and took no notice of Agnes. "I swear it on your Bible-book. I found the letter in my brother's tent, the day after he perished. Hearne, for Hearne he was, and a gentle Romany also, read the letter, saying that the raclan, his own romi, was running away with you."

"Who wrote the letter?" demanded Agnes indignantly.

This time Chaldea answered her fiercely. "You did, my Gorgious rani, and lie as you may, it's the truth I tell."

Ill as he was, Lambert could not endure seeing the girl insult Agnes. With unexpected strength he rose from his chair and took her by the shoulders to turn her out of the room. Chaldea laughed wildly, but did not resist. It was Agnes who intervened. "Let her stay until we learn the meaning of these things, Noel," she said rapidly in French.

"She insults you," he replied, in the same tongue, but released the girl.

"Never mind; never mind." Agnes turned to Chaldea and reverted to English. "Girl, you are playing a dangerous game. I wrote no letter to the man you call Hearne, and who was my husband—Sir Hubert Pine."

Chaldea laughed contemptuously. "Avali, that is true. The letter was written by you to my precious rye here, and Hearne's dukkerin brought it his way."

"How did he get it?"

"Those who know, know," retorted Chaldea indifferently. "Hearne's breath was out of him before I could ask."

"Why do you say that I wrote the letter?"

"The tiny rye swore by his God that you did."

"It is absolutely false!"

"Oh, my mother, there are liars about," jeered the gypsy sceptically. "Catch you blabbing your doings on the crook, my rani, Chore mandy—"

"Speak English," interrupted Agnes, who was quivering with rage.

"You can't cheat me," translated Chaldea sulkily. "You write my rye, here, the letter swearing to run world-wide with him, and let it fall into your rom's hands, so as to fetch him to the big house. Then did you, my cunning gentleman," she whirled round on the astounded Lambert viciously, "hide so quietly in the bushes to shoot. Hai! it is so, and I love you for the boldness, my Gorgious one."

"It is absolutely false," cried Lambert, echoing Agnes.

"True! true! and twice times true. May I go crazy, Meg, if it isn't. You wanted the raclan as your romi, and so plotted my brother's death. But your sweet one will go before the Poknees, and with irons on her wrists, and a rope round her—"

"You she-devil!" shouted Lambert in a frenzy of rage, and forgetting in his anger the presence of Agnes.

"Words of honey under the moon," mocked the girl, then suddenly became tender. "Let her go, rye, let her go. My love is all for you, and when we pad the hoof together, those who hate us shall take off the hat."

Lambert sat glaring at her furiously, and Agnes glided between him and the girl, fearful lest he should spring up and insult her. But she addressed her words to Chaldea. "Why do you think I got Mr. Lambert to kill my husband?" she asked, wincing at having to put the question, but seeing that it was extremely necessary to learn all she could from the gypsy.

The other woman drew her shawl closely round her fine form and snapped her fingers contemptuously. "It needs no chovihani to tell. Hearne the Romany was poor, Pine the Gentile chinked gold in his pockets. Says you to yourself, 'He I love isn't him with money.' And says you, 'If I don't get my true rom, the beauty of the world will clasp him to her breast.' So you goes for to get Hearne out of the flesh, to wed the rye here on my brother's rich possessions. Avali," she nodded vigorously. "That is so, though 'No' you says to me, for wisdom. Red money you have gained, my daring sister, for the blood of a Romany chal has changed the color. But I'm no—"

How long she would have continued to rage at Lady Agnes it is impossible to say, for the invalid, with the artificial strength of furious anger, sprang from his chair to turn her out of the room. Chaldea dodged him in the alert way of a wild animal.

"That's no love-embrace, my rye," she jibed, retreating swiftly. "Later, later, when the moon rises, my angel," and she slipped deftly through the door with a contemptuous laugh. Lambert would have followed, but that Agnes caught his arm, and with tears in her eyes implored him to remain.

"But what can we do in the face of such danger?" she asked him when he was quieter, and breaking down, she sobbed bitterly.

"We must meet it boldly. Silver has the forged letter: he must be arrested."

"But the scandal, Noel. Dare we—"

"Agnes, you are innocent: I am innocent. Innocence can dare all things."

Both sick, both troubled, both conscious of the dark clouds around them, they looked at one another in silence. Then Lambert repeated his words with conviction, to reassure himself as much as to comfort her.

"Innocence can dare all things," said Lambert, positively.

CHAPTER XIII

A FRIEND IN NEED

It was natural that Lambert should talk of having Silver arrested, as in the first flush of indignation at his audacious attempt to levy blackmail, this appeared the most reasonable thing to do. But when Agnes went back to The Manor, and the sick man was left alone to struggle through a long and weary night, the reaction suggested a more cautious dealing with the matter. Silver was a venomous little reptile, and if brought before a magistrate would probably produce the letter which he offered for sale at so ridiculous a price. If this was made public, Agnes would find herself in an extremely unpleasant position. Certainly the letter was forged, but that would not be easy to prove. And even if it were proved and Agnes cleared her character, the necessary scandal connected with the publicity of such a defence would be both distressing and painful. In wishing to silence Silver, and yet avoid the interference of the police, Lambert found himself on the horns of a dilemma.

Having readjusted the situation in his own mind, Lambert next day wrote a lengthy letter to Agnes, setting forth his objections to drastic measures. He informed her—not quite truthfully—that he hoped to be on his feet in twenty-four hours, and then would personally attend to the matter, although he could not say as yet what he intended to do. But five out of the seven days of grace allowed by the blackmailer yet remained, and much could be done in that time. "Return to town and attend to your own and to your brother's affairs as usual," concluded the letter. "All matters connected with Silver can be left in my hands, and should he attempt to see you in the meantime, refer him to me." The epistle ended with the intimation that Agnes was not to worry, as the writer would take the whole burden on his own shoulders. The widow felt more cheerful after this communication, and went back to her town house to act as her lover suggested. She had every belief in Lambert's capability to deal with the matter.

The young man was more doubtful, for he could not see how he was to begin unravelling this tangled skein. The interview with Chaldea had proved futile, as she was plainly on the side of the enemy, and to apply to Silver for information as to his intentions would merely result in a repetition of what he had said to Lady Agnes. It only remained to lay the whole matter before Inspector

Darby, and Lambert was half inclined to go to Wanbury for this purpose. He did not, however, undertake the journey, for two reasons. Firstly, he wished to avoid asking for official assistance until absolutely forced to do so; and secondly, he was too ill to leave the cottage. The worry he felt regarding Agnes's perilous position told on an already weakened frame, and the invalid grew worse instead of better.

Finally, Lambert decided to risk a journey to the camp, which was not so very far distant, and interview Mother Cockleshell. The old lady had no great love for Chaldea, who flouted her authority, and would not, therefore, be very kindly disposed towards the girl. The young man believed, in some vague way, that Chaldea had originated the conspiracy which had to do with the letter, and was carrying her underhand plans to a conclusion with the aid of Silver. Mother Cockleshell, who was very shrewd, might have learned or guessed the girl's rascality, and would assuredly thwart her aims if possible. Also the gypsy-queen would probably know a great deal about Pine in his character of Ishmael Hearne, since she had been acquainted with him intimately during the early part of his life. But, whatever she knew, or whatever she did not know, Lambert considered that it would be wise to enlist her on his side, as the mere fact that Chaldea was one of the opposite party would make her fight like a wild cat. And as the whole affair had to do with the gypsies, and as Gentilla Stanley was a gypsy, it was just as well to apply for her assistance. Nevertheless, Lambert was quite in the dark, as to what assistance could be rendered.

In this way the young man made his plans, only to be thwarted by the weakness of his body. He could crawl out of bed and sit before the fire, but in spite of all his will-power, he could not crawl as far as the camp. Baffled in this way, he decided to send a note asking Mother Cockleshell to call on him, although he knew that if Chaldea learned about the visit—which she was almost certain to do—she would be placed on her guard. But this had to be risked, and Lambert, moreover, believed that the old woman was quite equal to dealing with the girl. However, Fate took the matter out of his hands, and before he could even write the invitation, a visitor arrived in the person of Miss Greeby, who suggested a way out of the difficulty, by offering her services. Matters came to a head within half an hour of her presenting herself in the sitting-room.

Miss Greeby was quite her old breezy, masculine self, and her presence in the cottage was like a breath of moorland air blowing through the languid atmosphere of a hot-house. She was arrayed characteristically in a short-skirted, tailor-made gown of a brown hue and bound with brown leather, and wore in addition a man's cap, dog-skin gloves, and heavy laced-up boots fit to tramp miry country roads. With her fresh complexion and red hair, and a large frame instinct with vitality, she looked aggressively healthy, and Lambert with his failing life felt quite a weakling beside this magnificent goddess.

"Hallo, old fellow," cried Miss Greeby in her best man-to-man style, "feeling chippy? Why, you do look a wreck, I must say. What's up?"

"The fever's up and I'm down," replied Lambert, who was glad to see her, if only to distract his painful thoughts. "It's only a touch of malaria, my dear Clara. I shall be all right in a few days."

"You're hopeful, I must say, Lambert. What about a doctor?"

"I don't need one. Mrs. Tribb is nursing me."

"Coddling you," muttered Miss Greeby, planting herself manfully in an opposite chair and crossing her legs in a gentlemanly manner. "Fresh air and exercise, beefsteaks and tankards of beer are what you need. Defy Nature and you get the better of her. Kill or cure is my motto."

"As I have strong reasons to remain alive, I shan't adopt your prescription, Dr. Greeby," said Lambert, dryly. "What are you doing in these parts? I thought you were shooting in Scotland."

"So I was," admitted the visitor, frankly and laying her bludgeon—she still carried it—across her knee. "But I grew sick of the sport. Knocked over the birds too easy, Lambert, so there was no fun. The birds are getting as silly as the men."

"Well, women knock them over easy enough."

"That's what I mean," said Miss Greeby, vigorously. "It's a rotten world, this, unless one can get away into the wilds."

"Why don't you go there?"

"Well," Miss Greeby leaned forward with her elbows on her knees, and dandled the bludgeon with both hands. "I thought I'd like a change from the rough and ready. This case of Pine's rather puzzled me, and so I'm on the trail as a detective."

Lambert was rather startled. "That's considerably out of your line, Clara."

Miss Greeby nodded. "Exactly, and so I'm indulging in the novelty. One must do something to entertain one's self, you know, Lambert. It struck me that the gypsies know a lot more about the matter than they chose to say, so I came down yesterday, and put up at the Garvington Arms in the village. Here I'm going to stay until I can get at the root of the matter."

"What root?"

"I wish to learn who murdered Pine, poor devil."

"Ah," Lambert smiled. "You wish to gain the reward."

"Not me. I've got more money than I know what to do with, as it is. Silver is more anxious to get the cash than I am."

"Silver! Have you seen him lately?"

"A couple of days ago," Miss Greeby informed him easily. "He's my secretary now, Lambert. Yes! The poor beast was chucked out of his comfortable billet by the death of Pine, and hearing that I wanted some one to write my letters and run my errands, and act like a tame cat generally, he applied to me. Since I knew him pretty well through Pine, I took him on. He's a cunning little fox, but all right when he's kept in order. And I find him pretty useful, although I've only had him as a secretary for a fortnight."

Lambert did not immediately reply. The news rather amazed him, as it had always been Miss Greeby's boast that she could manage her own business. It was queer that she should have changed her mind in this respect, although she was woman enough to exercise that very feminine prerogative. But the immediate trend of Lambert's thoughts were in the direction of seeking aid from his visitor. He could not act himself because he was sick, and he knew that she was a capable person in dealing with difficulties. Also, simply for the sake of something to do she had become an amateur detective and was hunting for the trail of Pine's assassin. It seemed to Lambert that it would not be a bad idea to tell her of his troubles. She would, as he knew, be only too willing to assist, and in that readiness lay his hesitation. He did not wish, if possible, to lie under any obligation to Miss Greeby lest she should demand in payment that he should become her husband. And yet he believed that by this time she had overcome her desires in this direction. To make sure, he ventured on a few cautious questions.

"We're friends, aren't we, Clara?" he asked, after a long pause.

"Sure," said Miss Greeby, nodding heartily. "Does it need putting into words?"

"I suppose not, but what I mean is that we are pals." He used the word which he knew most appealed to her masculine affectations.

"Sure," said Miss Greeby again, and once more heartily. "Real, honest pals. I never believed in that stuff about the impossibility of a man and woman being pals unless there's love rubbish about the business. At one time, Lambert, I don't deny but what I had a feeling of that sort for you."

"And now?" questioned the young man with an uneasy smile.

"Now it's gone, or rather my love has become affection, and that's quite a different thing, old fellow. I want to see you happy, and you aren't now. I daresay you're still crying for the moon. Eh?" she looked at him sharply.

"You asked me that before when you came here," said Lambert, slowly. "And I refused to answer. I can answer now. The moon is quite beyond my reach, so I have dried my tears."

Miss Greeby, who was lighting a cigarette, threw away the match and stared hard at his haggard face. "Well, I didn't expect to hear that, now we know how the moon—"

"Call things by their right name," interrupted Lambert, sharply. "Agnes is now a widow, if that's what you mean."

"It is, if you call Agnes a thing. Of course, you'll marry her since the barrier has been removed?"

"Meaning Pine? No! I'm not certain on that point. She is a rich widow and I'm a poor artist. In honor bound I can't allow her to lose her money by becoming my wife."

Miss Greeby stared at the fire. "I heard about that beastly will," she said, frowning. "Horribly unfair, I call it. Still, I believed that you loved the moon—well, then, Agnes, since you wish us to be plain—and would carry her off if you had the pluck."

"I have never been accused of not having pluck, Clara. But there's another thing to be considered, and that's honor."

"Oh, bosh!" cried Miss Greeby, with boyish vigor. "You love her and she loves you, so why not marry?"

"I'm not worth paying two million for, Clara."

"You are, if she loves you."

"She does and would marry me to-morrow if I would let her. The hesitation is on my part."

"More fool you. If I were in her position I'd soon overcome your scruples."

"I think not," said Lambert delicately.

"Oh, I think so," she retorted. "A woman always gets her own way."

"And sometimes wrecks continents to get it."

"I'd wreck this one, anyhow," said Miss Greeby dryly. "However, we're pals, and if there's anything I can do—"

"Yes, there is," said Lambert abruptly, and making up his mind to trust her, since she showed plainly that there was no chance of love on her part destroying friendship. "I'm sick here and can't move. Let me engage you to act on my behalf."

"As what, if you don't mind my asking, Lambert?"

"As what you are for the moment, a detective."

"Ho!" said Miss Greeby in a guttural manner. "What's that?"

"I want you to learn on my behalf, and as my deputy, who murdered Pine."

"So that you can marry Agnes?"

"No. The will has stopped my chances in that direction. Her two million forms quite an insurmountable barrier between us now, as the fact of her being Pine's wife did formerly. Now you understand the situation, and that I am prevented by honor from making her my wife, don't let us talk any more on that especial subject."

"Right you are," assented Miss Greeby affably. "Only I'll say this, that you are too scrupulous, and if I can help you to marry Agnes I shall do so."

"Why?" demanded Lambert bluntly.

"Because I'm your pal and wish to see you happy. You won't be happy, like the Pears soap advertisement, until you get it. Agnes is the 'it.'"

"Well, then, leave the matter alone, Clara," said Lambert, taking the privilege of an invalid and becoming peevish. "As things stand, I can see no chance of marrying Agnes without violating my idea of honor."

"Then why do you wish me to help you?" demanded Miss Greeby sharply.

"How do I wish you to help me, you mean."

"Not at all. I know what you wish me to do; act as detective; I know about it, my dear boy."

"You don't," retorted Lambert, again fractious. "But if you listen I'll tell you exactly what I mean."

Miss Greeby made herself comfortable with a fresh cigarette, and nodded in an easy manner, "I'm all attention, old boy. Fire away!"

"You must regard my confidence as sacred."

"There's my hand on it. But I should like to know why you desire to learn who murdered Pine."

"Because if you don't track down the assassin, Agnes will get into trouble."

"Ho!" ejaculated Miss Greeby, guttural again. "Go on."

Lambert wasted no further time in preliminary explanations, but plunged into the middle of things. In a quarter of an hour his auditor was acquainted with the facts of a highly unpleasant case, but exhibited no surprise when she heard what her secretary had to do with the matter. In fact, she rather appeared to admire his acuteness in turning such shady knowledge to his own advantage. At the same time, she considered that Agnes had behaved in a decidedly weak manner. "If I'd been in her shoes I'd have fired the beast out in double-quick time," said Miss Greeby grimly. "And I'd have belted him over the head in addition."

"Then he would have gone straight to the police."

"Oh, no he wouldn't. One thousand reward against twenty-five thousand blackmail isn't good enough."

"He won't get his blackmail," said Lambert, tightening his lips.

"You bet he won't now that I've come into the matter. But there's no denying he's got the whip-hand so far."

"Agnes never wrote the letter," said Lambert quickly.

"Oh, that goes without the saying, my dear fellow. Agnes knew that if she became a rich widow, your uneasy sense of honor would never let you marry her. She had no reason to get rid of Pine on that score."

"Or on any score, you may add."

Miss Greeby nodded. "Certainly! You and Agnes should have got married and let Garvington get out of his troubles as best he could. That's what I should have done, as I'm not an aristocrat, and can't see the use of becoming the sacrifice for a musty, fusty old family. However, Agnes made her bargain and kept to it. She's all right, although other people may be not of that opinion."

"There isn't a man or woman who dare say a word against Agnes."

"A good many will say lots of words, should what you have told me get into print," rejoined Miss Greeby dryly.

"I agree with you. Therefore do I ask for your assistance. What is best to be done, Clara?"

"We must get the letter from Silver and learn who forged it. Once that is made plain, the truth will come to light, since the individual who forged and sent that letter must have fired the second shot."

"Quite so. But Silver won't give up the letter."

"Oh, yes, he will. He's my secretary, and I'll make him."

"Even as your secretary he won't," said Lambert, dubiously.

"We'll see about that, old boy. I'll heckle and harry and worry Silver on to the gallows if he doesn't do what he's told."

"The gallows. You don't think—"

"Oh, I think nothing. It was to Silver's interest that Pine should live, so I don't fancy he set the trap. It was to Chaldea's interest that Pine should not live, since she loves you, and I don't think she is to blame. Garvington couldn't have done it, as he has lost a good friend in Pine, and—and—go on Lambert, suggest some one else."

"I can't. And two out of three you mention were inside The Manor when the second shot was fired, so can prove an alibi."

"I'm not bothering about who fired the second shot," said Miss Greeby leisurely, "but as to who wrote that letter. Once we find the forger, we'll soon discover the assassin."

"True; but how are you going about it?"

"I shall see Silver and force him to give me the letter."

"If you can."

"Oh, I'll manage somehow. The little beast's a coward, and I'll bully him into compliance." Miss Greeby spoke very confidently. "Then we'll see the kind of paper the letter is written on, and there may be an envelope which would show where it was posted. Of course, the forger must be well acquainted with Agnes's handwriting."

"That's obvious," said Lambert promptly. "Well, I suppose that your way of starting the matter is the best. But we have only four days before Silver makes his move."

"When I get the letter he won't make any move," reported Miss Greeby, and she looked very determined.

"Let us hope so. But, Clara, before you return to town I wish you would see Mother Cockleshell."

"That old gypsy fortune-teller, who looks like an almshouse widow? Why?"

"She hates Chaldea, and I suspect that Chaldea has something to do with the matter of this conspiracy."

"Ha!" Miss Greeby rubbed her aquiline nose. "A conspiracy. Perhaps you may be right. But its reason?"

Lambert colored. "Chaldea wants me to marry her, you know."

"The minx! I know she does. I warned you against having her to sit for you, Lambert. But there's no sense in your suggestion, my boy. It wasn't any catch for her to get Pine killed and leave his wife free to marry you."

"No. And yet—and yet—hang it," the young man clutched his hair in desperation and glared at the fire, "I can't see any motive."

"Nor can I. Unless it is to be found in the City."

"Gypsies are more lawless than City men," observed the other quickly, "and Hearne would have enemies rather than Pine."

"I don't agree with you," said Miss Greeby, rising and getting ready to go away. "Hearne was nobody: Pine was a millionaire. Successful men have enemies all over the shop."

"At the inquest it was said that Pine had no enemies."

"Oh, rubbish. A strong man like that couldn't make such a fortune without exciting envy. I'll bet that his assassin is to be found in a frock coat and a silk hat. However, I'll look up Mother Cockleshell, as it is just as well to know what she thinks of this pretty gypsy hussy of yours."

"Not of mine. I don't care for her in the least."

"As if that mattered. There is always one who loves and one who is loved, as Heine says, and that is the cause of all life's tragedies. Of this tragedy maybe, although I think some envious stockbroker may have shot Pine as a too successful financial rival. However, we shall see about it."

"And see about another thing, Clara," said Lambert quickly. "Call on Agnes and tell her that she need not worry over Silver. She expects the Deluge in a few days, remember."

"Write and tell her that I have the case in hand and that she needn't trouble about Silver. I'll straighten him out."

"I fear you are too hopeful."

"I don't fear anything of the sort. I'll break his neck if he doesn't obey me. I wouldn't hesitate to do it, either."

Lambert ran his eyes over her masculine personality and laughed. "I quite believe that, Clara. But, I say, won't you have some tea before you go?"

"No, thanks. I don't eat between meals."

"Afternoon tea is a meal."

"Nonsense. It's a weakness. I'm not Garvington. By the way, where is he?"

"In Paris, but he returns in a few days."

"Then don't let him meddle with this matter, or he'll put things wrong."

"I shall allow no one but yourself to meddle, Clara, Garvington shan't know a single thing."

Miss Greeby nodded. "Right. All we wish kept quiet would be in the papers if Garvington gets hold of our secrets. He's a loose-tongued little glutton. Well, good-bye, old chap, and do look after yourself. Good people are scarce."

Lambert gripped her large hand. "I'm awfully obliged to you, Clara."

"Wait until I do something before you say that, old son," she laughed and strode towards the door. "By the way, oughtn't I to send the doctor in?"

"No. Confound the doctor! I'm all right. You'll see me on my legs in a few days."

"Then we can work together at the case. Keep your flag flying, old chap, for I'm at the helm to steer the bark." And with this nautical farewell she went off with a manly stride, whistling a gay tune.

Left alone, the invalid looked into the fire, and wondered if he had been right to trust her. After some thought, he concluded that it was the best thing he could have done, since, in his present helpless state, he needed some one to act as his deputy. And there was no doubt that Miss Greeby had entirely overcome the passion she had once entertained for him.

"I hope Agnes will think so also," thought Lambert, when he began a letter to the lady. "She was always rather doubtful of Clara."

CHAPTER XIV

MISS GREEBY, DETECTIVE

As Miss Greeby had informed Lambert, she intended to remain at the Garvington Arms until the mystery of Pine's death was solved. But her interview with him necessitated a rearrangement of plans, since the incriminating letter appeared to be such an important piece of evidence. To obtain it, Miss Greeby had decided to return to London forthwith, in order to compel its surrender. Silver would undoubtedly show fight, but his mistress was grimly satisfied that she would be able to manage him, and quite counted upon gaining her end by bullying him into compliance. When in possession of the letter she decided to submit it to Agnes and hear what that lady had to say about it as a dexterous piece of forgery. Then, on what was said would depend her next move in the complicated game. Meanwhile, since she was on the spot and desired to gather all possible evidence connected with Chaldea's apparent knowledge of the crime, Miss Greeby went straight from Lambert's cottage to the gypsy camp.

Here she found the community of vagrants in the throes of an election, or rather their excitement was connected with the deposition of Gentilla Stanley from the Bohemian throne, and the elevation of Chaldea. Miss Greeby mixed with the throng, dispensed a few judicious shillings and speedily became aware of what was going on. It appeared that Chaldea, being pretty and unscrupulous, and having gained, by cunning, a wonderful influence amongst the younger members of the tribe, was insisting that she should be elected its head. The older men and women, believing wisely that it was better to have an experienced ruler than a pretty figurehead, stood by Mother Cockleshell, therefore the camp was divided into two parties. Tongues were used freely, and occasionally fists came into play, while the gypsies gathered round the tent of the old woman and listened to the duet between her and the younger aspirant to this throne of Brentford. Miss Greeby, with crossed legs and leaning on her bludgeon, listened to the voluble speech of Mother Cockleshell, which was occasionally interrupted by Chaldea. The oration was delivered in Romany, and Miss Greeby only understood such scraps of it as was hastily translated to her by a wild-eyed girl to whom she had given a shilling. Gentilla, less like a sober pew-opener, and more resembling the Hecate of some witch-gathering, screamed objurgations at the pitch of her crocked voice, and waved her skinny arms to emphasize her words, in a most dramatic fashion.

"Oh, ye Romans," she screeched vehemently, "are ye not fools to be gulled by a babe with her mother's milk—and curses that it fed her—scarcely dry on her living lips? Who am I who speak, asses of the common? Gentilla Stanley, whose father was Pharaoh before her, and who can call up the ghosts of dead Egyptian kings, with a tent for a palace, and a cudgel for a sceptre, and the wisdom of our people at the service of all."

"Things have changed," cried out Chaldea with a mocking laugh. "For old wisdom is dead leaves, and I am the tree which puts forth the green of new truths to make the Gorgios take off their hats to the Romans."

"Oh, spawn of the old devil, but you lie. Truth is truth and changes not. Can you read the hand? can you cheat the Gentile? do you know the law of the Poknees, and can you diddle them as has money? Says you, 'I can!' And in that you lie, like your mother before you. Bless your wisdom"—Mother Cockleshell made an ironical curtsey. "Age must bow before a brat."

"Beauty draws money to the Romans, and wheedles the Gorgios to part with red gold. Wrinkles you have, mother, and weak wits to—"

"Weak wits, you drab? My weakest wits are your strongest. 'Wrinkles,' says you in your cunning way, and flaunts your brazen smoothness. I spit on you for a fool." The old woman suited her action to the word. "Every wrinkle is the mark of lessons learned, and them is wisdom which the Romans take from my mouth."

"Hear the witchly hag," cried Chaldea in her turn. "She and her musty wisdom that puts the Romans under the feet of the Gentiles. Are not three of our brothers in choky? have we not been turned off common and out of field? Isn't the fire low and the pot empty, and every purse without gold? Bad luck she has brought us," snarled the girl, pointing an accusing finger. "And bad luck we Romans will have till she is turned from the camp."

"Like a dog you would send me away," shrieked Mother Cockleshell, glancing round and seeing that Chaldea's supporters outnumbered her own. "But I'm dangerous, and go I shall as a queen should, at my own free will. I cast a shoe amongst you,"—she flung one of her own, hastily snatched off her foot—"and curses gather round it. Under its heels shall you lie, ye Romans, till time again and time once more be accomplished. I go on my own," she turned and walked to the door of her tent. "Alone I go to cheat the Gentiles and win my food. Take your new queen, and with her sorrow and starvation, prison, and the kicks of the Gorgios. So it is, as I have said, and so it shall be."

She vanished into the tent, and the older members of the tribe, shaking their heads over the ill-omen of her concluding words, withdrew sorrowfully to their various habitations, in order to discuss the situation. But the young men and women bowed down before Chaldea and forthwith elected her their ruler, fawning on her, kissing her hands and invoking blessings on her pretty face, that face which they hoped and believed would bring prosperity to them. And there was no doubt that of late, under Mother Cockleshell's leadership, the tribe had been unfortunate in many ways. It was for this reason that Chaldea had raised the standard of rebellion, and for this reason also she gained her triumph. To celebrate her coronation she gave Kara, who hovered constantly at her elbow, a couple of sovereigns, and told him to buy food and drink. In a high state of enjoyment the gypsies dispersed in order to prepare for the forthcoming festivity, and Chaldea, weary but victorious, stood alone by the steps of the caravan, which was her perambulating home. Seizing her opportunity, Miss Greeby approached.

"My congratulations to your majesty," she said ironically. "I'm sorry not to be able to stay for your coronation, which I presume takes place to-night. But I have to go back to London to see a friend of yours."

"I have no friends, my Gentile lady," retorted Chaldea, with a fiery spark in each eye. "And what do you here amongst the gentle Romany?"

"Gentle," Miss Greeby chuckled, "that's a new word for the row that's been going on, my girl. Do you know me?"

"As I know the road and the tent and the art of dukkerhin. You stay at the big house, and you love the rye who lived in the wood."

"Very clever of you to guess that," said Miss Greeby coolly, "but as it happens, you are wrong. The rye is not for me and not for you. He marries the lady he worships on his knees. Forgive me for speaking in this high-flowing manner," ended Miss Greeby apologetically, "but in romantic situations one must speak romantic words."

Chaldea did not pay attention to the greater part of this speech, as only one statement appealed to her. "The rye shall not marry the Gentile lady," she said between her white teeth.

"Oh, I think so, Chaldea. Your plotting has all been in vain."

"My plotting. What do you know of that?"

"A certain portion, my girl, and I'm going to know more when I see Silver."

Chaldea frowned darkly. "I know nothing of him."

"I think you do, since you gave him a certain letter."

"Patchessa tu adove?" asked Chaldea scornfully; then, seeing that her visitor did not understand her, explained: "Do you believe in that?"

"Yes," said Miss Greeby alertly. "You found the letter in Pine's tent when he was camping here as Hearne, and passed it to Silver so that he might ask money for it."

"It's a lie. I swear it's a lie. I ask no money. I told the tiny rye—"

"Silver, I presume," put in Miss Greeby carelessly.

"Aye: Silver is his name, and a good one for him as has no gold."

"He will get gold from Lady Agnes for the letter."

"No. Drodi—ah bah!" broke off Chaldea. "You don't understand Romanes. I speak the Gorgio tongue to such as you. Listen! I found the letter which lured my brother to his death. The rani wrote that letter, and I gave it to the tiny rye, saying: 'Tell her if she gives up the big rye free she shall go; if not take the letter to those who deal in the law.'"

"The police, I suppose you mean," said Miss Greeby coolly. "A very pretty scheme, my good girl. But it won't do, you know. Lady Agnes never wrote that letter, and had nothing to do with the death of her husband."

"She set a trap for him," cried Chaldea fiercely, "and Hearne walked into it like a rabbit into a snare. The big rye waited outside and shot—"

"That's a lie," interrupted Miss Greeby just as fiercely, and determined to defend her friend. "He would not do such a thing."

"Ha! but I can prove it, and will when the time is ripe. He becomes my rom does the big rye, or round his neck goes the rope; and she dances long-side, I swear."

"What a bloodthirsty idea, you savage devil! And how do you propose to prove that Mr. Lambert shot the man?"

"Aha," sneered Chaldea contemptuously, "you take me for a fool, saying more than I can do. But know this, my precious angel"—she fumbled in her pocket and brought out a more or less formless piece of lead—"what's this, may I ask? The bullet which passed through Hearne's heart, and buried itself in a tree-trunk."

Miss Greeby made a snatch at the article, but Chaldea was too quick for her and slipped it again into her pocket. "You can't prove that it is the bullet," snapped Miss Greeby glaring, for she dreaded lest its production should incriminate Lambert, innocent though she believed him to be.

"Kara can prove it. He went to where Hearne was shot and saw that there was a big tree by the blue door, and before the shrubbery. A shot fired from behind the bushes would by chance strike the tree. The bullet which killed my brother was not found in the heart. It passed through and was in the tree-trunk. Kara knifed it out and brought it to me. If this," Chaldea held up the bullet again jeeringly, "fits the pistol of the big rye he will swing for sure. The letter hangs her and the bullet hangs him. I want my price."

"You won't get it, then," said Miss Greeby, eyeing the pocket into which the girl had again dropped the bullet. "Mr. Lambert was absent in London on that night. I heard that by chance."

"Then you heard wrong, my Gentile lady. Avali, quite wrong. The big rye returned on that very night and went to Lundra again in the morning."

"Even if he did," said Miss Greeby desperately, "he did not leave the cottage. His housekeeper can prove—"

"Nothing," snapped Chaldea triumphantly. "She was in her bed and the golden rye was in his bed. My brother was killed after midnight, and if the rye took a walk then, who can say where he was?"

"You have to prove all this, you know."

Chaldea snapped her fingers. "First, the letter to shame her; then the bullet to hang him. The rest comes after. My price, you know, my Gorgious artful. I toves my own gad. It's a good proverb, lady, and true Romany."

"What does it mean?"

"I wash my own shirt," said Chaldea, significantly, and sprang up the steps of her gaily-painted caravan to shut herself in.

"What a fool I am not to take that bullet from her," thought Miss Greeby, standing irresolutely before the vehicle, and she cast a glance around to see if such an idea was feasible. It was not, as she speedily decided, for a single cry from Chaldea would bring the gypsies round to protect their new queen. It was probable also that the girl would fight like a wild cat; although Miss Greeby felt that she could manage her so far. But she was not equal to fighting the whole camp of vagrants, and so was compelled to abandon her scheme. In a somewhat discontented mood, she turned away, feeling that, so far, Chaldea had the whip-hand.

Then it occurred to her that she had not yet examined Mother Cockleshell as had been her original intention when she came to the camp. Forthwith she passed back to the tent under the elm, to interview the deposed queen. Here, she found Gentilla Stanley placing her goods in an untidy bundle on the back of a large gray donkey, which was her private property. The old creature's eyes were red with weeping and her gray hair had fallen down, so that she presented a somewhat wild appearance. This, in connection with her employment, reminded Miss Greeby—whose reading was wide—of a similar scene in Borrow's "Lavengro," when Mrs. Pentulengro's mother shifted herself. And for the moment Mother Cockleshell had just the hairy looks of Mrs. Hern, and also at the moment, probably had the same amiable feelings.

Feeling that the old woman detested her successful rival, Miss Greeby approached, guessing that now was the right moment to work on her mind, and thus to learn what she could of Chaldea's underhand doings. She quite expected a snub, as Gentilla could scarcely be expected to answer questions when taken up with her own troubles. But the artful creature, seeing by a side-glance that Miss Greeby was a wealthy Gentile lady, dropped one of her almshouse curtseys when she approached, and bundled up her hair. A change passed over her withered face, and Miss Greeby found herself addressing not so much a fallen queen, as a respectable old woman who had known better days.

"And a blessing on your sweet face, my angel," mumbled Mother Cockleshell. "For a heart you have to feel for my sorrows."

"Here is a sign of my feelings," said Miss Greeby, handing over a sovereign, for she rightly judged that the gypsy would only appreciate this outward symbol of sympathy. "Now, what do you know of Pine's murder?"

Mother Cockleshell, who was busy tying up the sovereign in a corner of her respectable shawl, after biting it to make sure it was current gold, looked up with a vacant expression. "Murder, my lady, and what should I know of that?"

Miss Greeby looked at her straightly. "What does Chaldea know of it?"

A vicious pair of devils looked out of the decent widow's eyes in a moment, and at once she became the Romany. "Hai! She knows, does she, the drab! I hope to see her hanged."

"For what?"

"For killing of Hearne, may his bones rest sweetly."

Miss Greeby suppressed an exclamation. "She accuses Lady Agnes of laying a trap by writing a letter, and says that Mr. Lambert fired the shot."

"Avali! Avali!" Mother Cockleshell nodded vigorously, but did not interrupt her preparations for departure. "That she would say, since she loves the Gorgio, and hates the rani. A rope round her neck to set the rye free to make Chaldea—my curses on her—his true wife."

"She couldn't have fired the shot herself, you know," went on

Miss Greeby in a musing manner. "For then she would remove an obstacle to Mr. Lambert marrying Lady Agnes."

"Blessings on her for a kind, Gentile lady," said Gentilla, piously, and looking more respectable than ever, since the lurking devils had disappeared. "But Chaldea is artful, and knows the rye."

"What do you mean?"

"This, my lady. Hearne, who was the Gorgio Pine, had the angel to wife, but he did not hope to live long because of illness."

Miss Greeby nodded. "Consumption, Pine told me."

"If he had died natural," pursued Mother Cockleshell, pulling hard at a strap, "maybe the Gentile lady would have married the golden rye, whom she loves. But by the violent death, Chaldea has tangled up both in her knots, and if they wed she will make trouble."

"So she says. But can she?"

"Hai! But she's a deep one, ma'am, believe me when I say so," Mother Cockleshell nodded sapiently. "But foolish trouble has she given herself, when the death of Hearne natural, or by the pistol-shot would stop the marriage."

"What do you mean?" inquired Miss Greeby once more.

"You Gentiles are fools," said Gentilla, politely. "For you put other things before true love. Hearne, as Pine, had much gold, and that he left to his wife should she not marry the golden rye."

"How do you know that?"

"Chaldea was told so by the dead, and told me, my lady. Now the angel of the big house would give up the gold to marry the rye, for her heart is all for him. 'But,' says he, and tell me if I'm wrong. Says he, 'No. If I make you my romi that would beggar you and fair it would not be, for a Romany rye to do!' So, my lady, the red gold parts them, because it's red money."

"Red money?"

"Blood money. The taint of blood is on the wealth of the dead one, and so it divides by a curse the true hearts of the living. You see, my lady?"

Miss Greeby did see, and the more readily, since she had heard Lambert express exactly the sentiments with which the old gypsy credited him. An overstrained feeling of honor prevented him in any case from making Agnes his wife, whether the death had come by violence or by natural causes. But it was amazing that Gentilla should know this, and Miss Greeby wonderingly asked her how she came by such knowledge. The respectable widow chuckled.

"I have witchly ways, ma'am, and the golden rye has talked many a time to me in my tent, when I told him of the Gorgious lady's goodness to me when ill. They love—aye, that is sure—but the money divides their hearts, and that is foolish. Chaldea had no need to shoot to keep them apart."

"How do you know she shot Pine?"

"Oh, I can say nothing the Poknees would listen to," said Mother Cockleshell readily. "For I speak only as I think, and not as I know. But the child was impatient for joy, and hoped by placing the cruel will between true hearts to gain that of the golden rye for her own part. But that she will not. Ha! Ha! Nor you, my lady, nor you."

"Me?" Miss Greeby colored even redder than she was by nature.

Gentilla looked at her shrewdly. "La! La! La! La!" she croaked. "Age brings a mighty wisdom. They were fools to throw me out," and she jerked her grizzled head in the direction of the caravans and tents.

"Don't talk rubbish, you old donkey! Mr. Lambert is only my friend."

"You're a woman and he's a man," said Mother Cockleshell sententiously.

"We are chums, pals, whatever you like to call us. I want to see him happy."

"He will never be happy, my lady, unless he marries the rani. And death, by bringing the money between their true love, has divided them forever, unless the golden rye puts his heart before his fear of silly chatter for them he moves amongst. The child was right to shoot Hearne, so far, although she could have waited and gained the same end. The rye is free to marry her, or to marry you, ma'am, but never to marry the angel, unless—" Mother Cockleshell adjusted the bundle carefully on the donkey, and then cut a long switch from the tree.

"I don't want to marry Mr. Lambert," said Miss Greeby decisively. "And I'll take care that Chaldea doesn't!"

Gentilla chuckled again. "Oh, trust you for that."

"As to Chaldea shooting Pine—"

"Leave it to me, leave it to me, ma'am," said the old gypsy with a grandiloquent wave of her dirty hand.

"But I wish to learn the truth and save Lady Agnes from this trouble."

"You wish to save her?" chuckled Mother Cockleshell. "And not the golden rye? Ah well, my angel, there are women, and women." She faced round, and the humor died out of her wrinkled face. "You wish for help and so have come to see me? Is it not so?"

"Yes," said Miss Greeby tartly. "Chaldea will make trouble."

"The child won't. I can manage her."

Miss Greeby hitched up her broad shoulders contemptuously. "She has managed you just now."

"There are ways and ways, and when the hour arrives, the sun rises to scatter the darkness," said Gentilla mystically. "Let the child win for the moment, for my turn comes."

"Then you know something?"

"What I know mustn't be said till the hour strikes. But content yourself, my Gorgious lady, with knowing that the child will make no trouble."

"She has parted with the letter?"

"I know of that letter. Hearne showed it to me, and would make for the big house, although I told him fair not to doubt his true wife."

"How did he get the letter?"

"That's tellings," said Mother Cockleshell with a wink of her lively eye.

"I've a good mind to take you to the police, and then you'd be forced to say what you know," said Miss Greeby crossly, for the vague hints irritated her not a little.

The old woman cackled in evident enjoyment. "Do that, and the pot will boil over, ma'am. I wish to help the angel rani who nursed me when I was sick, and I have debts to pay to Chaldea. Both I do in my own witchly way."

"You will help me to learn the truth?"

"Surely! Surely! my Gorgious one. And now," Mother Cockleshell gave a tug at the donkey's mouth, "I goes my ways."

"But where can I find you again?"

"When the time comes the mouth will open, and them as thinks they're high will find themselves in the dust. Aye, and maybe lower, if six feet of good earth lies atop, and them burning in lime, uncoffined and unblessed."

Miss Greeby was masculine and fearless, but there was something so weird about this mystic sentence, which hinted at capital punishment, that she shrank back nervously. Mother Cockleshell, delighted to see that she had made an impression, climbed on to the gray donkey and made a progress through the camp. Passing by Chaldea's caravan she spat on it and muttered a word or so, which did not indicate that she wished a blessing to rest on it. Chaldea did not show herself, so the deposed queen was accompanied to the outskirts of the wood by the elder gypsies, mourning loudly. But when they finally halted to see the last of Mother Cockleshell, she raised her hand and spoke authoritatively.

"I go and I come, my children. Forget not, ye Romans, that I say so much. When the seed needs rain it falls. Sarishan, brothers and sisters all." And with this strange speech, mystical to the last, she rode away into the setting sun, on the gray donkey, looking more like an almshouse widow than ever.

As for Miss Greeby, she strode out of the camp and out of the Abbot's Wood, and made for the Garvington Arms, where she had left her baggage. What Mother Cockleshell knew, she did not guess; what Mother Cockleshell intended to do, she could not think; but she was satisfied that Chaldea would in some way pay for her triumph. And the downfall of the girl was evidently connected with the unravelling of the murder mystery. In a witchly way, as the old woman would have said herself, she intended to adjust matters.

"I'll leave things so far in her hands," thought Miss Greeby. "Now for Silver."

CHAPTER XV

GUESSWORK

Whether Miss Greeby found a difficulty, as was probable, in getting Silver to hand over the forged letter, or whether she had decided to leave the solution of this mystery to Mother Cockleshell, it is impossible to say. But she certainly did not put in an appearance at Lady Agnes Pine's town house to report progress until after the new year. Nor in the meantime did she visit Lambert, although she wrote to say that she induced the secretary to delay his threatened exposure. The position of things was therefore highly unsatisfactory, since the consequent suspense was painful both to Agnes and her lover. And of course the widow had been duly informed of the interview at the cottage, and naturally expected events to move more rapidly.

However, taking the wise advice of Isaiah to "Make no haste in time of trouble," Agnes possessed her soul in patience, and did not seek out Miss Greeby in any way, either by visiting or by letter. She attended at her lawyers' offices to supervise her late husband's affairs, and had frequent consultations with Garvington's solicitors in connection with the freeing of the Lambert estates. Everything was going on very satisfactorily, even to the improvement of Lambert's health, so Agnes was not at all so ill at ease in her mind as might have been expected. Certainly the sword of Damocles still dangled over her head, and over the head of Lambert, but a consciousness that they were both innocent, assured her inwardly that it would not fall. Nevertheless the beginning of the new year found her in anything but a placid frame of mind. She was greatly relieved when Miss Greeby at last condescended to pay her a visit.

Luckily Agnes was alone when the lady arrived, as Garvington and his wife were both out enjoying themselves in their several ways. The pair had been staying with the wealthy widow for Christmas, and had not yet taken their departure, since Garvington always tried to live at somebody's expense if possible. He had naturally shut up The Manor during the festive season, as the villagers expected coals and blankets and port wine and plum-puddings, which he had neither the money nor the inclination to supply. In fact, the greedy little man considered that they should ask for nothing and pay larger rents than they did. By deserting them when peace on earth and goodwill to men prevailed, or ought to have prevailed, he disappointed them greatly and chuckled over their lamentations. Garvington was very human in some ways.

However, both the corpulent little lord and his untidy wife were out of the way when Miss Greeby was announced, and Agnes was thankful that such was the case, since the interview was bound to be an important one. Miss Greeby, as usual, looked large and aggressively healthy, bouncing into the room like an india-rubber ball. Her town dress differed very little from the garb she wore in the country, save that she had a feather-trimmed hat instead of a man's cap, and carried an umbrella in place of a bludgeon. A smile, which showed all her strong white teeth in a somewhat carnivorous way, overspread her face as she shook hands vigorously with her hostess. And Miss Greeby's grip was so friendly as to be positively painful.

"Here you are, Agnes, and here am I. Beastly day, ain't it? Rain and rain and rain again. Seems as though we'd gone back to Father Noah's times, don't it?"

"I expected you before, Clara," remarked Lady Agnes rather hurriedly, and too full of anxiety to discuss the weather.

"Well, I intended to come before," confessed Miss Greeby candidly. "Only, one thing and another prevented me!" Agnes noticed that she did not specify the hindrances. "It was the deuce's own job to get that letter. Oh, by the way, I suppose Lambert told you about the letter?"

"Mr. Silver told me about it, and I told Noel," responded Agnes gravely. "I also heard about your interview with—"

"Oh, that's ages ago, long before Christmas. I should have gone and seen him, to tell about my experiences at the gypsy camp, but I thought that I would learn more before making my report as a detective. By the way, how is Lambert, do you know?"

"He is all right now, and is in town."

"At his old rooms, I suppose. For how long? I want to see him."

"For an indefinite period. Garvington has turned him out of the cottage."

"The deuce! What's that for?"

"Well," said Agnes, explaining reluctantly, "you see Noel paid no rent, as Garvington is his cousin, and when an offer came along offering a pound a week for the place, Garvington said that he was too poor to refuse it. So Noel has taken a small house in Kensington, and Mrs. Tribb has been installed as his housekeeper. I wonder you didn't know these things."

"Why should I?" asked Miss Greeby, rather aggressively.

"Because it is Mr. Silver who has taken the cottage."

Miss Greeby sat up alertly. "Silver. Oh, indeed. Then that

explains why he asked me for leave to stay in the country. Said his health required fresh air, and that London got on his nerves. Hum! hum!" Miss Greeby bit the handle of her umbrella. "So he's taken the Abbot's Wood Cottage, has he? I wonder what that's for?"

"I don't know, and I don't care," said Agnes restlessly. "Of course I could have prevented Garvington letting it to him, since he tried to blackmail me, but I thought it was best to see the letter, and to understand his meaning more thoroughly before telling my brother about his impertinence. Noel wanted me to tell, but I decided not to—in the meantime at all events."

"Silver's meaning is not hard to understand," said Miss Greeby, drily and feeling in her pocket. "He wants to get twenty-five thousand pounds for this." She produced a sheet of paper dramatically. "However, I made the little animal give it to me for nothing. Never mind what arguments I used. I got it out of him, and brought it to show you."

Agnes, paling slightly, took the letter and glanced over it with surprise.

"Well," she said, drawing a long breath, "if I had not been certain that I never wrote such a letter, I should believe that I did. My handwriting has certainly been imitated in a wonderfully accurate way."

"Who imitated it?" asked Miss Greeby, who was watching her eagerly.

"I can't say. But doesn't Mr. Silver—"

"Oh, he knows nothing, or says that he knows nothing. All he swears to is that Chaldea found the letter in Pine's tent the day after his murder, and before Inspector Darby had time to search. The envelope had been destroyed, so we don't know if the letter was posted or delivered by hand."

"If I had written such a letter to Noel," said Agnes quietly, "it certainly would have been delivered by hand."

"In which case Pine might have intercepted the messenger," put in Miss Greeby. "It couldn't have been sent by post, or Pine would not have got hold of it, unless he bribed Mrs. Tribb into giving it up."

"Mrs. Tribb is not open to bribery, Clara. And as to the letter, I never wrote it, nor did Noel ever receive it."

"It was written from The Manor, anyhow," said Miss Greeby bluntly. "Look at the crest and the heading. Someone in the house wrote it, if you didn't."

"I'm not so sure of that. The paper might have been stolen."

"Well." Miss Greeby again bit her umbrella handle reflectively. "There's something in that, Agnes. Chaldea told Mrs. Belgrove's fortune in the park, and afterwards she came to the drawing-room to tell it again. I wonder if she stole the paper while she was in the house."

"Even if she did, an uneducated gypsy could not have forged the letter."

"She might have got somebody to do so," suggested Miss Greeby, nodding.

"Then the somebody must be well acquainted with my handwriting," retorted Lady Agnes, and began to study the few lines closely.

She might have written it herself, so much did it resemble her style of writing. The terse communication stated that the writer, who signed herself "Agnes Pine," would meet "her dearest Noel" outside the blue door, shortly after midnight, and hoped that he would have the motor at the park gates to take them to London en route to Paris. "Hubert is sure to get a divorce," ended the letter, "and then we can marry at once and be happy ever more."

It was certainly a silly letter, and Agnes laughed scornfully.

"I don't express myself in that way," she said contemptuously, and still eyeing the writing wonderingly. "And as I respected my husband and respect myself, I should never have thought of eloping with my cousin, especially from Garvington's house, when I had much better and safer chances of eloping in town. Had Noel received this, he would never have believed that I wrote it, as I assuredly did not. And a 'motor at the park gates,'" she read. "Why not at the postern gate, which leads to the blue door? that would have been safer and more reasonable. Pah! I never heard such rubbish," and she folded up the letter to slip it into her pocket.

Miss Greeby looked rather aghast. "Oh, you must give it back to me," she said hurriedly. "I have to look into the case, you know."

"I shall not give it back to you," said Agnes in a determined manner. "It is in my possession and shall remain there. I wish to show it to Noel."

"And what am I to say to Silver?"

"Whatever you like. You can manage him, you know."

"He'll make trouble."

"Now that he has lost this weapon"—Agnes touched her pocket—"he can't."

"Well"—Miss Greeby shrugged her big shoulders and stood up—"just as you please. But it would be best to leave the letter and the case in my hands."

"I think not," rejoined Agnes decisively. "Noel is now quite well again, and I prefer him to take charge of the matter himself."

"Is that all the thanks I get for my trouble?"

"My dear Clara," said the other cordially, "I am ever so much obliged to you for robbing Mr. Silver of this letter. But I don't wish to put you to any more trouble."

"Just as you please," said Miss Greeby again, and rather sullenly. "I wash my hands of the business, and if Silver makes trouble you have only yourself to thank. I advise you also, Agnes, to see Mother Cockleshell and learn what she has to say."

"Does she know anything?"

"She gave me certain mysterious hints that she did. But she appears to have a great opinion of you, my dear, so she may be more open with you than she was with me."

"Where is she to be found?"

"I don't know. Chaldea is queen of the tribe, which is still camped on the outskirts of Abbot's Wood. Mother Cockleshell has gone away on her own. Have you any idea who wrote the letter?"

Agnes took out the forged missive again and studied it. "Not in the least," she said, shaking her head.

"Do you know of any one who can imitate your handwriting?"

"Not that I know—oh," she stopped suddenly and grew as white as the widow's cap she wore. "Oh," she said blankly.

"What is it?" demanded Miss Greeby, on fire with curiosity. "Have you thought of any one?"

Agnes shook her head again and placed the letter in her pocket. "I can think of no one," she said in a low voice.

Miss Greeby did not entirely believe this, as the sudden hesitation and the paleness hinted at some unexpected thought, probably connected with the forgery. However, since she had done all she could, it was best, as she judged, to leave things in the widow's hands. "I'm tired of the whole business," said Miss Greeby carelessly. "It wouldn't do for me to be a detective, as I have no staying power, and get sick of things. Still, if you want me, you know where to send for me, and at all events I've drawn Silver's teeth."

"Yes, dear; thank you very much," said Agnes mechanically, so the visitor took her leave, wondering what was rendering her hostess so absent-minded. A very persistent thought told her that Agnes had made a discovery in connection with the letter, but since she would not impart that thought there was no more to be said.

When Miss Greeby left the house and was striding down the street, Agnes for the third time took the letter from her pocket and studied every line of the writing. It was wonderfully like her own, she thought again, and yet wondered both at the contents and at the signature. "I should never have written in this way to Noel," she reflected. "And certainly I should never have signed myself 'Agnes

Pine' to so intimate a note. However, we shall see," and with this cryptic thought she placed the letter in her desk.

When Garvington and his wife returned they found Agnes singularly quiet and pale. The little man did not notice this, as he never took any interest in other people's emotions, but his wife asked questions to which she received no answers, and looked at Agnes uneasily, when she saw that she did not eat any dinner to speak of. Lady Garvington was very fond of her kind-hearted sister-in-law, and would have been glad to know what was troubling her. But Agnes kept her worries to herself, and insisted that Jane should go to the pantomime, as she had arranged with some friends instead of remaining at home. But when Garvington moved to leave the drawing-room, after drinking his coffee, his sister detained him.

"I want you to come to the library to write a letter for me, Freddy," she said in a tremulous voice.

"Can't you write it yourself?" said Garvington selfishly, as he was in a hurry to get to his club.

"No, dear. I am so tired," sighed Agnes, passing her hand across her brow.

"Then you should have kept on Silver as your secretary," grumbled Garvington. "However, if it won't take long, I don't mind obliging you." He followed her into the library, and took his seat at the writing table. "Who is the letter to?" he demanded, taking up a pen in a hurry.

"To Mr. Jarwin. I want him to find out where Gentilla Stanley is. It's only a formal letter, so write it and sign it on my behalf."

"Like an infernal secretary," sighed Garvington, taking paper and squaring his elbows. "What do you want with old Mother Cockleshell?"

"Miss Greeby was here to-day and told me that the woman knows something about poor Hubert's death."

Garvington's pen halted for a moment, but he did not look round. "What can she possibly know?" he demanded irritably.

"That's what I shall find out when Mr. Jarwin discovers her," said Agnes, who was in a low chair near the fire. "By the way, Freddy, I am sorry you let the Abbot's Wood Cottage to Mr. Silver."

"Why shouldn't I?" growled Garvington, writing industriously. "Noel didn't pay me a pound a week, and Silver does."

"You might have a more respectable tenant," said Agnes scathingly.

"Who says Silver isn't respectable?" he asked, looking round.

"I do, and I have every reason to say so."

"Oh, nonsense!" Garvington began to write again. "Silver was Pine's secretary, and now he's Miss Greeby's. They wouldn't have engaged him unless he was respectable, although he did start life as a pauper toymaker. I suppose that is what you mean, Agnes. I'm surprised at your narrowness."

"Ah, we have not all your tolerance, Freddy. Have you finished that letter?"

"There you are." Garvington handed it over. "You don't want me to address the envelope?"

"Yes, I do," Agnes ran her eyes over the missive; "and you can add a postscript to this, telling Mr. Jarwin he can take my motor to look for Gentilla Stanley if he chooses."

Garvington did as he was asked reluctantly. "Though I don't see why Jarwin can't supply his own motors," he grumbled, "and ten to one he'll only put an advertisement in the newspapers."

"As if Mother Cockleshell ever saw a newspaper," retorted his sister. "Oh, thank you, Freddy, you are good," she went on when he handed her the letter in a newly addressed envelope; "no, don't go, I want to speak to you about Mr. Silver."

Garvington threw himself with a growl into a chair. "I don't know anything about him except that he's my tenant," he complained.

"Then it is time you did. Perhaps you are not aware that Mr. Silver tried to blackmail me."

"What?" the little man grew purple and exploded. "Oh, nonsense!"

"It's anything but nonsense." Agnes rose and went to her desk to get the forged letter. "He came to me a long time before Christmas and said that Chaldea found this," she flourished the letter before her brother's eyes, "in Hubert's tent when he was masquerading as Hearne."

"A letter? What does it say?" Garvington stretched out his hand.

Agnes drew back and returned to her seat by the fire. "I can tell you the contents," she said coolly, "it is supposed to be written by me to Noel and makes an appointment to meet him at the blue door on the night of Hubert's death in order to elope."

"Agnes, you never wrote such a letter," cried Garvington, jumping up with a furious red face.

His sister did not answer for a moment. She had taken the letter just written to Jarwin by Garvington and was comparing it with that which Miss Greeby had extorted from Silver. "No," she said in a strange voice and becoming white, "I never wrote such a letter; but I should be glad to know why you did."

"I did?" Garvington retreated and his face became as white as that of the woman who confronted him, "what the devil do you mean?"

"I always knew that you were clever at imitating handwriting, Freddy," said Agnes, while the two letters shook in her grasp, "we used to make a joke of it, I remember. But it was no joke when you altered that check Hubert gave you, and none when you imitated his signature to that mortgage about which he told me."

"I never—I never!" stammered the detected little scoundrel, holding on to a chair for support. "I never—"

"Spare me these lies," interrupted his sister scornfully, "Hubert showed the mortgage, when it came into his possession, to me. He admitted that his signature was legal to spare you, and also, for my sake, hushed up the affair of the check. He warned you against playing with fire, Freddy, and now you have done so again, to bring about his death."

"It's a damned lie."

"It's a damned truth," retorted Agnes fiercely. "I got you to write the letter to Mr. Jarwin so that I might compare the signature to the one in the forged letter. Agnes Pine in one and Agnes Pine in the other, both with the same twists and twirls—very, very like my signature and yet with a difference that I alone can detect. The postscript about the motor I asked you to write because the word occurs in the forged letter. Motor and motor—both the same."

"It's a lie," denied Garvington again. "I have not imitated your handwriting in the letter to Jarwin."

"You unconsciously imitated the signature, and you have written the word motor the same in both letters," said Agnes decisively. "I suddenly thought of your talent for writing like other people when Clara Greeby asked me to-day if I could guess who had forged the letter. I laid a trap for you and you have fallen into it. And you"—she took a step forward with fiery glance so that Garvington, retreating, nearly tumbled over a chair—"you laid a trap for Hubert into which he fell."

"I never did—I never did!" babbled Garvington, gray with fear.

"Yes, you did. I swear to it. Now I understand why you threatened to shoot any possible burglar who should come to The Manor. You learned, in some way, I don't know how, that Hubert was with the gypsies, and, knowing his jealous nature, you wrote this letter and let it fall into his hands, so that he might risk being shot as a robber and a thief."

"I—I—I—didn't shoot him," panted the man brokenly.

"It was not for the want of trying. You broke his arm, and probably would have followed him out to inflict a mortal wound if your accomplice in the shrubbery had not been beforehand with you."

"Agnes, I swear that I took Pine for a burglar, and I don't know who shot him. Really, I don't!"

"You liar!" said Agnes with intense scorn. "When you posted your accompl—"

She had no chance to finish the word, for Garvington broke in furiously and made a great effort to assert himself. "I had no accomplice. Who shot Pine I don't know. I never wrote the letter; I never lured him to his death; he was more good to me alive than dead. He never—"

"He was not more good to you alive than dead," interrupted Lady Agnes in her turn. "For Hubert despised you for the way in which you tried to trick him out of money. He thought you little better than a criminal, and only hushed up your wickedness for my sake. You would have got no more money out of him, and you know that much. By killing him you hoped that I would get the fortune and then you could plunder me at your leisure. Hubert was hard to manage, and you thought that I would be easy. Well, I have got the money and you have got rid of Hubert. But I shall punish you."

"Punish me?" Garvington passed his tongue over his dry lips, and looked as though in his terror he would go down on his knees to plead.

"Oh, not by denouncing you to the police," said his sister contemptuously. "For, bad as you are, I have to consider our family name. But you had Hubert shot so as to get the money through me, and now that I am in possession I shall surrender it to the person named in the sealed envelope."

"No! No! No! No! Don't—don't—"

"Yes, I shall. I can do so by marrying Noel. I shall no longer consider the financial position of the family. I have sacrificed enough, and I shall sacrifice no more. Hubert was a good husband to me, and I was a good and loyal wife to him; but his will insults me, and you have made me your enemy by what you have done."

"I did not do it. I swear I did not do it."

"Yes, you did; and no denial on your part will make me believe otherwise. I shall give you a few days to think over the necessity of making a confession, and in any case I shall marry Noel."

"And lose the money. You shan't!"

"Shan't!" Agnes stepped forward and looked fairly into his shifty eyes. "You are not in a position to say that, Freddy. I am mistress both of the situation and of Hubert's millions. Go away," she pushed him toward the door. "Take time to think over your position, and confess everything to me."

Garvington got out of the room as swiftly as his shaky legs could carry him, and paused at the door to turn with a very evil face.

"You daren't split on me," he screeched. "I defy you! I defy you! You daren't split on me."

Alas! Agnes knew that only too well, and when he disappeared she wept bitterly, feeling her impotence.

CHAPTER XVI

THE LAST STRAW

Lady Agnes was inaccurate when she informed Miss Greeby that her cousin had taken a house in Kensington, since, like many women, she was accustomed to speak in general terms, rather than in a precise way. The young man certainly did live in the suburb she mentioned, but he had simply rented a furnished flat in one of the cheaper streets. He was the poorest of all the Lamberts, and could scarcely pay his club subscriptions, much less live in the style his ancient name demanded. The St. James's chambers had merely been lent to him by a friend, and when the owner returned, the temporary occupant had to shift. Therefore, on the score of economy, he hired the dingy flat and brought up Mrs. Tribb to look after it. The little woman, on her master's account, was disgusted with the mean surroundings.

"When you ought to be living in a kind of Buckingham Palace, Master Noel, as I should declare with my dying breath," she said indignantly. "And have the title, too, if things was as they ought to be."

"I shouldn't be much better off if I did have the title, Mrs. Tribb," replied Lambert with a shrug. "It's common knowledge that Garvington can scarcely keep his head above water. As an old family servant you should know."

"Ah, Master Noel, there's many things as I know, as I'm sorry I do know," said Mrs. Tribb incoherently. "And them lords as is dead and buried did waste the money, there's no denying. But some of your cousins, Master Noel, have gone into trade and made money, more shame to them."

"I don't see that, Mrs. Tribb. I'd go into trade myself if I had any head for figures. There's no disgrace in trade."

"Not for them as isn't Lamberts, Master Noel, and far be it from me to say so, gentry not being so rich as they used to be when my mother was a gal. I don't hold with it though for you, sir. But now Lady Agnes having millions and billions will make things easier for you."

"Certainly not, Mrs. Tribb. How could I take money from her?"

"And why not, Master Noel? if you'll excuse my making so free. As a child she'd give you anything in the way of toys, and as a grown-up, her head is yours if not her heart, as is—"

"There! there! Don't talk any more," said Lambert, coloring and vexed.

"I haven't annoyed you, sir, I hope. It's my heart as speaks."

"I appreciate the interest you take in the family, Mrs. Tribb, but you had better leave some things unsaid. Now, go and prepare tea, as Lady Agnes has written saying she will be here this afternoon."

"Oh, Master Noel, and you only tell me now. Then there ain't time to cook them cakes she dotes on."

But Lambert declined to argue further, and Mrs. Tribb withdrew, murmuring that she would have to make shift with sardine sandwiches. Her tongue was assuredly something of a nuisance, but the young man knew how devoted she was to the family, and, since she had looked after him when he was a child, he sanctioned in her a freedom he would not have permitted any one else to indulge in. And it is to be feared, that the little woman in her zeal sometimes abused her privileges.

The sitting room was small and cramped, and atrociously furnished in an overcrowded way. There were patterns on the wallpaper, on the carpet, on the tablecloth and curtains, until the eye ached for a clean surface without a design. And there were so many ill-matched colors, misused for decorative purposes, that Lambert shuddered to the core of his artistic soul when he beheld them. To neutralize the glaring tints, he pulled down the blinds of the two windows which looked on to a dull suburban roadway, and thus shut out the weak sunshine. Then he threw himself into an uncomfortable arm-chair and sought solace in his briar root. The future was dark, the present was disagreeable, and the past would not bear thinking about, so intimately did it deal with the murder of Pine, the threats of Silver, and the misery occasioned by the sacrifice of Agnes to the family fetish. It was in the young man's mind to leave England forthwith and begin a new life, unhampered by former troubles and present grievances. But Agnes required help and could not be left to struggle unaided, so Lambert silently vowed again, as he had vowed before, to stand by her to the end. Yet so far he was unable to see what the end would be.

While he thus contemplated the unpleasantness of life he became aware that the front door bell was ringing, and he heard Mrs. Tribb hurrying along the passage. So thin were the walls, and so near the door that he heard also the housekeeper's effusive welcome, which was cut short by a gasp of surprise. Lambert idly wondered what caused the little woman's astonishment, but speedily learned when Agnes appeared in the room. With rare discretion Mrs. Tribb ushered in the visitor and then fled to the kitchen to wonder why the widow had discarded her mourning.

"And him only planted six months, as you might say," murmured the puzzled woman. "Whatever will Master Noel say to such goings on?"

Master Noel said nothing, because he was too astonished to speak, and Agnes, seeing his surprise, and guessing its cause, waited, somewhat defiantly, for him to make an observation. She was dressed in a gray silk frock, with a hat and gloves, and shoes to match, and drew off a fur-lined cloak of maroon-colored velvet, when she entered the room. Her face was somewhat pale and her eyes looked unnaturally large, but she had a resolute expression about her mouth, which showed that she had made up her mind. Lambert, swift, from long association, to read her moods, wondered what conclusion she had arrived at, and proceeded to inquire.

"Whatever is the meaning of this?" he demanded, considerably startled.

"This dress?"

"Of course. Where is your widow's cap and—"

"In the fire, and there they can remain until they are burned to ashes."

Lambert stared harder than ever. "What does it mean?" he asked again.

"It means," said Agnes, replying very directly, "that the victim is no longer decked out for the sacrifice. It means, that as Hubert insulted me by his will, I no longer intend to consider his memory."

"But, Agnes, you respected him. You always said that you did?"

"Quite so, until his will was read. Then when I found that his mean jealousy—which was entirely unreasonable—had arranged to rob me of my income by preventing my marriage with you, I ceased to have any regard for him. Hubert knew that I loved you, and was content to take me on those terms so long as I was loyal to him. I was loyal, and did what I could to show him gratitude for the way in which he helped the family. Now his will has broken the bargain I respect him no longer, and for that reason I refuse to pose any longer as a grieving widow."

"I wonder, with these thoughts, that you posed at all," said Lambert gloomily, and pushed forward a chair.

"I could not make up my mind until lately what to do," explained Agnes, sitting down gracefully, "and while I accepted his money it appeared to me that I ought to show his memory the outward respect of crape and all the rest of it. Now," she leaned forward and spoke meaningly, "I am resolved to surrender the money. That breaks the link between us. The will! the will!" she tapped an impatient foot on the carpet. "How could you expect any woman to put up with such an insult?"

Lambert dropped on the sofa and looked at her hard. "What's up?" he asked anxiously. "I never saw you like this before."

"I was not free when you last saw me," she replied dryly.

"Oh, yes; you were a widow."

"I mean free, in my own mind, to marry you. I am now. I don't intend to consider the family or society, or Mr. Silver's threats, or anything else. I have shaken off my fetters; I have discarded my ring." She violently pulled off her glove to show that the circle of gold was absent. "I am free, and I thank God that I am free."

"Agnes! Agnes! I can't reduce you to poverty by marrying you. It would not be honorable of me."

"And would it be honorable on my part for me to keep the money of a man I despise because his will insults me?" she retorted.

"We argued all this before."

"Yes, we did, and concluded to wait until we saw how the estates could be freed before we came to any conclusion."

"And do you see now how the estates can be freed without using Pine's money, Agnes?" asked Lambert anxiously.

"No. Things are ever so much worse than I thought. Garvington can hold out for another year, but at the end of twelve months the estates will be sold up by the person whose name is in the sealed envelope, and he will be reduced to some hundreds a year. The Lamberts!" she waved her arm dramatically, "are ruined, my dear; entirely ruined!"

"And for the simple reason that you wish us to place love before duty."

Agnes leaned forward and took his hand firmly. "Noel, you love me?"

"Of course I do."

"Do you love the family name better?"

"In one way I wish to save it, in another I am willing to let it go hang."

"Yes. Those were my views until three or four days ago."

"And what caused you to change your mind, dear?"

"A visit which Clara Greeby paid me."

"Oh." Lambert sat up very straight. "She hasn't been making mischief, has she?"

"Not at all. On the contrary, she has done both of us a great service."

Lambert nodded thankfully. He felt doubtful as to whether Miss Greeby really had meant to renounce her absurd passion for himself, and it was a relief to find that she had been acting honestly. "Has she then learned who killed Pine?" he asked cautiously.

Lady Agnes suddenly rose and began to pace the room, twisting her gloves and trying to control herself. Usually she was so composed that Lambert wondered at this restlessness. He wondered still more when she burst into violent tears, and therefore hastened to draw her back to the chair. When she was seated he knelt beside her and passed his arm round her neck, as distressed as she was. It was so unlike Agnes to break down in this way, and more unlike her to sob brokenly. "Oh, I'm afraid—I'm afraid."

"Afraid of what, darling?"

"I'm afraid to learn who killed my husband. He might have done so, and yet he only fired the first shot—"

"Agnes," Lambert rose up suddenly, "are you talking of Garvington?"

"Yes." She leaned back and dried her tears. "In spite of what he says, I am afraid he may be guilty."

Lambert's heart seemed to stand still. "You talk rubbish!" he cried angrily.

"I wish it was. Oh, how I wish it was rubbish! But I can't be sure. Of course, he may have meant what he says—"

"What does he say? Tell me everything. Oh, heavens!" Lambert clutched his smooth hair. "What does it all mean?"

"Ruin to the Lambert family. I told you so."

"You have only told me scraps so far. I don't understand how you can arrive at the conclusion that Garvington is guilty. Agnes, don't go on crying in so unnecessary a way. If things have to be faced, surely we are strong enough to face them. Don't let our emotions make fools of us. Stop it! Stop it!" he said sharply and stamping. "Dry your eyes and explain matters."

"I—I can't help my feelings," faltered Agnes, beginning to respond to the spur, and becoming calmer.

"Yes, you can. I don't offer you brandy or smelling salts, or anything of the sort, because I know you to be a woman with a firm mind. Exert your will, and compel your nerves to be calm. This exhibition is too cheap."

"Oh," cried Agnes indignantly, and this feeling was the one Lambert wished to arouse, "how can you talk so?"

"Because I love you and respect you," he retorted.

She knew that he meant what he said, and that her firmness of mind and self-control had always appealed to him, therefore she made a great effort and subdued her unruly nerves. Lambert gave her no assistance, and merely walked up and down the room while waiting for her to recover. It was not easy for her to be herself immediately, as she really was shaken, and privately considered that he expected too much. But pride came to her aid, and she gradually became more composed. Meanwhile Lambert pulled up the blind to display the ugly room in all its deformity, and the sight—as he guessed it would—extorted an exclamation from her.

"Oh, how can you live in this horrid place?" she asked irrelevantly.

"Necessity knows no law. Are you better?"

"Yes; I am all right. But you are brutal, Noel."

"I wouldn't have been brutal to a weaker woman," he answered. "And by acting as I have done, I show how much I think of you."

"Rather a strange way of showing approval. But your drastic methods have triumphed. I am quite composed, and shall tell you of our disgrace in as unemotional a manner as if I were reckoning pounds, shillings and pence."

"Disgrace?" Lambert fastened on the one word anxiously. "To us?"

"To Garvington in the first place. But sit down and listen. I shall tell you everything, from the moment Clara came to see me."

Lambert nodded and resumed his seat. Agnes, with wonderful coolness, detailed Miss Greeby's visit and production of the letter. Thence she passed on to explain how she had tricked Garvington into confession. "But he did not confess," interrupted Lambert at this point.

"Not at the moment. He did yesterday in a letter to me. You see, he left my house immediately and slept at his club. Then he went down to The Manor and sent for Jane, who, by the way, knows nothing of what I have explained. Here are two letters," added Agnes, taking an envelope out of her pocket. "One is the forged one, and the other came from Garvington yesterday. Even though he is not imitating my writing, you can see every now and then the similarity. Perhaps there is a family resemblance in our caligraphy." Her cousin examined the two epistles with a rather scared look, for there was no doubt that things looked black against the head of the family. However, he did not read Garvington's letter, but asked Agnes to explain. "What excuse does he make for forging your name?" asked Lambert in a business-like way, for there was no need to rage over such a worm as Freddy.

"A very weak one," she replied. "So weak that I scarcely believe him to be in earnest. Besides, Freddy always was a liar. He declares that when he went to see about getting the gypsies turned off the land, he caught sight of Hubert. He did not speak to him, but learned the truth from Mr. Silver, whom he forced to speak. Then he wrote the letter and let it purposely fall into Mr. Silver's hands, and by Mr. Silver it was passed on to Hubert. Freddy writes that he only wanted to hurt Hubert so that he might be laid up in bed at The

Manor. When he was weak—Hubert, I mean—Freddy then intended to get all the money he could out of him."

"He did not wish to kill Pine, then?"

"No. And all the evidence goes to show that he only broke Hubert's arm."

"That is true," murmured Lambert thoughtfully, "for the evidence of the other guests and of the servants showed plainly at the inquest that the second shot was fired outside while Garvington was indoors."

Agnes nodded. "Yes; it really seems as though Freddy for once in his life is telling the exact truth."

Her cousin glanced at Garvington's lengthy letter of explanation. "Do you really believe that he hoped to manage Pine during the illness?"

"Well," said Agnes reluctantly, "Freddy has tremendous faith in his powers of persuasion. Hubert would do nothing more for him since he was such a cormorant for money. But if Hubert had been laid up with a broken arm, it is just possible that he might have been worried into doing what Freddy wanted, if only to get rid of his importunity."

"Hum! It sounds weak. Garvington certainly winged Pine, so that seems to corroborate the statement in this letter. He's such a good shot that he could easily have killed Pine if he wanted to."

"Then you don't think that Freddy is responsible for the death?" inquired Agnes with a look of relief.

Lambert appeared worried. "I think not, dear. He lured Hubert into his own private trap so as to get him laid up and extort money. Unfortunately, another person, aware of the trap, waited outside and killed your poor husband."

"According to what Freddy says, Mr. Silver knew of the trap, since he delivered the letter to Hubert. And Mr. Silver knew that Freddy had threatened to shoot any possible burglar. It seems to me," ended Agnes deliberately, "that Mr. Silver is guilty."

"But why should he shoot Pine, to whom he owed so much?"

"I can't say."

"And, remember, Silver was inside the house."

"Yes," assented Lady Agnes, in dismay. "That is true. It is a great puzzle, Noel. However, I am not trying to solve it. Clara says that Mr. Silver will hold his tongue, and certainly as the letter is now in my possession he cannot bring forward any evidence to show that I am inculpated in the matter. I think the best thing to do is to let Freddy and Mr. Silver fight out the matter between them, while we are on our honeymoon."

Lambert started. "Agnes! What do you mean?"

She grew impatient. "Oh, what is the use of asking what I mean when you know quite well, Noel? Hubert insulted me in his will, and cast a slur on my character by forbidding me to marry you. Freddy—although he did not fire the second shot—certainly lured Hubert to his death by forging that letter. I don't intend to consider my husband's memory any more, nor my brother's position. I shall never speak to him again if I can help it, as he is a wicked little animal. I have sacrificed myself sufficiently, and now I intend to take my own way. Let the millions go, and let Freddy be ruined, if only to punish him for his wickedness."

"But, dear, how can I ask you to share my poverty?" said Lambert, greatly distressed. "I have only five hundred a year, and you have been accustomed to such luxury."

"I have another five hundred a year of my own," said Agnes obstinately, "which Hubert settled on me for pin money. He refused to make any other settlements. I have a right to that money, since I sacrificed so much, and I shall keep it. Surely we can live on one thousand a year."

"In England?" inquired Lambert doubtfully. "And after you have led such a luxurious life?"

"No," she said quickly. "I mean in the Colonies. Let us go to Australia, or Canada, or South Africa, I don't care which, and cut ourselves off from the past. We have suffered enough; let us now think of ourselves."

"But are we not selfish to let the family name be disgraced?"

"Freddy is selfish, and will disgrace it in any case," said Agnes, with a contemptuous shrug. "What's the use of pulling him out of the mud, when he will only sink back into it again? No, Noel, if you love me you will marry me within the week."

"But it's so sudden, dear," he urged, more and more distressed. "Take time to consider. How can I rob you of millions?"

"You won't rob me. If you refuse, I shall make over the money to some charity, and live on my five hundred a year. Remember, Noel, what people think of me: that I married Hubert to get his money and to become your wife when he died, so that we could live on his wealth. We can only prove that belief to be false by surrendering the millions and marrying as paupers."

"You may be right, and yet—"

"And yet, and yet—oh," she cried, wounded, "you don't love me."

The man did not answer, but stood looking at her with all his soul in his eyes, and shaking from head to foot. Never before had she looked so desirable, and never before had he felt the tides of love surge to so high a Water-mark. "Love you!" he said in a hoarse voice. "Agnes, I would give my soul for you."

"Then give it." She wreathed her arms round his neck and whispered with her warm lips close to his ear, "Give me all of you."

"But two millions—"

"You are worth it."

"Darling, you will repent."

"Repent!" She pressed him closer to her. "Repent that I exchange a lonely life for companionship with you? Oh, my dear, how can you think so? I am sick of money and sick of loneliness. I want you, you, you! Noel, Noel, it is your part to woo, and here am I making all the love."

"It is such a serious step for you to take."

"It is the only step that I can take. I am known as a mercenary woman, and until we marry and give up the money, everybody will think scornfully of me. Besides, Freddy must be punished, and in no other way can I make him suffer so much as by depriving him of the wealth he sinned to obtain."

"Yes. There is that view, certainly. And," Lambert gasped, "I love you—oh, never doubt that, my darling."

"I shall," she whispered ardently, "unless you get a special license and marry me straightaway."

"But Garvington and Silver—"

"And Clara Greeby and Chaldea, who both love you," she mocked. "Let them all fight out their troubles alone. I have had enough suffering; so have you. So there's no more to be said. Now, sir," she added playfully, "wilt thou take this woman to be thy wedded wife?"

"Yes," he said, opening his arms and gathering Agnes to his heart. "But what will people say of your marrying so soon after Pine's death?"

"Let them say what they like and do what they like. We are going to the Colonies and will be beyond reach of slanderous tongues. Now, let us have tea, Noel, for I am hungry and thirsty, and quite tired out with trying to convince you of my earnestness."

Lambert rang for the tea. "Shall we tell Jarwin that we intend to marry?"

"No. We shall tell no one until we are married," she replied, and kissed him once, twice, thrice, and again, until Mrs. Tribb entered with the tray. Then they both sat demurely at the first of many meals which they hoped would be the start of a new Darby and Joan existence.

And the outcome of the interview and of the decision that was arrived at appeared in a letter to Mr. Jarwin, of Chancery Lane. A week later he received a communication signed by Agnes Lambert, in which she stated that on the preceding day she had married her cousin by special license. Mr. Jarwin had to read the epistle twice before he could grasp the astounding fact that the woman had paid two millions for a husband.

"She's mad, crazy, silly, insane," murmured the lawyer, then his eyes lighted up with curiosity. "Now I shall know the name of the person in the sealed letter who inherits," and he forthwith proceeded to his safe.

CHAPTER XVII

ON THE TRAIL

Great was the excitement in society when it became known—through the medium of a newspaper paragraph—that Lady Agnes Pine had surrendered two millions sterling to become Mrs. Noel Lambert. Some romantic people praised her as a noble woman, who placed love above mere money, while others loudly declared her to be a superlative fool. But one and all agreed that she must have loved her cousin all the time, and that clearly the marriage with the deceased millionaire had been forced on by Garvington, for family reasons connected with the poverty of the Lamberts. It was believed that the fat little egotist had obtained his price for selling his sister, and that his estates had been freed from all claims through the generosity of Pine. Of course, this was not the case; but the fact was unknown to the general public, and Garvington was credited with an income which he did not possess.

The man himself was furious at having been tricked. He put it in this way, quite oblivious to his own actions, which had brought about such a result. He could not plead ignorance on this score, as Agnes had written him a letter announcing her marriage, and plainly stating her reasons for giving up her late husband's fortune. She ironically advised him to seek out the person to whom the money would pass, and to see if he could not plunder that individual. Garvington, angry as he was, took the advice seriously, and sought out Jarwin. But that astute individual declined to satisfy his curiosity, guessing what use he would make of the information. In due time, as the solicitor said, the name of the lucky legatee would be made public, and with this assurance Garvington was obliged to be content.

Meanwhile the happy pair—and they truly were extremely happy—heard nothing of the chatter, and were indifferent to either praise or blame. They were all in all to one another, and lived in a kind of Paradise, on the south coast of Devonshire. On one of his sketching tours Lambert had discovered a picturesque old-world village, tucked away in a fold of the moorlands, and hither he brought his wife for the golden hours of the honeymoon. They lived at the small inn and were attended to by a gigantic landlady, who made them very comfortable. Mrs. "Anak," as Noel called her, took the young couple for poor but artistic people, since Agnes had dropped her title, as unsuited to her now humble position.

"And in the Colonies," she explained to her husband, during a moorland ramble, "it would be absurd for me to be called 'my lady.' Mrs. Noel Lambert is good enough for me."

"Quite so, dear, if we ever do go to the Colonies."

"We must, Noel, as we have so little to live on."

"Oh, one thousand a year isn't so bad," he answered good-humoredly. "It may seem poverty to you, who have been used to millions, my darling; but all my life I have been hard up, and I am thankful for twenty pounds a week."

"You speak as though I had been wealthy all my life, Noel. But remember that I was as hard up as you before I married Hubert, poor soul."

"Then, dear, you must appreciate the fact that we can never starve. Besides I hope to make a name as a painter."

"In the Colonies?"

"Why not? Art is to be found there as in England. Change of scene does not destroy any talent one may possess. But I am not so sure, darling, if it is wise to leave England—at least until we learn who murdered Pine."

"Oh, my dear, do let us leave that vexed question alone. The truth will never become known."

"It must become known, Agnes," said Lambert firmly. "Remember that Silver and Chaldea practically accuse us of murdering your husband."

"They know it is a lie, and won't proceed further," said Agnes hopefully.

"Oh, yes, they will, and Miss Greeby also."

"Clara! Why, she is on our side."

"Indeed she is not. Your guess that she was still in love with me turns out to be quite correct. I received a letter from her this morning, which was forwarded from Kensington. She reproaches me with marrying you after the trouble she took in getting the forged letter back from Silver."

"But you told me that she said she would help you as a friend."

"She did so, in order—to use an expressive phrase—to pull the wool over my eyes. But she intended—and she puts her intention plainly in her letter—to help me in order to secure my gratitude, and then she counted upon my making her my wife."

Agnes flushed. "I might have guessed that she would act in that way. When you told me that she was helping I had a suspicion what she was aiming at. What else does she say?"

"Oh, all manner of things, more or less silly. She hints that I have acted meanly in causing you to forfeit two millions, and says that no man of honor would act in such a way."

"I see," said Mrs. Lambert coolly. "She believed that my possession of the money would be even a greater barrier to our coming together than the fact of my being married to Hubert. Well, dear, what does it matter?"

"A great deal, Agnes," replied Noel, wrinkling his brows. "She intends to make mischief, and she can, with the aid of Silver, who is naturally furious at having lost his chance of blackmail. Then there's Chaldea—"

"She can do nothing."

"She can join forces with Miss Greeby and the secretary, and they will do their best to get us into trouble. To defend ourselves we should have to explain that Garvington wrote the letter, and then heaven only knows what disgrace would befall the name."

"But you don't believe that Freddy is guilty?" asked Agnes anxiously.

"Oh, no. Still, he wrote that letter which lured Pine to his death, and if such a mean act became known, he would be disgraced forever."

"Freddy has such criminal instincts," said Mrs. Lambert gloomily, "that I am quite sure he will sooner or later stand in the dock."

"We must keep him out of it as long as we can," said Noel decisively. "For that reason I intend to leave you here and go to Garvington."

"To see Freddy?"

"Yes, and to see Chaldea, and to call on Silver, who is living in my old cottage. Also I wish to have a conversation with Miss Greeby. In some way, my dear, I must settle these people, or they will make trouble. Have you noticed, Agnes, what a number of gypsies seem to cross our path?"

"Yes; but there are many gypsies in Devonshire."

"No doubt, but many gypsies do not come to this retired spot as a rule, and yet they seem to swarm. Chaldea is having us watched."

"For what reason?" Agnes opened her astonished eyes.

"I wish to learn. Chaldea is now a queen, and evidently has sent instructions to her kinsfolk in this county to keep an eye on us."

Agnes ruminated for a few minutes. "I met Mother Cockleshell yesterday," she observed; "but I thought nothing of it, as she belongs to Devonshire."

"I believe Mother Cockleshell is on our side, dear, since she is so grateful to you for looking after her when she was sick. But Kara has been hovering about, and we know that he is Chaldea's lover."

"Then," said Mrs. Lambert, rising from the heather on which they had seated themselves, "it will be best to face Mother Cockleshell and Kara in order to learn what all this spying means."

Lambert approved of this suggestion, and the two returned to Mrs. "Anak's" abode to watch for the gypsies. But, although they saw two or three, or even more during the next few days, they did not set eyes on the Servian dwarf, or on Gentilla Stanley. Then—since it never rains but it pours—the two came together to the inn. Agnes saw them through the sitting-room window, and walked out boldly to confront them. Noel was absent at the moment, so she had to conduct the examination entirely alone.

"Gentilla, why are you spying on me and my husband?" asked Agnes abruptly.

The respectable woman dropped a curtsey and clutched the shoulder of Kara, who showed a disposition to run away. "I'm no spy, my angel," said the old creature with a cunning glint in her eyes. "It's this one who keeps watch."

"For what reason?"

"Bless you, my lady—"

"Don't call me by my title. I've dropped it."

"Only for a time, my dear. I have read your fortune in the stars, my Gorgio one, and higher you will be with money and rank than ever you have been in past days. But not with the child's approval."

"The child. What child?"

"Chaldea, no less. She's raging mad, as the golden rye has made you his romi, my sweet one, and she has set many besides Kara to overlook you."

"So Mr. Lambert and I thought. And Chaldea's reason?"

"She would make trouble," replied Mother Cockleshell mysteriously. "But Kara does not wish her to love the golden rye—as she still does—since he would have the child to himself." She turned and spoke rapidly in Romany to the small man in the faded green coat.

Kara listened with twinkling eyes, and pulling at his heavy beard with one hand, while he held the neck of his violin with the other. When Mother Cockleshell ceased he poured out a flood of the kalo jib with much gesticulation, and in a voice which boomed like a gong. Of course, Mrs. Lambert did not understand a word of his speech, and looked inquiringly at Gentilla.

"Kara says," translated the woman hurriedly, "that he is your friend, since he is glad you are the golden rye's romi. Ever since you left Lundra the child has set him and others to spy on you. She makes mischief, does the child in her witchly way."

"Ask him," said Agnes, indicating the dwarf, "if he knows who murdered my late husband?"

Gentilla asked the question and translated the reply. "He knows nothing, but the child knows much. I go back to the wood in Hengishire, my dear, to bring about much that will astonish Chaldea—curses on her evil heart. Tell the rye to meet me at his old cottage in a week. Then the wrong will be made right," ended Mother Cockleshell, speaking quite in the style of Meg Merrilees, and very grandiloquently. "And happiness will be yours. By this and this I bless you, my precious lady," making several mystical signs, she turned away, forcing the reluctant Kara to follow her.

"But, Gentilla?" Agnes hurried in pursuit.

"No! no, my Gorgious. It is not the time. Seven days, and seven hours, and seven minutes will hear the striking of the moment. Sarishan, my deary."

Mother Cockleshell hobbled away with surprising alacrity, and Mrs. Lambert returned thoughtfully to the inn. Evidently the old woman knew of something which would solve the mystery, else she would scarcely have asked Noel to meet her in Hengishire. And being an enemy to Chaldea, who had deposed her, Agnes was quite sure that Gentilla would work her hardest to thwart the younger gypsy's plans. It flashed across her mind that Chaldea herself might have murdered Pine. But since his death would have removed the barrier between Lambert and herself, Agnes could not believe that Chaldea was guilty. The affair seemed to become more involved every time it was looked into.

However, Mrs. Lambert related to her husband that same evening all that had taken place, and duly delivered the old gypsy's message. Noel listened quietly and nodded. He made up his mind to keep the appointment in Abbot's Wood the moment he received the intelligence. "And you can stay here, Agnes," he said.

"No, no," she pleaded. "I wish to be beside you."

"There may be danger, my dear. Chaldea will not stick at a trifle to revenge herself, you know."

"All the more reason that I should be with you," insisted Agnes. "Besides, these wretches are plotting against me as much as against you, so it is only fair that I should be on the spot to defend myself."

"You have a husband to defend you now, Agnes. Still, as I know you will be anxious if I leave you in this out-of-the-way place, it will be best for us both to go to London. There is a telephone at Wanbury, and I can communicate with you at once should it be necessary."

"Of course it will be necessary," said Mrs. Lambert with fond impatience. "I shall worry dreadfully to think that you are in danger. I don't wish to lose you now that we are together."

"You can depend upon my keeping out of danger, for your sake, dear," said the young man, caressing her. "Moreover, Mother Cockleshell will look after me should Chaldea try any of her Romany tricks. Stay in town, darling."

"Oh, dear me, that flat is so dingy, and lonely, and disagreeable."

"You shan't remain at the flat. There's a very pleasant hotel near Hyde Park where we can put up."

"It's so expensive."

"Never mind the expense, just now. When everything is square we can consider economy. But I shall not be easy in my mind until poor Pine's murderer is in custody."

"I only hope Garvington won't be found to be an accomplice," said Agnes, with a shiver. "Bad as he is, I can't help remembering that he is my brother."

"And the head of the Lamberts," added her husband gravely. "You may be sure that I shall try and save the name from disgrace."

"It's a dismal ending to our honeymoon."

"Let us look upon it as the last hedge of trouble which has to be jumped."

Agnes laughed at this quaint way of putting things, and cheered up. For the next few days they did their best to enjoy to the full the golden hours of love, and peace which remained, and then departed, to the unfeigned regret of Mrs. "Anak." But present pleasure meant future trouble, so the happy pair—and they were happy in spite of the lowering clouds—were forced to leave their temporary paradise in order to baffle their enemies. Miss Greeby, Chaldea, Silver, and perhaps Garvington, were all arrayed against them, so a conflict could not possibly be avoided.

Agnes took up her abode in the private hotel near the Park which Lambert had referred to, and was very comfortable, although she did not enjoy that luxury with which Pine's care had formerly surrounded her. Having seen that she had all she required, Noel took the train to Wanbury, and thence drove in a hired fly to Garvington, where he put up at the village inn. It was late at night when he arrived, so it might have been expected that few would have noted his coming. This was true, but among the few was Chaldea, who still camped with her tribe in Abbot's Wood. Whosoever now owned the property on mortgage, evidently did not desire to send the gypsies packing, and, of course, Garvington, not having the power, could not do so.

Thus it happened that while Lambert was breakfasting next

morning, somewhere about ten o'clock, word was brought to him by the landlady that a gypsy wished to see him. The young man at once thought that Mother Cockleshell had called to adjust the situation, and gave orders that she should be admitted. He was startled and ill-pleased when Chaldea made her appearance. She looked as handsome as ever, but her face wore a sullen, vicious look, which augured ill for a peaceful interview.

"So you cheated me after all, rye?" was her greeting, and her eyes sparkled with anger at the sight of the man she had lost.

"Don't be a fool, girl," said Lambert, purposely rough, for her persistence irritated him. "You know that I never loved you."

"Am I so ugly then?" demanded the girl bitterly.

"That remark is beside the point," said the man coldly. "And I am not going to discuss such things with you. But I should like to know why you set spies on me when I was in Devonshire?"

Chaldea's eyes sparkled still more, and she taunted him. "Oh, the clever one that you are, to know that I had you watched. Aye, and I did, my rye. From the time you left the cottage you were under the looks of my people."

"Why, may I ask?"

"Because I want revenge," cried Chaldea, stepping forward and striking so hard a blow on the table that the dishes jumped. "You scorned me, and now you shall pay for that scorn."

"Don't be melodramatic, please. What can you do to harm me, I should like to know, you silly creature?"

"I can prove that you murdered my brother Hearne."

"Oh, can you, and in what way?"

"I have the bullet which killed him," said the gypsy, speaking very fast so as to prevent interruption. "Kara knifed it out of the tree-trunk which grows near the shrubbery. If I take it to the police and it fits your pistol, then where will you be, my precious cheat?"

Lambert looked at her thoughtfully. If she really did possess the bullet he would be able to learn if Garvington had fired the second shot, since it would fit the barrel of his revolver. So far as he was concerned, when coming to live in the Abbot's Wood Cottage, he had left all his weapons stored in London, and would be able to prove that such was the case. He did not fear for himself, as Chaldea's malice could not hurt him in this way, but he wondered if it would be wise to take her to The Manor, where Garvington was in residence, in order to test the fitting of the bullet. Finally, he decided to risk doing so, as in this way he might be able to force the girl's hand and learn how much she really knew. If aware that Garvington was the culprit, she would exhibit no surprise did the bullet fit the barrel of that gentleman's revolver. And should it be proved that she knew the truth, she would not dare to say anything to the police, lest she should be brought into the matter, as an accomplice after the fact. Chaldea misunderstood his silence, while he was thinking in this way, and smiled mockingly with a toss of her head.

"Ah, the rye is afraid. His sin has come home to him," she sneered. "Hai, you are at my feet now, my Gorgious one."

"I think not," said Lambert coolly, and rose to put on his cap. "Come with me, Chaldea. We go to The Manor."

"And what would I do in the boro rye's ken, my precious?"

Lambert ignored the question. "Have you the bullet with you?"

"Avali," Chaldea nodded. "It lies in my pocket."

"Then we shall see at The Manor if it fits the pistol."

"Hai! you have left the shooter at the big house," said the girl, falling into the trap, and thereby proved—to Lambert at least—that she was really in the dark as regards the true criminal.

"Lord Garvington has a revolver of mine," said the young man evasively, although the remark was a true one, since he had presented his cousin with a brace of revolvers some twelve months before.

Chaldea looked at him doubtfully. "And if the bullet fits—"

"Then you can do what you like," retorted Lambert tartly. "Come on. I can't wait here all day listening to the rubbish you talk."

The gypsy followed him sullenly enough, being overborne by his peremptory manner, and anxious, if possible, to bring home the crime to him. What she could not understand, for all her cleverness, was, why he should be so eager to condemn himself, and so went to The Manor on the lookout for treachery. Chaldea always judged other people by herself, and looked upon treachery as quite necessary on certain occasions. Had she guessed the kind of trap which Lambert was laying for her, it is questionable if she would have fallen into it so easily. And Lambert, even at this late hour, could not be certain if she really regarded him as guilty, or if she was only bluffing in order to gain her ends.

Needless to say, Garvington did not welcome his cousin enthusiastically when he entered the library to find him waiting with Chaldea beside him. The fat little man rushed in like a whirlwind, and, ignoring his own shady behavior, heaped reproaches on Lambert's head.

"I wonder you have the cheek to come here," he raged. "You and this beast of a girl. I want no gypsies in my house, I can tell you. And you've lost me a fortune by your selfish behavior."

"I don't think we need talk of selfishness when you are present, Garvington."

"Why not? By marrying Agnes you have made her give up the money."

"She wished to give it up to punish you," said Lambert rebukingly.

"To punish me!" Garvington's gooseberry eyes nearly fell out of his head. "And what have I done?"

Lambert laughed and shrugged his shoulders. In the face of this dense egotism, it was impossible to argue in any way. He dismissed the subject and got to business, as he did not wish to remain longer in Garvington's society than was absolutely necessary.

"This girl," he said abruptly, indicating Chaldea, who stood passively at his elbow, "has found the bullet with which Pine was shot."

"Kara found it, my boro rye," put in the gypsy quickly, and addressing Lord Garvington, who gurgled out his surprises, "in the tree-trunk."

"Ah, yes," interrupted the other. "The elm which is near the shrubbery. Then why didn't you give the bullet to the police?"

"Do you ask that, Garvington?" inquired Lambert meaningly, and the little man whirled round to answer with an expression of innocent surprise.

"Of course I do," he vociferated, growing purple with resentment. "You don't accuse me of murdering the man who was so useful to me, I hope?"

"I shall answer that very leading question when you bring out the revolver with which you shot Pine on that night."

"I only winged him," cried Garvington indignantly. "The second shot was fired by some unknown person, as was proved clearly enough at the inquest."

"All the same, I wish you to produce the revolver."

"Why?" The host looked suspicious and even anxious.

It was Chaldea who replied, and when doing so she fished out the battered bullet. "To see if this fits the barrel of the pistol which the golden rye gave you, my great one," said she significantly.

Garvington started, his color changed and he stole a queer look at the impassive face of his cousin. "The pistol which the golden rye gave me?" he repeated slowly and weighing the words. "Did you give me one, Noel?"

"I gave you a couple in a case," answered Lambert without mentioning the date of the present. "And if this bullet fits the one you used—"

"It will prove nothing," interrupted the other hurriedly, and with a restless movement. "I fired from the doorstep, and my bullet, after breaking Pine's arm, must have vanished into the beyond. The shot which killed him was fired from the shrubbery, and, it is quite easy to guess how it passed through him and buried itself in the tree which was in the line of fire."

"I want to see the pistols," said Lambert insistently, and this time Chaldea looked at him, wondering why he was so anxious to condemn himself.

"Oh, very well," snapped Garvington, with some reluctance, and walked toward the door. There he paused, and evidently awaited to arrive at some conclusion, the nature of which his cousin could not guess. "Oh, very well," he said again, and left the room.

"He thinks that you are a fool, as I do, my Gorgious," said Chaldea scornfully. "You wish to hang yourself it seems, my rye."

"Oh, I don't think that I shall be the one to be hanged. Tell me, Chaldea, do you really believe that I am guilty?"

"Yes," said the girl positively. "And if you had married me I should have saved you."

Lambert laughed, but was saved the trouble of a reply by the return of Garvington, who trotted in to lay a mahogany case on the table. Opening this, he took out a small revolver of beautiful workmanship. Chaldea, desperately anxious to bring home the crime to Lambert, hastily snatched the weapon from the little man's hand and slipped the bullet into one of the chambers. It fitted—making allowance for its battered condition—precisely. She uttered a cry of triumph. "So you did shoot the Romany, my bold one," was her victorious speech.

"Because the bullet fits the barrel of a revolver I gave to my cousin some twelve months ago?" he inquired, smiling.

Chaldea's face fell. "Twelve months ago!" she echoed, greatly disappointed.

"Yes, as Lord Garvington can swear to. So I could not have used the weapon on that night, you see."

"I used it," admitted Garvington readily enough. "And winged Pine."

"Exactly. But I gave you a brace of revolvers of the same make. The bullet which would fit one—as it does—would fit the other. I see there is only one in the case. Where is the other?"

Garvington's color changed and he shuffled with his feet. "I lent it to Silver," he said in a low voice, and reluctantly.

"Was it in Silver's possession on the night Pine was shot?"

"Must have been. He borrowed it a week before because he feared burglars."

"Then," said Lambert coolly, and drawing a breath of relief, for the tension had been great, "the inference is obvious. Silver shot Hubert Pine."

CHAPTER XVIII

AN AMAZING ACCUSATION

"Beng in tutes bukko!" swore Chaldea in good Romany, meaning that she wished the devil was in some one's body. And she heartily meant what she said, and cared little which of the two men's interior was occupied by the enemy of mankind, since she hated both. The girl was disappointed to think that Lambert should escape from her snare, and enraged that Garvington's production of one revolver and his confession that Silver had the other tended to this end. "May the pair of you burn in hell," she cried, taking to English, so that they could understand the insult. "Ashes may you be in the Crooked One's furnace."

Lambert shrugged his shoulders, as he quite understood her feelings, and did not intend to lower himself by correcting her. He addressed himself to his cousin and turned his back on the gypsy. "Silver shot Hubert Pine," he repeated, with his eyes on Garvington's craven face.

"It's impossible—impossible!" returned the other hurriedly. "Silver was shut up in the house with the rest. I saw to the windows and doors myself, along with the butler and footmen. At the inquest—"

"Never mind about the inquest. I know what you said there, and I am now beginning to see why you said it."

"What the devil do you mean?"

"I mean," stated the other, staring hard at him, "that you knew Silver was guilty when the inquest took place, and screened him for some reason."

"I didn't know; I swear I didn't know!" stuttered Garvington, wiping his heated face, and with his lower lip trembling.

"You must have done so," replied Lambert relentlessly. "This bullet will fit both the revolvers I gave you, and as you passed on one to Silver—"

"Rubbish! Bosh! Nonsense!" babbled the little man incoherently. "Until you brought the bullet I never knew that it would fit the revolver."

This was true, as Lambert admitted. However, he saw that Garvington was afraid for some reason, and pressed his advantage. "Now that you see how it fits, you must be aware that it could only have been fired from the revolver which you gave Silver."

"I don't see that," protested Garvington. "That bullet may fit many revolvers."

Lambert shook his head. "I don't think so. I had that brace of revolvers especially manufactured, and the make is peculiar. I am quite prepared to swear that the bullet would fit no other weapon. And—and"—he hesitated, then faced the girl, who lingered, sullen and disappointed. "You can go, Chaldea," said Lambert, pointing to the French window of the library, which was wide open.

The gypsy sauntered toward it, clutching her shawl and gritting her white teeth together. "Oh, I go my ways, my rye, but I have not done with you yet, may the big devil rack my bones if I have. You win to-day—I win to-morrow, and so good day to you, and curses on you for a bad one. The devil is a nice character—and that's you!" she screamed, beside herself with rage. "The puro beng is a fino mush, if you will have the kalo jib!" and with a wild cry worthy of a banshee she disappeared and was seen running unsteadily across the lawn. Lambert shrugged his shoulders again and turned to his miserable cousin, who had sat down with a dogged look on his fat face. "I have got rid of her because I wish to save the family name from disgrace," said Lambert quietly.

"There is no disgrace on my part. Remember to whom you are speaking."

"I do. I speak to the head of the family, worse luck! You have done your best to trail our name in the mud. You altered a check which Pine gave you so as to get more money; you forged his name to a mortgage—"

"Lies, lies, the lies of Agnes!" screamed Garvington, jumping up and shaking his fist in puny anger. "The wicked—"

"Speak properly of my wife, or I'll wring your neck," said Lambert sharply. "As to what she told me being lies, it is only too true, as you know. I read the letter you wrote confessing that you had lured Pine here to be shot by telling falsehoods about Agnes and me."

"I only lured him to get his arm broken so that I might nurse him when he was ill and get some money," growled Garvington, sitting down again.

"I am well aware of what you did and how you did it. But you gave that forged letter to Silver so that it might be passed on to Pine."

"I didn't! I didn't! I didn't! I didn't!"

"You did. And because Silver knew too much you gave him the Abbot's Wood Cottage at a cheap rent, or at no rent at all, for all I know. To be quite plain, Garvington, you conspired with Silver to have Pine killed."

"Winged—only winged, I tell you. I never shot him."

"Your accomplice did."

"He's not my accomplice. He was in the house—everything was locked up."

"By you," said Lambert quickly. "So it was easy for you to leave a window unfastened, so that Silver might get outside to hide in the shrubbery."

"Oh!" Garvington jumped up again, looking both pale and wicked. "You want to put a rope round my neck, curse you."

"That's a melodramatic speech which is not true," replied the other coldly. "For I want to save you, or, rather, our name, from disgrace. I won't call in the police"—Garvington winced at this word—"because I wish to hush the matter up. But since Chaldea and Silver accuse me and accuse Agnes of getting rid of Pine so that we might marry, it is necessary that I should learn the exact truth."

"I don't know it. I know nothing more than I have confessed."

"You are such a liar that I can't believe you. However, I shall go at once to Silver and you shall come with me."

"I shan't!" Garvington, who was overfed and flabby and unable to hold his own against a determined man, settled himself in his chair and looked as obstinate as a battery mule.

"Oh, yes, you will, you little swine," said Lambert freezingly cold.

"How dare you call me names?"

"Names! If I called you those you deserved I should have to annex the vocabulary of a Texan muledriver. How such a beast as you ever got into our family I can't conceive."

"I am the head of the family and I order you to leave the room."

"Oh, you do, do you? Very good. Then I go straight to Wanbury and shall tell what I have discovered to Inspector Darby."

"No! No! No! No!" Garvington, cornered at last, sprang from his chair and made for his cousin with unsteady legs. "It might be unpleasant."

"I daresay—to you. Well, will you come with me to Abbot's Wood?"

"Yes," whimpered Garvington. "Wait till I get my cap and stick, curse you, for an interfering beast. You don't know what you're doing."

"Ah! then you do know something likely to reveal the truth."

"I don't—I swear I don't! I only—"

"Oh, damn you, get your cap, and let us be off," broke in Lambert angrily, "for I can't be here all day listening to your lies."

Garvington scowled and ambled out of the room, closely followed by his cousin, who did not think it wise to lose sight of so shifty a person. In a few minutes they were out of the house and took the path leading from the blue door to the postern gate in the brick wall surrounding the park. It was a frosty, sunny day, with a hard blue sky, overarching a wintry landscape. A slight fall of snow had powdered the ground with a film of white, and the men's feet drummed loudly on the iron earth, which was in the grip of the frost. Garvington complained of the cold, although he had on a fur overcoat which made him look like a baby bear.

"You'll give me my death of cold, dragging me out like this," he moaned, as he trotted beside his cousin. "I believe you want me to take pneumonia so that I may die and leave you the title."

"I should at least respect it more than you do," said Lambert with scorn. "Why can't you be a man instead of a thing on two legs? If you did die no one would miss you but cooks and provision dealers."

Garvington gave him a vicious glance from his little pig's eyes, and longed to be tall, and strong, and daring, so that he might knock him down. But he knew that Lambert was muscular and dexterous, and would probably break his neck if it came to a tussle. Therefore, as the stout little lord had a great regard for his neck, he judged it best to yield to superior force, and trotted along obediently enough. Also he became aware within himself that it would be necessary to explain to Silver how he had come to betray him, and that would not be easy. Silver would be certain to make himself extremely disagreeable. Altogether the walk was not a pleasant one for the sybarite.

The Abbot's Wood looked bare and lean with the leaves stripped from its many trees. Occasionally there was a fir, clothed in dark green foliage, but for the most part the branches of the trees were naked, and quivered constantly in the chilly breeze. Even on the outskirts of the wood one could see right into the centre where the black monoliths—they looked black against the snow—reared themselves grimly. To the right there was a glimpse of gypsy fires and tents and caravans, and the sound of the Romany tongue was borne toward them through the clear atmosphere. On such a day it was easy both to see and hear for long distances, and for this reason Chaldea became aware that the two men were walking toward the cottage.

The girl, desperately angry that she had been unable to bring Lambert to book, had sauntered back to the camp, but had just reached it when she caught sight of the tall figure and the short one. In a moment she knew that Lambert and his cousin were making for Silver's abode, which was just what she had expected them to do. At once she determined to again adopt her former tactics, which had been successful in enabling her to overhear the conversation between Lambert and Lady Agnes, and, following at a respectful distance, she waited for her chance. It came when the pair entered the cottage, for then Chaldea ran swiftly in a circle toward the monoliths, and crouched down behind one. While peering from behind this shelter, she saw Silver pass the window of the studio, and felt certain that the interview, would take place in that room. Like a serpent, as she was, the girl crawled and wriggled through the frozen vegetation and finally managed to get under the window without being observed. The window was closed, but by pressing her ear close to the woodwork she was enabled to hear a great deal, if not all. Candidly speaking, Chaldea had truly believed that Lambert had shot Pine, but now that he had disproved the charge so easily, she became desperately anxious to learn the truth. Lambert had escaped her, but she thought that it might be possible to implicate his wife in the crime, which would serve her purpose of injuring him just as well.

Silver was not surprised to see his landlord, as it seemed that Garvington paid him frequent visits. But he certainly showed an uneasy amazement when Lambert stalked in behind the fat little man. Silver was also small, and also cowardly, and also not quite at rest in his conscience, so he shivered when he met the very direct gaze of his unwelcome visitor.

"You have come to look at your old house, Mr. Lambert," he remarked, when the two made themselves comfortable by the studio fire.

"Not at all. I have come to see you," was the grim response.

"That is an unexpected honor," said Silver uneasily, and his eyes sought those of Lord Garvington, who was spreading out his hands to the blaze, looking blue with cold. He caught Silver's inquiring look.

"I couldn't help it," said Garvington crossly. "I must look after myself."

Silver's smooth, foxy face became livid, and he could scarcely speak. When he did, it was with a sickly smile. "Whatever are you talking about, my lord?"

"Oh, you know, d—— you! I did give you that revolver, you know."

"The revolver?" Silver stared. "Yes, why should I deny it? I suppose you have come to get it back?"

"I have come to get it, Mr. Silver," put in Lambert politely. "Hand it over to me, if you please."

"If you like. It certainly has your name on the handle," said the secretary so quietly that the other man was puzzled. Silver did not seem to be so uncomfortable as he might have been.

"The revolver was one of a pair which I had especially made when I went to Africa some years ago," explained Lambert elaborately, and determined to make his listener understand the situation thoroughly. "On my return I made them a present to my cousin. I understand, Mr. Silver, that Lord Garvington lent you one—"

"And kept the other," interrupted the man sharply. "That is true. I was afraid of burglars, since Lord Garvington was always talking about them, so I asked him to lend me a weapon to defend myself with."

"And you used it to shoot Pine," snapped Garvington, anxious to end his suspense and get the interview over as speedily as possible.

Silver rose from his seat in an automatic manner, and turned delicately pale. "Are you mad?" he gasped, looking from one man to the other.

"It's all very well you talking," whimpered Garvington with a shiver; "but Pine was shot with that revolver I lent you."

"It's a lie!"

"Oh, I knew you'd say that," complained Garvington, shivering again. "But I warned you that there might be trouble, since you carried that letter for me, so that it might fall by chance into Pine's hands."

"Augh!" groaned Silver, sinking back into his chair and passing his tongue over a pair of dry, gray lips. "Hold your tongue, my lord."

"What's the use? He knows," and Garvington jerked his head in the direction of his cousin. "The game's up, Silver—the game's up!"

"Oh!" Silver's eyes flashed, and he looked like a rat at bay. "So you intend to save yourself at my expense. But it won't do, my lord. You wrote that letter, if I carried it to the camp."

"I have admitted to my sister and to Lambert, here, that I wrote the letter, Silver. I had to, or get into trouble with the police, since neither of them will listen to reason. But you suggested the plan to get Pine winged so that he might be ill in my house, and then we could both get money out of him. You invented the plot, and I only wrote the letter."

"Augh! Augh!" gulped Silver, unable to speak plainly.

"Do you confess the truth of Lord Garvington's statement?" inquired Lambert suavely, and fixing a merciless eye on the trapped fox.

"No—that is—yes. He swings on the same hook as I do."

"Indeed. Then Lord Garvington was aware that you shot Pine?"

"I was not! I was not!" screamed the head of the Lambert family, jumping up and clenching his hands. "I swear I never knew the truth until you brought the bullet to the library to fit the revolver."

"The—the—bullet!" stammered Silver, whose smooth red hair was almost standing on end from sheer fright.

"Yes," said Lambert, addressing him sharply. "Kara, under the direction of Chaldea, found the bullet in the trunk of the elm tree which was in the line of fire. She came with me to The Manor this morning, and we found that it fitted the barrel of Lord Garvington's revolver. At the inquest, and on unimpeachable evidence, it was proved that he fired only the first shot, which disabled Pine without killing him. The second shot, which pierced the man's heart, could only have come from the second revolver, which was, and is, in your possession, Mr. Silver. The bullet found in the tree trunk will fit no other barrel of no other weapon. I'm prepared to swear to this."

Silver covered his face with his hands and looked so deadly white that Lambert believed he would faint. However, he pulled himself together, and addressed Garvington anxiously. "You know, my lord, that you locked up the house on that night, and that I was indoors."

"Yes," admitted the other hesitating. "So far as I knew you certainly were inside. It is true, Noel," he added, catching his cousin's eye. "Even to save myself I must admit that."

"Oh, you'd admit anything to save yourself," retorted his cousin contemptuously, and noting the mistake in the wording of the sentence. "But admitting that Silver was within doors doesn't save you, so far as I can see."

"There is no need for Lord Garvington to excuse himself," spoke up Silver, attempting to enlist the little man on his side by defending him. "It was proved at the inquest, as you have admitted, Mr. Lambert, that he only fired the first shot."

"And you fired the second."

"I never did. I was inside and in bed. I only came down with the rest of the guests when I heard the firing. Is that not so, my lord?"

"Yes," admitted Garvington grudgingly. "So far as I know you had nothing to do with the second shot."

Silver turned a relieved face toward Lambert. "I shall confess this much, sir," he said, trying to speak calmly and judicially. "Pine treated me badly by taking my toy inventions and by giving me very little money. When I was staying at The Manor I learned that Lord Garvington had also been treated badly by Pine. He said if we could get money that we should go shares. I knew that Pine was jealous of his wife, and that you were at the cottage here, so I suggested that, as Lord Garvington could imitate handwriting, he should forge a letter purporting to come from Lady Agnes to you, saying that she intended to elope on a certain night. Also I told Lord Garvington to talk a great deal about shooting burglars, so as to give color to his shooting Pine."

"It was arranged to shoot him, then?"

"No, it wasn't," cried Garvington, glaring at Silver. "All we wanted to do was to break Pine's arm or leg so that he might be laid up in The Manor."

"Yes, that is so," said Silver feverishly, and nodding. "I fancied—and for this reason I suggested the plot—that when Pine was ill, both Lord Garvington and myself could deal with him in an easier manner. Also—since the business would be left in my hands—I hoped to take out some money from various investments, and share it with Lord Garvington. We never meant that Pine should be killed, but only reduced to weakness so that we might force him to give us both money."

"A very ingenious plot," said Lambert grimly and wondering how much of the story was true. "And then?"

"Then Lord Garvington wrote the letter, and when seeing Pine, I gave it to him saying that while keeping watch on his wife—as he asked me to," said Silver with an emphasis which made Lambert wince, "I had intercepted the letter. Pine was furious, as I knew he would be, and said that he would come to the blue door at the appointed time to prevent the supposed elopement. I told Lord Garvington, who was ready, and—"

"And I went down, pretending that Pine was a burglar," said Lord Garvington, continuing the story in a most shameless manner. "I opened the door quite expecting to find him there. He rushed me, believing in his blind haste that I was Agnes coming to elope with you. I shot him in the arm, and he staggered away, while I shut the door again. Whether, on finding his mistake, and knowing that he had met me instead of Agnes, he intended to go away, I can't say, as I was on the wrong side of the door. But Agnes, attracted to the window by the shot, declared—and you heard her declare it at the inquest, Noel—that Pine walked rapidly away and was shot just as he came abreast of the shrubbery. That's all."

"And quite enough, too," said Lambert savagely. "You tricky pair of beasts; I suppose you hoped to implicate me in the crime?"

"It wasn't a crime," protested Silver; "but only a way to get money. By going up to London you certainly delayed what we intended to do, since we could not carry out our plan until you returned. You did for one night, as Chaldea, who was on the watch for you, told us, and then we acted."

"Did Chaldea know of the trap?"

"No! She knew nothing save that I"—it was Silver who spoke—"wanted to know about your return. She found the letter in Pine's tent, and really believed that Lady Agnes had written it, and that you had shot Pine. It was to force you by threats to marry her that she gave the letter to me."

"And she instructed you to show it to the police," said Lambert between his teeth, "whereas you tried to blackmail Lady Agnes."

"I had to make my money somehow," said Silver insolently. "Pine was dead and Lady Agnes had the coin."

"You were to share in the twenty-five thousand pounds, I suppose?" Lambert asked his cousin indignantly.

"No; Silver blackmailed on his own. I hoped to get money from Agnes in another way—as her hard-up brother that is. And if—"

"Oh, shut up! You make me sick," interrupted Lambert, suppressing a strong desire to choke his cousin. "You are as bad as Silver."

"And Silver is as innocent as Lord Garvington," struck in that gentleman, whose face was recovering its natural color.

Lambert turned on him sharply. "I don't agree with that. You shot Pine!"

Silver sprang up with a hysterical cry. He had judged like Agag that the bitterness of death was past, but found that he was not yet safe. "I did not shoot Pine," he declared, wringing his hands. "Oh, why can't you believe me."

"Because Garvington gave you the second revolver and with that—on the evidence of the bullet—Pine was murdered."

"That might be so, but—but—" Silver hesitated, and shivered and looked round with a hunted expression in his eyes.

"But what? You may as well explain to me."

"I shan't—I refuse to. I am innocent! You can't hurt me!"

Lambert brushed aside this puny rage. "Inspector Darby can. I shall go to Wanbury this evening and tell him all."

"No; don't do that!" cried Garvington, greatly agitated. "Think of me—think of the family!"

"I think of Justice! You two beasts aren't fit to be at large. I'm off," and he made for the door.

In a moment Silver was clutching his coat. "No, don't!" he screamed. "I am innocent! Lord Garvington, say that I am innocent!"

"Oh, —— you, get out of the hole as best you can! I'm in as big a mess as you are, unless Lambert acts decently."

"Decently, you wicked little devil," said Lambert scornfully. "I only propose to do what any decent man would do. You trapped Pine by means of the letter, and Silver shot him."

"I didn't! I didn't!"

"You had the revolver!"

"I hadn't. I gave it away! I lent it!" panted Silver, crying with terror.

"You lent it—you gave it—you liar! Who to?"

Silver looked round again for some way of escape, but could see none. "To Miss Greeby. She—she—she—she shot Pine. I swear she did."

CHAPTER XIX

MOTHER COCKLESHELL

It was late in the afternoon when Lambert got back to the village inn, and he felt both tired and bewildered. The examination of Silver had been so long, and what he revealed so amazing, that the young man wished to be alone, both to rest and to think over the situation. It was a very perplexing one, as he plainly saw, since, in the light of the new revelations, it seemed almost impossible to preserve the name of the family from disgrace. Seated in his sitting room, with his legs stretched out and his hands in his pockets, Lambert moodily glared at the carpet, recalling all that had been confessed by the foxy secretary of Miss Greeby. That he should accuse her of committing the crime seemed unreasonable.

According to Silver, the woman had overheard by chance the scheme to lure Pine to The Manor. Knowing that the millionaire was coming to Abbot's Wood, the secretary had propounded the plan to Garvington long before the man's arrival. Hence the constant talk of the host about burglars and his somewhat unnecessary threat to shoot any one who tried to break into the house. The persistence of this remark had roused Miss Greeby's curiosity, and noting that Silver and his host were frequently in one another's company, she had seized her opportunity to listen. For some time, so cautious were the plotters, she had heard nothing particular, but after her recognition of Hearne as Pine when she visited the gypsy camp she became aware that these secret talks were connected with his presence. Then a chance remark of Garvington's—he was always loose-tongued—gave her the clue, and by threats of exposure she managed to make Silver confess the whole plot. Far from thwarting it she agreed to let them carry it out, and promised secrecy, only extracting a promise that she should be advised of the time and place for the trapping of the millionaire. And it was this acquiescence of Miss Greeby's which puzzled Lambert.

On the face of it, since she was in love with him, it was better for her own private plans that Pine should remain alive, because the marriage placed Agnes beyond his reach. Why, then, should Miss Greeby have removed the barrier—and at the cost of being hanged for murder? Lambert had asked Silver this question, but had obtained no definite answer, since the secretary protested that she had not explained her reasons. Jokingly referring to possible burglars, she had borrowed the revolver from Silver which he had obtained from Garvington, and it was this action which first led the little secretary to suspect her. Afterward, knowing that she had met Pine in Abbot's Wood, he kept a close watch on her every action to see if she intended to take a hand in the game. But Silver protested that he could see no reason for her doing so, and even up to the moment when he confessed to Lambert could not conjecture why she had acted in such a manner.

However, it appeared that she was duly informed of the hour when Pine would probably arrive to prevent the pretended elopement, and also learned that he would be hanging about the blue door. When Silver retired for the night he watched the door of her bedroom—which was in the same wing of the mansion of his own. Also he occasionally looked out to see if Pine had arrived, as the window of his room afforded a fair view of the blue door and the shrubbery. For over an hour—as he told Lambert—he divided his attention between the passage and the window. It was while looking out of the last, and after midnight, that he saw Miss Greeby climb out of her room and descend to the ground by means of the ivy which formed a natural ladder. Her window was no great height from the ground, and she was an athletic woman much given to exercise. Wondering what she intended to do, yet afraid—because of Pine's expected arrival—to leave the house, Silver watched her cautiously. She was arrayed in a long black cloak with a hood, he said, but in the brilliant moonlight he could easily distinguish her gigantic form as she slipped into the shrubbery. When Pine arrived, Silver saw him dash at the blue door when it was opened by Garvington, and saw him fall back after the first shot. Then he heard the shutting of the door; immediately afterward the opening of Lady Agnes's window, and noted that Pine ran quickly and unsteadily down the path. As he passed the shrubbery, the second shot came—at this point Silver simply gave the same description as Lady Agnes did at the inquest—and then Pine fell. Afterward Garvington and his guests came out and gathered round the body, but Miss Greeby, slipping along the rear of the shrubbery, doubled back to the shadow at the corner of the house. Silver, having to play his part, did not wait to see her re-enter the mansion, but presumed she did so by clambering up the ivy. He ran down and mingled with the guests and servants, who were clustered round the dead man, and finally found Miss Greeby at his elbow, artlessly inquiring what had happened. For the time being he accepted her innocent attitude.

Later on, when dismissed by Jarwin and in want of funds, he sought out Miss Greeby and accused her. At first she denied the story, but finally, as she judged that he could bring home the crime to her, she compromised with him by giving him the post of her secretary at a good salary. When he obtained the forged letter from Chaldea—and she learned this from Lambert when he was ill—Miss Greeby made him give it to her, alleging that by showing it to Agnes she could the more positively part the widow from her lover. Miss Greeby, knowing who had written the letter, counted upon Agnes guessing the truth, and had she not seen that it had entered her mind, when the letter was brought to her, she would have given a hint as to the forger's name. But Agnes's hesitation and sudden paleness assured Miss Greeby that she guessed the truth, so the letter was left to work its poison. Silver, of course, clamored for his blackmail, but Miss Greeby promised to recompense him, and also threatened if he did not hold his tongue that she would accuse him and Garvington of the murder. Since the latter had forged the letter and the former had borrowed the revolver which had killed Pine, it would have been tolerably easy for Miss Greeby to substantiate her accusation. As to her share in the crime, all she had to do was to deny that Silver had passed the borrowed revolver on to her, and there was no way in which he could prove that he had done so. On the whole, Silver had judged it best to fall in with Miss Greeby's plans, and preserve silence, especially as she was rich and could supply him with whatever money he chose to ask for. She was in his power, and he was in her power, so it was necessary to act on the golden rule of give and take.

And the final statement which Silver made to Lambert intimated that Garvington was ignorant of the truth. Until the bullet was produced in the library to fit the revolver it had never struck Garvington that the other weapon had been used to kill Pine. And he had honestly believed that Silver—as was actually the case—had remained in his bedroom all the time, until he came downstairs to play his part. As to Miss Greeby being concerned in the matter, such an idea had never entered Garvington's head. The little man's hesitation in producing the revolver, when he got an inkling of the truth, was due to his dread that if Silver was accused of the murder—and at the time it seemed as though the secretary was guilty—he might turn king's evidence to save his neck, and explain the very shady plot in which Garvington had been engaged. But Lambert had forced his cousin's hand, and Silver had been brought to book, with the result that the young man now sat in his room at the inn, quite convinced that Miss Greeby was guilty, yet wondering what motive had led her to act in such a murderous way.

Also, Lambert wondered what was best to be done, in order to save the family name. If he went to the police and had Miss Greeby arrested, the truth of Garvington's shady dealings would certainly come to light, especially as Silver was an accessory after the fact. On the other hand, if he left things as they were, there was always a chance that hints might be thrown out by Chaldea—who had everything to gain and nothing to lose—that he and Agnes were responsible for the death of Pine. Of course, Lambert, not knowing that Chaldea had been listening to the conversation in the cottage, believed that the girl was ignorant of the true state of affairs, and he wondered how he could inform her that the actual criminal was known without risking her malignity. He wanted to clear his character and that of his wife; likewise he wished to save the family name. But it seemed to him that the issue of these things lay in the hands of Chaldea, and she was bent upon injuring him if she could. It was all very perplexing.

It was at this point of his meditation that Mother Cockleshell arrived at the inn. He heard her jovial voice outside and judged from its tone that the old dame was in excellent spirits. Her visit seemed to be a hint from heaven as to what he should do. Gentilla hated Chaldea and loved Agnes, so Lambert felt that she would be able to help him. As soon as possible he had her brought into the sitting room, and, having made her sit down, closed both the door and the window, preparatory to telling her all that he had learned. The conversation was, indeed, an important one, and he was anxious that it should take place without witnesses.

"You are kind, sir," said Mother Cockleshell, who had been supplied with a glass of gin and water. "But it ain't for the likes of me to be sitting down with the likes of you."

"Nonsense! We must have a long talk, and I can't expect you to stand all the time—at your age."

"Some Gentiles ain't so anxious to save the legs of old ones," remarked Gentilla Stanley cheerfully. "But I always did say as you were a golden one for kindness of heart. Well, them as does what's unexpected gets what they don't hope for."

"I have got my heart's desire, Mother," said Lambert, sitting down and lighting his pipe. "I am happy now."

"Not as happy as you'd like to be, sir," said the old woman, speaking quite in the Gentile manner, and looking like a decent charwoman. "You've a dear wife, as I don't deny, Mr. Lambert, but money is what you want."

"I have enough for my needs."

"Not for her needs, sir. She should be wrapped in cloth of gold and have a path of flowers to tread upon."

"It's a path of thorns just now," muttered Lambert moodily.

"Not for long, sir; not for long. I come to put the crooked straight and to raise a lamp to banish the dark. Very good this white satin is," said Mother Cockleshell irrelevantly, and alluding to the gin. "And terbaccer goes well with it, as there's no denying. You wouldn't mind my taking a whiff, sir, would you?" and she produced a blackened clay pipe which had seen much service. "Smoking is good for the nerves, Mr. Lambert."

The young man handed her his pouch. "Fill up," he said, smiling at the idea of his smoking in company with an old gypsy hag.

"Bless you, my precious!" said Mother Cockleshell, accepting the offer with avidity, and talking more in the Romany manner. "I allers did say as you were what I said before you were, and that's golden, my Gorgious one. Ahime!" she blew a wreath of blue smoke from her withered lips, "that's food to me, my dearie, and heat to my old bones."

Lambert nodded. "You hinted, in Devonshire, that you had something to say, and a few moments ago you talked about putting the crooked straight."

"And don't the crooked need that same?" chuckled Gentilla, nodding. "There's trouble at hand, my gentleman. The child's brewing witch's broth, for sure."

"Chaldea!" Lambert sat up anxiously. He mistrusted the younger gypsy greatly, and was eager to know what she was now doing.

"Aye! Aye! Aye!" Mother Cockleshell nodded three times like a veritable Macbeth witch. "She came tearing, rampagious-like, to the camp an hour or so back and put on her fine clothes—may they cleave with pain to her skin—to go to the big city. It is true, rye. Kara ran by the side of the donkey she rode upon—may she have an accident—to Wanbury."

"To Wanbury?" Lambert looked startled as it crossed his mind, and not unnaturally, that Chaldea might have gone to inform Inspector Darby about the conversation with Garvington in the library.

"To Wanbury first, sir, and then to Lundra."

"How can you be certain of that?"

"The child treated me like the devil's calls her," said Gentilla Stanley, shaking her head angrily. "And I have no trust in her, for a witchly wrong 'un she is. When she goes donkey-wise to Wanbury, I says to a chal, says I, quick-like, 'Follow and watch her games!' So the chal runs secret, behind hedges, and comes on the child at the railway line making for Lundra. And off she goes on wheels in place of tramping the droms in true Romany style."

"What the deuce has she gone to London for?" Lambert asked himself in a low voice, but Gentilla's sharp ears overheard.

"Mischief for sure, my gentleman. Hai, but she's a bad one, that same. But she plays and I play, with the winning for me—since the good cards are always in the old hand. Fear nothing, my rye. She cannot hurt, though snake that she is, her bite stings."

The young man did not reply. He was uneasy in one way and relieved in another. Chaldea certainly had not gone to see Inspector Darby, so she could not have any intention of bringing the police into the matter. But why had she gone to London? He asked himself this question and finally put it to the old woman, who watched him with bright, twinkling eyes.

"She's gone for mischief," answered Gentilla, nodding positively. "For mischief's as natural to her as cheating is to a Romany chal. But I'm a dealer of cards myself, rye, and I deal myself the best hand."

"I wish you'd leave metaphor and come to plain speaking," cried Lambert in an irritable tone, for the conversation was getting on his nerves by reason of its prolixity and indirectness.

Mother Cockleshell laughed and nodded, then emptied the ashes out of her pipe and spoke out, irrelevantly as it would seem: "The child has taken the hearts of the young from me," said she, shaking her grizzled head; "but the old cling to the old. With them as trusts my wisdom, my rye, I goes across the black water to America and leaves the silly ones to the child. She'll get them into choky and trouble, for sure. And that's a true dukkerin."

"Have you the money to go to America?"

"Money?" The old woman chuckled and hugged herself. "And why not, sir, when Ishmael Hearne was my child. Aye, the child of my child, for I am the bebee of Hearne, bebee being grandmother in our Romany tongue, sir."

Lambert started from his seat, almost too astonished to speak. "Do you mean to say that you are Pine's grandmother?"

"Pine? Who is Pine? A Gentile I know not. Hearne he was born and Hearne he shall be to me, though the grass is now a quilt for him. Ohone! Hai mai! Ah, me! Woe! and woe, my gentleman. He was the child of my child and the love of my heart," she rocked herself to and fro sorrowfully, "like a leaf has he fallen from the tree; like the dew has he vanished into the blackness of the great shadow. Hai mai! Hai mai! the sadness of it."

"Hearne your grandson?" murmured Lambert, staring at her and scarcely able to believe her.

"True. Yes; it is true," said Gentilla, still rocking. "He left the road, and the tent, and the merry fire under a hedge for your Gentile life. But a born Romany he was and no Gorgio. Ahr-r-r!" she shook herself with disgust. "Why did he labor for gold in the Gentile manner, when he could have chored and cheated like a true-hearted black one?"

Her allusions to money suddenly enlightened the young man. "Yours is the name mentioned in the sealed letter held by Jarwin?" he cried, with genuine amazement written largely on his face. "You inherit the millions?"

Mother Cockleshell wiped her eyes with a corner of her shawl and chuckled complacently. "It is so, young man, therefore can I take those who hold to my wisdom to the great land beyond the water. Ah, I am rich now, sir, and as a Gorgious one could I live beneath a roof-tree. But for why, I asks you, my golden rye, when I was bred to the open and the sky? In a tent I was born; in a tent I shall die. Should I go, Gentile, it's longing for the free life I'd be, since Romany I am and ever shall be. As we says in our tongue, my dear, 'It's allers the boro matcho that pet-a-lay 'dree the panni,' though true gypsy lingo you can't call it for sure."

"What does it mean?" demanded Lambert, staring at the dingy possessor of two millions sterling.

"It's allers the largest fish that falls back into the water," translated Mrs. Stanley. "I told that to Leland, the boro rye, and he goes and puts the same into a book for your readings, my dearie!" then she uttered a howl and flung up her arms. "But what matter I am rich, when my child's child's blood calls out for vengeance. I'd give all the red gold—and red money it is, my loved one," she added, fixing a bright pair of eyes on Lambert, "if I could find him as shot the darling of my heart."

Knowing that he could trust her, and pitying her obvious sorrow, Lambert had no hesitation in revealing the truth so far as he knew it. "It wasn't a him who shot your grandson, but a her."

"Hai!" Gentilla flung up her arms again, "then I was right. My old eyes did see like a cat in the dark, though brightly shone the moon when he fell."

"What? You know?" Lambert started back again at this second surprise.

"If it's a Gentile lady, I know. A red one large as a cow in the meadows, and fierce as an unbroken colt."

"Miss Greeby!"

"Greeby! Greeby! So your romi told me," shrieked the old woman, throwing up her hands in ecstasy. "Says I to her, 'Who's the foxy one?' and says she, smiling like, 'Greeby's her name!'"

"Why did you ask my wife that?" demanded Lambert, much astonished.

"Hai, she was no wife of yours then, sir. Why did I ask her? Because I saw the shooting—"

"Of Pine—of Hearne—of your son?"

"Of who else? of who else?" cried Mother Cockleshell, clapping her skinny hand and paddling on the floor with her feet. "Says Ishmael to me, 'Bebee,' says he, 'my romi is false and would run away with the golden rye this very night as ever was.' And says I to him, 'It's not so, son of my son, for your romi is as true as the stars and purer than gold.' But says he, 'There's a letter,' he says, and shows it to me. 'Lies, son of my son,' says I, and calls on him to play the trustful rom. But he pitches down the letter, and says he, 'I go this night to stop them from paddling the hoof,' and says I to him, 'No! No!' says I. 'She's a true one.' But he goes, when all in the camp are sleeping death-like, and I watches, and I follers, and I hides."

"Where did you hide?"

"Never mind, dearie. I hides securely, and sees him walking up and down biting the lips of him and swinging his arms. Then I sees—for Oliver was bright, and Oliver's the moon, lovey—the big Gentile woman come round and hide in the bushes. Says I to myself, says I, 'And what's your game?' I says, not knowing the same till she shoots and my child's child falls dead as a hedgehog. Then she runs and I run, and all is over."

"Why didn't you denounce her, Gentilla?"

"And for why, my precious heart? Who would believe the old gypsy? Rather would the Poknees say as I'd killed my dear one. No! no! Artful am I and patient in abiding my time. But the hour strikes, as I said when I spoke to your romi in Devonshire no less, and the foxy moll shall hang. You see, my dear, I waited for some Gentile to speak what I could speak, to say as what I saw was truth for sure. You speak, and now I can tell my tale to the big policeman at Wanbury so that my son's son may sleep quiet, knowing that the evil has come home to her as laid him low. But, lovey, oh, lovey, and my precious one!" cried the old woman darting forward to caress Lambert's hand in a fondling way, "tell me how you know and what you learned. At the cottage you were, and maybe out in the open watching the winder of her you loved."

"No," said Lambert sharply, "I was at the cottage certainly, but in bed and asleep. I did not hear of the crime until I was in London. In this way I found out the truth, Mother!" and he related rapidly all that had been discovered, bringing the narrative right up to the confession of Silver, which he detailed at length.

The old woman kept her sharp eyes on his expressive face and hugged his hand every now and then, as various points in the narrative struck her. At the end she dropped his hand and returned back to her chair chuckling. "It's a sad dukkerin for the foxy lady," said Gentilla, grinning like the witch she was. "Hanged she will be, and rightful it is to be so!"

"I agree with you," replied Lambert relentlessly. "Your evidence and that of Silver can hang her, certainly. Yet, if she is arrested, and the whole tale comes out in the newspapers, think of the disgrace to my family."

Mother Cockleshell nodded. "That's as true as true, my golden rye," she said pondering. "And I wish not to hurt you and the rani, who was kind to me. I go away," she rose to her feet briskly, "and I think. What will you do?"

"I can't say," said Lambert, doubtfully and irresolutely. "I must consult my wife. Miss Greeby should certainly suffer for her crime, and yet—"

"Aye! Aye! Aye! The boro rye," she meant Garvington, "is a bad one for sure, as we know. Shame to him is shame to you, and I wouldn't have the rani miserable—the good kind one that she is. Wait! aye, wait, my precious gentleman, and we shall see."

"You will say nothing in the meantime," said Lambert, stopping her at the door, and anxious to know exactly what were her intentions.

"I have waited long for vengeance and I can wait longer, sir," said Mother Cockleshell, becoming less the gypsy and more the respectable almshouse widow. "Depend upon my keeping quiet until—"

"Until what? Until when?"

"Never you mind," said the woman mysteriously. "Them as sins must suffer for the sin. But not you and her as is innocent."

"No violence, Gentilla," said the young man, alarmed less the lawless gypsy nature should punish Miss Greeby privately.

"I swear there shall be no violence, rye. Wait, for the child is making mischief, and until we knows of her doings we must be silent. Give me your gripper, my dearie," she seized his wrist and bent back the palm of the hand to trace the lines with a dirty finger. "Good fortune comes to you and to her, my golden rye," she droned in true gypsy fashion. "Money, and peace, and honor, and many children, to carry on a stainless name. Your son shall you see, and your son's son, my noble gentleman, and with your romi shall you go with happiness to the grave," she dropped the hand. "So be it for a true dukkerin, and remember Gentilla Stanley when the luck comes true."

"But Mother, Mother," said Lambert, following her to the door, as he was still doubtful as to her intentions concerning Miss Greeby.

The gypsy waved him aside solemnly. "Never again will you see me, my golden rye, if the stars speak truly, and if there be virtue in the lines of the hand. I came into your life: I go out of your life: and what is written shall be!" she made a mystic sign close to his face and then nodded cheerily.

"Duveleste rye!" was her final greeting, and she disappeared swiftly, but the young man did not know that the Romany farewell meant, "God bless you!"

CHAPTER XX

THE DESTINED END

As might have been anticipated, Lord Garvington was in anything but a happy frame of mind. He left Silver in almost a fainting condition, and returned to The Manor feeling very sick himself. The two cowardly little men had not the necessary pluck of conspirators, and now that there seemed to be a very good chance that their nefarious doings would be made public they were both in deadly fear of the consequences. Silver was in the worst plight, since he was well aware that the law would consider him to be an accessory after the fact, and that, although his neck was not in danger, his liberty assuredly was. He was so stunned by the storm which had broken so unexpectedly over his head, that he had not even the sense to run away. All manly grit—what he possessed of it—had been knocked out of him, and he could only whimper over the fire while waiting for Lambert to act.

Garvington was not quite so downhearted, as he knew that his cousin was anxious to consider the fair fame of the family. Thinking thus, he felt a trifle reassured, for the forged letter could not be made public without a slur being cast on the name. Then, again, Garvington knew that he was innocent of designing Pine's death, and that, even if Lambert did inform the police, he could not be arrested. It is only just to say that had the little man known of Miss Greeby's intention to murder the millionaire, he would never have written the letter which lured the man to his doom. And for two reasons: in the first place he was too cowardly to risk his neck; and in the second Pine was of more value to him alive than dead. Comforting himself with this reflection, he managed to maintain a fairly calm demeanor before his wife.

But on this night Lady Garvington was particularly exasperating, for she constantly asked questions which the husband did not feel inclined to answer. Having heard that Lambert was in the village, she wished to know why he had not been asked to stay at The Manor, and defended the young man when Garvington pointed out that an iniquitous person who had robbed Agnes of two millions could not be tolerated by the man—Garvington meant himself—he had wronged. Then Jane inquired why Lambert had brought Chaldea to the house, and what had passed in the library, but received no answer, save a growl. Finally she insisted that Freddy had lost his appetite, which was perfectly true.

"And I thought you liked that way of dressing a fish so much, dear," was her wail. "I never seem to quite hit your taste."

"Oh, bother: leave me alone, Jane. I'm worried."

"I know you are, for you have eaten so little. What is the matter?"

"Everything's the matter, confound your inquisitiveness. Hasn't Agnes lost all her money because of this selfish marriage with Noel, hang him? How the dickens do you expect us to carry on unless we borrow?"

"Can't you get some money from the person who now inherits?"

"Jarwin won't tell me the name."

"But I know who it is," said Lady Garvington triumphantly. "One of the servants who went to the gypsy camp this afternoon told my maid, and my maid told me. The gypsies are greatly excited, and no wonder."

Freddy stared at her. "Excited, what about?"

"Why, about the money, dear. Don't you know?"

"No, I don't!" shouted Freddy, breaking a glass in his irritation. "What is it? Bother you, Jane. Don't keep me hanging on in suspense."

"I'm sure I never do, Freddy, dear. It's Hubert's money which has gone to his mother."

Garvington jumped up. "Who—who—who is his mother?" he demanded, furiously.

"That dear old Gentilla Stanley."

"What! What! What!"

"Oh, Freddy," said his wife plaintively. "You make my head ache. Yes, it's quite true. Celestine had it from William the footman. Fancy, Gentilla having all that money. How lucky she is."

"Oh, damn her; damn her," growled Garvington, breaking another glass.

"Why, dear. I'm sure she's going to make good use of the money. She says—so William told Celestine—that she would give a million to learn for certain who murdered poor Hubert."

"Would she? would she? would she?" Garvington's gooseberry eyes nearly dropped out of his head, and he babbled, and burbled, and choked, and spluttered, until his wife was quite alarmed.

"Freddy, you always eat too fast. Go and lie down, dear."

"Yes," said Garvington, rapidly making up his mind to adopt a certain course about which he wished his wife to know nothing. "I'll lie down, Jane."

"And don't take any more wine," warned Jane, as she drifted out of the dining-room. "You are quite red as it is, dear."

But Freddy did not take this advice, but drank glass after glass until he became pot-valiant. He needed courage, as he intended to go all by himself to the lonely Abbot's Wood Cottage and interview Silver. It occurred to Freddy that if he could induce the secretary to give up Miss Greeby to justice, Mother Cockleshell, out of gratitude, might surrender to him the sum of one million pounds. Of course, the old hag might have been talking all round the shop, and her offer might be bluff, but it was worth taking into consideration. Garvington, thinking that there was no time to lose, since his cousin might be beforehand in denouncing the guilty woman, hurried on his fur overcoat, and after leaving a lying statement with the butler that he had gone to bed, he went out by the useful blue door. In a few minutes he was trotting along the well-known path making up his mind what to say to Silver. The interview did not promise to be an easy one.

"I wish I could do without him," thought the treacherous little scoundrel as he left his own property and struck across the waste ground beyond the park wall. "But I can't, dash it all, since he's the only person who saw the crime actually committed. 'Course he'll get jailed as an accessory-after-the-fact: but when he comes out I'll give him a thousand or so if the old woman parts. At all events, I'll see what Silver is prepared to do, and then I'll call on old Cockleshell and make things right with her. Hang it," Freddy had a qualmish feeling. "The exposure won't be pleasant for me over that unlucky letter, but if I can snaffle a million, it's worth it. Curse the honor of the family, I've got to look after myself somehow. Ho! ho!" he chuckled as he remembered his cousin. "What a sell for Noel when he finds that I've taken the wind out of his sails. Serve him jolly well right."

In this way Garvington kept up his spirits during the walk, and felt entirely cheerful and virtuous by the time he reached the cottage. In the thin, cold moonlight, the wintry wood looked spectral and wan. The sight of the frowning monoliths, the gaunt, frozen trees and the snow-powdered earth, made the luxurious little man shiver. Also the anticipated conversation rather daunted him, although he decided that after all Silver was but a feeble creature who could be easily managed. What Freddy forgot was that he lacked pluck himself, and that Silver, driven into a corner, might fight with the courage of despair. The sight of the secretary's deadly white and terrified face as he opened the door sufficient to peer out showed that he was at bay.

"If you come in I'll shoot," he quavered, brokenly. "I'll—I'll brain you with the poker. I'll throw hot water on you, and—and scratch out your—your—"

"Come, come," said Garvington, boldly. "It's only me—a friend!"

Silver recognized the voice and the dumpy figure of his visitor. At once he dragged him into the passage and barred the door quickly, breathing hard meanwhile. "I don't mind you," he giggled, hysterically. "You're in the same boat with me, my lord. But I fancied when you knocked that the police—the police"—his voice died weakly in his throat: he cast a wild glance around and touched his neck uneasily as though he already felt the hangman's rope encircling it.

Garvington did not approve of this grim pantomime, and swore. "I'm quite alone, damn you," he said roughly. "It's all right, so far!" He sat down and loosened his overcoat, for the place was like a Turkish bath for heat. "I want a drink. You've been priming yourself, I see," and he pointed to a decanter of port wine and a bottle of brandy which were on the table along with a tray of glasses. "Silly ass you are to mix."

"I'm—I'm—keeping up my—my spirits," giggled Silver, wholly unnerved, and pouring out the brandy with a shaking hand. "There you are, my lord. There's water, but no soda."

"Keeping up your spirits by pouring spirits down," said Garvington, venturing on a weak joke. "You're in a state of siege, too."

Silver certainly was. He had bolted the shutters, and had piled furniture against the two windows of the room. On the table beside the decanter and bottles of brandy, lay a poker, a heavy club which Lambert had brought from Africa, and had left behind when he gave up the cottage, a revolver loaded in all six chambers, and a large bread knife. Apparently the man was in a dangerous state of despair and was ready to give the officers of the law a hostile welcome when they came to arrest him. He touched the various weapons feverishly.

"I'll give them beans," he said, looking fearfully from right to left. "Every door is locked; every window is bolted. I've heaped up chairs and sofas and tables and chests of drawers, and wardrobes and mattresses against every opening to keep the devils out. And the lamps—look at the lamps. Ugh!" he shuddered. "I can't bear to be in the dark."

"Plenty of light," observed Garvington, and spoke truly, for there must have been at least six lamps in the room—two on the table, two on the mantel-piece, and a couple on the sideboard. And amidst his primitive defences sat Silver quailing and quivering at every sound, occasionally pouring brandy down his throat to keep up his courage.

The white looks of the man, the disorder of the room, the glare of the many lights, and the real danger of the situation, communicated their thrill to Garvington. He shivered and looked into shadowy corners, as Silver did; then strove to reassure both himself and his companion. "Don't worry so," he said, sipping his brandy to keep him up to concert pitch, "I've got an idea which will be good for both of us."

"What is it?" questioned the secretary cautiously. He naturally did not trust the man who had betrayed him.

"Do you know who has inherited Pine's money?"

"No. The person named in the sealed envelope?"

"Exactly, and the person is Mother Cockleshell."

Silver was so amazed that he forgot his fright. "What? Is Gentilla Stanley related to Pine?"

"She's his grandmother, it seems. One of my servants was at the camp to-day and found the gypsies greatly excited over the old cat's windfall."

"Whew!" Silver whistled and drew a deep breath. "If I'd known that, I'd have got round the old woman. But it's too late now since all the fat is on the fire. Mr. Lambert knows too much, and you have confessed what should have been kept quiet."

"I had to save my own skin," said Garvington sullenly. "After all, I had nothing to do with the murder. I never guessed that you were so mixed up in it until Lambert brought that bullet to fit the revolver I lent you."

"And which I gave to Miss Greeby," snapped Silver tartly. "She is the criminal, not me. What a wax she will be in when she learns the truth. I expect your cousin will have her arrested."

"I don't think so. He has some silly idea in his head about the honor of our name, and won't press matters unless he is forced to."

"Who can force him?" asked Silver, looking more at ease, since he saw a gleam of hope.

"Chaldea! She's death on making trouble."

"Can't we silence her? Remember you swing on my hook."

"No, I don't," contradicted Garvington sharply. "I can't be arrested."

"For forging that letter you can!"

"Not at all. I did not write it to lure Pine to his death, but only wished to maim him."

"That will get you into trouble," insisted Silver, anxious to have a companion in misery.

"It won't, I tell you. There's no one to prosecute. You are the person who is in danger, as you knew Miss Greeby to be guilty, and are therefore an accessory after the fact."

"If Mr. Lambert has the honor of your family at heart he will do nothing," said the secretary hopefully; "for if Miss Greeby is arrested along with me the writing of that letter is bound to come out."

"I don't care. It's worth a million."

"What is worth a million?"

"The exposure. See here, Silver, I hear that Mother Cockleshell is willing to hand over that sum to the person who finds the murderer of her grandson. We know that Miss Greeby is guilty, so why not give her up and earn the money?"

The secretary rose in quivering alarm. "But I'd be arrested also. You said so; you know you said so."

"And I say so again," remarked Garvington, leaning back coolly. "You'd not be hanged, you know, although she would. A few years in prison would be your little lot and when you came out I could give you say—er—er—ten thousand pounds. There! That's a splendid offer."

"Where would you get the ten thousand? Tell me!" asked Silver with a curious look.

"From the million Mother Cockleshell would hand over to me."

"For denouncing me?"

"For denouncing Miss Greeby."

"You beast!" shrieked Silver hysterically. "You know quite well that if she is taken by the police I have no chance of escaping. I'd run away now if I had the cash. But I haven't. I count on your cousin keeping quiet because of your family name, and you shan't give the show away."

"But think," said Garvington, persuasively, "a whole million."

"For you, and only ten thousand for me. Oh, I like that."

"Well, I'll make it twenty thousand."

"No! no."

"Thirty thousand."

"No! no! no!"

"Forty, fifty, sixty, seventy—oh, hang it, you greedy beast! I'll give you one hundred thousand. You'd be rich for life then."

"Would I, curse you!" Silver clenched his fists and backed against the wall looking decidedly dangerous. "And risk a life-long sentence to get the money while you take the lion's share."

"You'd only get ten years at most," argued the visitor, annoyed by what he considered to be silly objections.

"Ten years are ten centuries at my time of life. You shan't denounce me."

Garvington rose. "Yes, I shall," he declared, rendered desperate by the dread lest he should lose the million. "I'm going to Wanbury to-night to tell Inspector Darby and get a warrant for Miss Greeby's arrest along with yours as her accomplice."

Silver flung himself forward and gripped Garvington's coat. "You daren't!"

"Yes, I dare. I can't be hurt. I didn't murder the man and I'm not going to lose a pile of money for your silly scruples."

"Oh, my lord, consider." Silver in a panic dropped on his knees. "I shall be shut up for years; it will kill me; it will kill me! And you don't know what a terrible and clever woman Miss Greeby is. She may deny that I gave her the revolver and I can't prove that I did. Then I might be accused of the crime and hanged. Hanged!" cried the poor wretch miserably. "Oh, you'll never give me away, my lord, will you."

"Confound you, don't I risk my reputation to get the money," raged Garvington, shaking off the trembling arms which were round his knees. "The truth of the letter will have to come out, and then I'm dished so far as society is concerned. I wouldn't do it—tell that is—but that the stakes are so large. One million is waiting to be picked up and I'm going to pick it up."

"No! no! no! no!" Silver grovelled on the floor and embraced Garvington's feet. But the more he wailed the more insulting and determined did the visitor become. Like all tyrants and bullies Garvington gained strength and courage from the increased feebleness of his victim. "Don't give me up," wept the secretary, nearly beside himself with terror; "don't give me up."

"Oh, damn you, get out of the way!" said Garvington, and made for the door. "I go straight to Wanbury," which statement was a lie, as he first intended to see Mother Cockleshell at the camp and make certain that the reward was safe. But Silver believed him and was goaded to frenzy.

"You shan't go!" he screamed, leaping to his feet, and before Garvington knew where he was the secretary had the heavy poker in his grasp. The little fat lord gave a cry of terror and dodged the first blow which merely fell on his shoulder. But the second alighted on his head and with a moan he dropped to the ground. Silver flung away the poker.

"Are you dead? are you dead?" he gasped, kneeling beside Garvington, and placed his hand on the senseless man's heart. It still beat feebly, so he arose with a sigh of relief. "He's only stunned," panted Silver, and staggered unsteadily to the table to seize a glass of brandy. "I'll, ah—ah—ah!" he shrieked and dropped the tumbler as a loud and continuous knocking came to the front door.

Naturally in his state of panic he believed that the police had actually arrived, and here he had struck down Lord Garvington. Even though the little man was not dead, Silver knew that the assault would add to his punishment, although he might have concluded that the lesser crime was swallowed up in the greater. But he was too terrified to think of doing anything save hiding the stunned man, and with a gigantic effort he managed to fling the body behind the sofa. Then he piled up rugs and cushions between the wall and the back of the sofa until Garvington was quite hidden and ran a considerable risk of being suffocated. All the time the ominous knocking continued, as though the gallows was being constructed. At least it seemed so to Silver's disturbed fancy, and he crept along to the door holding the revolver in an unsteady grip.

"Who—who—is—"

"Let me in; let me in," said a loud, hard voice. "I'm Miss Greeby. I have come to save you. Let me in."

Silver had no hesitation in obeying, since she was in as much danger as he was and could not hurt him without hurting herself. With trembling fingers he unbolted the door and opened it, to find her tall and stately and tremendously impatient on the threshold. She stepped in and banged the door to without locking it. Silver's teeth chattered so much and his limbs trembled so greatly that he could scarcely move or speak. On seeing this—for there was a lamp in the passage—Miss Greeby picked him up in her big arms like a baby and made for the sitting-room. When, within she pitched Silver on to the sofa behind which Garvington lay senseless, and placing her arms akimbo surveyed him viciously.

"You infernal worm!" said Miss Greeby, grim and savage in her looks, "you have split on me, have you?"

"How—how—how do you know?" quavered Silver mechanically, noting that in her long driving coat with a man's cap she looked more masculine than ever.

"How do I know? Because Chaldea was hiding under the studio window this afternoon and overheard all that passed between you and Garvington and that meddlesome Lambert. She knew that I was in danger and came at once to London to tell me since I had given her my address. I lost no time, but motored down here and dropped her at the camp. Now I've come to get you out of the country."

"Me out of the country?" stammered the secretary.

"Yes, you cowardly swine, although I'd rather choke the life out of you if it could be done with safety. You denounced me, you beast."

"I had to; my own neck was in danger."

"It's in danger now. I'd strangle you for two pins. But I intend to send you abroad since your evidence is dangerous to me. If you are out of the way there's no one else can state that I shot Pine. Here's twenty pounds in gold;" she thrust a canvas bag into the man's shaking hands; "get on your coat and cap and I'll take you to the nearest seaport wherever that is. My motor is on the verge of the wood. You must get on board some ship and sail for the world's end. I'll send you more money when you write. Come, come," she stamped, "sharp's the word."

"But—but—but—"

Miss Greeby lifted him off the sofa by the scruff of the neck. "Do you want to be killed?" she said between her teeth, "there's no time to be lost. Chaldea tells me that Lambert threatens to have me arrested."

The prospect of safety and prosperity in a distant land so appealed to Silver that he regained his courage in a wonderfully short space of time. Rising to his feet he hastily drained another glass of brandy and the color came back to his wan cheeks. But for all the quantity he had drank that same evening he was not in the least intoxicated. He was about to rush out of the room to get his coat and cap when Miss Greeby laid a heavy hand on his shoulder.

"Is there any one else in the house?" she asked suspiciously.

Silver cast a glance towards the sofa. "There's no servant," he said in a stronger voice. "I have been cooking and looking after myself since I came here. But—but—but—"

"But what, you hound?" she shook him fiercely.

"Garvington's behind the sofa."

"Garvington!" Miss Greeby was on the spot in a moment pulling away the concealing rugs and cushions. "Have you murdered him?" she demanded, drawing a deep breath and looking at the senseless man.

"No, he's only stunned. I struck him with the poker because he wanted to denounce me."

"Quite right." Miss Greeby patted the head of her accomplice as if he were a child, "You're bolder than I thought. Go on; hurry up! Before Garvington recovers his senses we'll be far enough away. Denounce me; denounce him, will you?" she said, looking at Garvington while the secretary slipped out of the room; "you do so at your own cost, my lord. That forged letter won't tell in your favor. Ha!" she started to her feet. "What's that! Who's here?"

She might well ask. There was a struggle going on in the passage, and she heard cries for help. Miss Greeby flung open the sitting-room door, and Silver, embracing Mother Cockleshell, tumbled at her feet. "She got in by the door you left open," cried Silver breathlessly, "hold her or we are lost; we'll never get away."

"No, you won't!" shouted the dishevelled old woman, producing a knife to keep Miss Greeby at bay. "Chaldea came to the camp and I learned through Kara how she'd brought you down, my Gentile lady. I went to tell the golden rye, and he's on the way here with the village policeman. You're done for."

"Not yet." Miss Greeby darted under the uplifted knife and caught Gentilla round the waist. The next moment the old woman was flung against the wall, breathless and broken up. But she still contrived to hurl curses at the murderess of her grandson.

"I saw you shoot him; I saw you shoot him," screamed Mother Cockleshell, trying to rise.

"Silver, make for the motor; it's near the camp; follow the path," ordered Miss Greeby breathlessly; "there's no time to be lost. As to this old devil—" she snatched up a lamp as the secretary dashed out of the house, and flung it fairly at Gentilla Stanley. In a moment the old woman was yelling with agony, and scrambled to her feet a pillar of fire. Miss Greeby laughed in a taunting manner and hurled another lamp behind the sofa. "You'd have given me up also, would you, Garvington?" she cried in her deep tone; "take that, and that, and that."

Lamp after lamp was smashed and burst into flames, until only one was left. Then Miss Greeby, seeing with satisfaction that the entire room was on fire and hearing the sound of hasty footsteps and the echoing of distant voices, rushed in her turn from the cottage. As she bolted the voice of Garvington screaming with pain and dread was heard as he came to his senses to find himself encircled by fire. And Mother Cockleshell also shrieked, not so much because of her agony as to stop Miss Greeby from escaping.

"Rye! Rye! she's running; catch her; catch her. Aha—aha—aha!" and she sank into the now blazing furnace of the room.

The walls of the cottage were of mud, the partitions and roof of wood and thatch, so the whole place soon burned like a bonfire. Miss Greeby shot out of the door and strode at a quick pace across the glade. But as she passed beyond the monoliths, Lambert, in company with a policeman, made a sudden appearance and blocked her way of escape. With a grim determination to thwart him she kilted up her skirts and leaped like a kangaroo towards the undergrowth beneath the leafless trees. By this time the flames were shooting through the thatched roof in long scarlet streamers and illuminated the spectral wood with awful light.

"Stop! stop!" cried Lambert, racing to cut off the woman's retreat, closely followed by the constable.

Miss Greeby laughed scornfully, and instead of avoiding them as they crossed her path, she darted straight towards the pair. In a moment, by a dexterous touch of her shoulders right and left, she knocked them over by taking them unawares, and then sprang down the path which curved towards the gypsies' encampment. At its end the motor was waiting, and so vivid was the light that she saw Silver's black figure bending down as he frantically strove to start the machine. She travelled at top speed, fearful lest the man should escape without her.

Then came an onrush of Romany, attracted to the glade by the fire. They guessed from Miss Greeby's haste that something was seriously wrong and tried to stop her. But, delivering blows straight from the shoulder, here, there, and everywhere, the woman managed to break through, and finally reached the end of the pathway. Here was the motor and safety, since she hoped to make a dash for the nearest seaport and get out of the kingdom before the police authorities could act.

But the stars in their course fought against her. Silver, having started the machinery, was already handling the steering gear, and bent only upon saving his own miserable self, had put the car in motion. He could only drive in a slip-slop amateur way and aimlessly zigzagged down the sloping bank which fell away to the high road. As the motor began to gather speed Miss Greeby ran for her life and liberty, ranging at length breathlessly alongside. The gypsies tailed behind, shouting.

"Stop, you beast!" screamed Miss Greeby, feeling fear for the first time, and she tried to grab the car for the purpose of swinging herself on board.

But Silver urged it to greater speed. "I save myself; myself," he shrieked shrilly and unhinged by deadly terror, "get away; get away."

In his panic he twisted the wheel in the wrong direction, and the big machine swerved obediently. The next moment Miss Greeby was knocked down and writhed under the wheels. She uttered a tragic cry, but little Silver cared for that. Rendered merciless with fear he sent the car right over her body, and then drove desperately down the hill to gain the hard road. Miss Greeby, with a broken back, lay on the ground and saw as in a ghastly dream her machine flash roaring along the highway driven by a man who could not manage it. Even in her pain a smile crept over her pale face.

"He's done for, the little beast," she muttered, "he'll smash. Lambert! Lambert!" The man whose name she breathed had arrived as she spoke; and knelt breathlessly beside her to raise her head. "You—you—oh, poor creature!" he gasped.

"I'm done for, Lambert," she panted in deadly pain, "back broken. I sinned for you, but—but you can't hang me. Look—look after Garvington—Cockleshell too—look—look—Augh!" and she moaned.

"Where are they?"

"In—in—the—cottage," murmured the woman, and fell back in a fainting condition with a would-be sneering laugh.

Lambert started to his feet with an oath, and leaving the wretched woman to the care of some gypsies, ran back to the glade. The cottage was a mass of streaming, crackling flames, and there was no water to extinguish these, as he realized with sudden fear. It was terrible to think that the old woman and Garvington were burning in that furnace, and desperately anxious to save at least one of the two, Lambert tried to enter the door. But the heat of the fire drove him back, and the flames seemed to roar at his discomfiture. He could do nothing but stand helplessly and gaze upon what was plainly Garvington's funeral pyre.

By this time the villagers were making for the wood, and the whole place rang with cries of excitement and dismay. The wintry scene was revealed only too clearly by the ruddy glare and by the same sinister light. Lambert suddenly beheld Chaldea at his elbow. Gripping his arm, she spoke hoarsely, "The tiny rye is dead. He drove the engine over a bank and it smashed him to a pulp."

"Oh! ah! And—and Miss Greeby?"

"She is dying."

Lambert clenched his hands and groaned, "Garvington and Mother Cockleshell?"

"She is dead and he is dead by now," said Chaldea, looking with a callous smile at the burning cottage, "both are dead—Lord Garvington."

"Lord Garvington?" Lambert groaned again. He had forgotten that he now possessed the title and what remained of the family estates.

"Avali!" cried Chaldea, clapping her hands and nodding toward the cottage with a meaning smile, "there's the bonfire to celebrate the luck."

CHAPTER XXI

A FINAL SURPRISE

A week later and Lambert was seated in the library of The Manor, looking worn and anxious. His wan appearance was not due so much to what he had passed through, trying as late events had been, as to his dread of what Inspector Darby was about to say. That officer was beside him, getting ready for an immediate conversation by turning over various papers which he produced from a large and well-filled pocket-book. Darby looked complacent and important, as an examination into the late tragedy had added greatly to his reputation as a zealous officer. Things were now more ship-shape, as Miss Greeby had died after making confession of her crime and had been duly buried by her shocked relatives. The ashes of Lord Garvington and Mother Cockleshell, recovered from the débris of the cottage, had also been disposed of with religious ceremonies, and Silver's broken body had been placed in an unwept grave. The frightful catastrophe which had resulted in the death of four people had been the talk of the United Kingdom for the entire seven days.

What Lambert was dreading to hear was the report of Miss Greeby's confession, which Inspector Darby had come to talk about. He had tried to see her himself at the village inn, whither she had been transferred to die, but she had refused to let him come to her dying bed, and therefore he did not know in what state of mind she had passed away. Judging from the vindictive spirit which she had displayed, Lambert fancied that she had told Darby the whole wretched story of the forged letter and the murder. The last was bound to be confessed, but the young man had hoped against hope that Miss Greeby would be silent regarding Garvington's share in the shameful plot. Wickedly as his cousin had behaved, Lambert did not wish his memory to be smirched and the family honor to be tarnished by a revelation of the little man's true character. He heartily wished that the evil Garvington had done might be buried with him, and the whole sordid affair forgotten.

"First, my lord," said Darby leisurely, when his papers were in order, "I have to congratulate your lordship on your accession to the title. Hitherto so busy have I been that there has been no time to do this."

"Thank you, Mr. Inspector, but I regret that I should have succeeded through so tragic a death."

"Yes, yes, my lord! the feeling does you honor," Darby nodded sympathetically; "but it must be some comfort for you to know that your poor cousin perished when on an errand of mercy, although his aim was not perhaps quite in accordance with strict justice."

Lambert stared. "I don't know what you mean," he remarked, being puzzled by this coupling of Garvington's name with any good deed.

"Of course you don't, my lord. But for you to understand I had better begin with Miss Greeby's confession. I must touch on some rather intimate things, however," said the inspector rather shyly.

"Meaning that Miss Greeby was in love with me."

"Exactly, my lord. Her love for you—if you will excuse my mentioning so private a subject—caused the whole catastrophe."

"Indeed," the young man felt a sense of relief, as if Darby put the matter in this way the truth about the forged letter could scarcely have come to light, "will you explain?"

"Certainly, my lord. Miss Greeby always wished to marry your lordship, but she knew that you loved your wife, the present Lady Garvington, who was then Lady Agnes Pine. She believed that you and Lady Agnes would sooner or later run away together."

"There was no reason she should think so," said Noel, becoming scarlet.

"Of course not, my lord. Pardon me again for speaking of such very private matters. But I can scarcely make your lordship understand how the late Sir Hubert Pine came by his death unless I am painfully frank."

"Go on, Mr. Inspector," Noel leaned back and folded his arms. "Be frank to the verge of rudeness, if you like."

"Oh, no, no, my lord; certainly not," Darby said in a shocked manner. "I will be as delicate as I possibly can. Well, then, my lord, Miss Greeby, thinking that you might elope with the then Lady Agnes Pine, resolved to place an even greater barrier between you than the marriage."

"What could be a possibly greater barrier?"

"Your honor, my lord, your strict sense of honor. Miss Greeby thought that if she got rid of Sir Hubert, and Lady Agnes was in possession of the millions, that you would never risk her losing the same for your sake."

"She was right in supposing that, Mr. Inspector, but how did Miss Greeby know that Lady Agnes would lose the money if she married me?"

"Sir Hubert told her so himself, my lord, when she discovered that he was at the Abbot's Wood camp under the name of Ishmael Hearne."

"His real name."

"Of course, my lord; of course. And having made this discovery and knowing how jealous Sir Hubert was of his wife—if you will pardon my mentioning the fact—Miss Greeby laid a trap to lure him to The Manor that he might be shot."

The listener moved uneasily, and he now quite expected to hear the revelation of Garvington's forgery. "Go on, Mr. Inspector."

"Miss Greeby," pursued the officer, glancing at his notes, "knew that the late Mark Silver, who was Sir Hubert's secretary, was not well disposed toward his employer, as he fancied that he had been cheated out of the proceeds of certain inventions. Miss Greeby worked on this point and induced Silver to forge a letter purporting to come from Lady Agnes to you saying that an elopement had been arranged."

"Oh," Lambert drew a breath of relief, "so Silver laid a trap, did he?"

"Yes, my lord, and a very clever one. The letter was arranged by Silver to fall into Sir Hubert's hands. That unfortunate gentleman came to the blue door at the appointed time, then Miss Greeby, who had climbed out of the window of her bedroom to hide in the shrubbery, shot the unsuspecting man. She then got back into her room—and a very clever climber she must have been, my lord—and afterward mingled with the guests."

"But why did she think of luring Sir Hubert to be shot?" asked Noel with feigned ignorance, "when she ran such a risk of being discovered?"

"Ah, my lord, therein lies the cleverness of the idea. Poor Lord Garvington had threatened to shoot any burglar, and that gave Miss Greeby the idea. It was her hope that your late cousin might kill Sir Hubert by mistaking him for a robber, and she only posted herself in the shrubbery to shoot if Sir Hubert was not killed. He was not, as we know that the shot fired by Lord Garvington only broke his arm. Miss Greeby made sure by killing him herself, and very cleverly she did so."

"And what about my late cousin's philanthropic visit to Silver?"

"Ah, my lord, that was a mistake. His lordship was informed of the forged letter by Chaldea the gypsy girl, who found it in Sir Hubert's tent, and for the sake of your family wished to get Silver out of the country. It would have been dreadful—as Lord Garvington rightly considered—that the name of his sister and your name should be mentioned in connection with an elopement even though it was untrue. He therefore went to induce Silver to leave the country, but the man, instead of being grateful, stunned his lordship with a blow from a poker which he had picked up."

"How was that known, Mr. Inspector?"

"Miss Greeby had the truth from his own lips. Silver threatened to denounce her, and knowing this Chaldea went to London to warn her."

"Oh," muttered Lambert, thinking of what Gentilla Stanley had said, "how did she find out?"

"She overheard a conversation between Silver and Lord Garvington in the cottage."

Lambert was relieved again, since Miss Greeby had not evidently mentioned him as being mixed up with the matter. "Yes, Mr. Inspector, I can guess the rest. This unfortunate woman came down to get Silver, who could have hanged her, out of the country, and he set fire to the cottage."

"She set fire to it," corrected Darby quickly, "by chance, as she told me, she overturned a lamp. Of course, Lord Garvington, being senseless, was burned to death. Gentilla Stanley was also burned."

"How did she come to be there?"

"Oh, it seems that Gentilla followed Hearne—he was her grandson I hear from the gypsies—to The Manor on that night and saw the shooting. But she said nothing, not feeling sure if her unsupported testimony would be sufficient to convict Miss Greeby. However, she watched that lady and followed her to the cottage to denounce her and prevent the escape of Silver—who knew the truth also, as she ascertained. Silver knocked the old woman down and stunned her, so she also was burned to death. Then Silver ran for the motor car and crushed Miss Greeby—since he could not manage the machine."

"Did he crush her on purpose, do you think?"

"No," said Darby after a pause, "I don't think so. Miss Greeby was rich, and if the pair of them had escaped Silver would have been able to extort money. He no more killed her than he killed himself by dashing into that chalk pit near the road. It was mismanagement of the motor in both cases."

Lambert was quiet for a time. "Is that all?" he asked, looking up.

"All, my lord," answered the inspector, gathering his papers together.

"Is anything else likely to appear in the papers?"

"No, my lord."

"I noted," said Lambert slowly, "that there was no mention of the forged letter made at the inquest."

Darby nodded. "I arranged that, my lord, since the forged letter made so free with your lordship's name and that of the present Lady Garvington. As you probably saw, it was only stated that the late Sir

Hubert had gone to meet his secretary at The Manor and that Miss Greeby, knowing of his coming, had shot him. The motive was ascribed as anger at the late Sir Hubert for having lost a great sum of money which Miss Greeby entrusted to him for the purpose of speculation."

"And is it true that such money was entrusted and lost?"

"Perfectly true, my lord. I saw in that fact a chance of hiding the real truth. It would do no good to make the forged letter public and would cast discredit both on the dead and the living. Therefore all that has been said does not even hint at the trap laid by Silver. Now that all parties concerned are dead and buried, no more will be heard of the matter, and your lordship can sleep in peace."

The young man walked up and down the room for a few minutes while the inspector made ready to depart. Noel was deeply touched by the man's consideration and made up his mind that he should not lose by the delicacy he had shown in preserving his name and that of Agnes from the tongue of gossips. He saw plainly that Darby was a man he could thoroughly trust and forthwith did so.

"Mr. Inspector," he said, coming forward to shake hands, "you have acted in a most kind and generous manner and I cannot show my appreciation of your behavior more than by telling you the exact truth of this sad affair."

"I know the truth," said Darby staring.

"Not the exact truth, which closely concerns the honor of my family. But as you have saved that by suppressing certain evidence it is only right that you should know more than you do know."

"I shall keep quiet anything that you tell me, my lord," said Darby greatly pleased; "that is, anything that is consistent with my official duty."

"Of course. Also I wish you to know exactly how matters stand, since there may be trouble with Chaldea."

"Oh, I don't think so, my lord. Chaldea has married that dwarf."

"Kara, the Servian gypsy?"

"Yes. She's given him a bad time, and he put up with it because he had no authority over her; but now that she's his romi—as these people call a wife—he'll make her dance to his playing. They left England yesterday for foreign parts—Hungary, I fancy, my lord. The girl won't come back in a hurry, for Kara will keep an eye on her."

Lambert drew a long breath of relief. "I am glad," he said simply, "as I never should have felt safe while she remained in England."

"Felt safe?" echoed the officer suspiciously.

His host nodded and told the man to take a seat again. Then, without wasting further time, he related the real truth about the forged letter. Darby listened to the recital in amazement and shook his head sadly over the delinquency of the late Lord Garvington.

"Well! Well!" said the inspector staring, "to think as a nobleman born and bred should act in this way."

"Why shouldn't a nobleman be wicked as well as the grocer?" said Lambert impatiently, "and according to the socialistic press all the evil of humanity is to be found in aristocratic circles. However, you know the exact truth, Mr. Inspector, and I have confided to you the secret which concerns the honor of my family. You won't abuse my confidence."

Darby rose and extended his hand. "You may be sure of that, my lord. What you have told me will never be repeated. Everything in connection with this matter is finished, and you will hear no more about it."

"I'm glad and thankful," said the other, again drawing a breath of relief, "and to show my appreciation of your services, Darby, I shall send you a substantial check."

"Oh, my lord, I couldn't take it. I only did my duty."

"I think you did a great deal more than that," answered the new Lord Garvington dryly, "and had you acted entirely on the evidence you gathered together, and especially on the confession of that miserable woman, you might have made public much that I would prefer to keep private. Take the money from a friend, Darby, and as a mark of esteem for a man."

"Thank you, my lord," replied the inspector straightly, "I don't deny but what my conscience and my duty to the Government will allow me to take it since you put it in that way. And as I am not a rich man the money will be welcome. Thank you!"

With a warm hand-shake the inspector took his departure and Noel offered up a silent prayer of thankfulness to God that things had turned out so admirably. His shifty cousin was now dead and there was no longer any danger that the honor of the family, for which so much had been sacrificed, both by himself and Agnes, would be smirched. The young man regretted the death of Mother Cockleshell, who had been so well disposed toward his wife and himself, but he rejoiced that Chaldea had left England under the guardianship of Kara, as henceforth—if he knew anything of the dwarf's jealous disposition—the girl would trouble him no more. And Silver was dead and buried, which did away with any possible trouble coming from that quarter. Finally, poor Miss Greeby, who had sinned for love, was out of the way and there was no need to be anxious on her account. Fate had made a clean sweep of all the actors in the tragedy, and Lambert hoped that this particular play was ended.

When the inspector went away, Lord Garvington sought out his wife and his late cousin's widow. To them he reported all that had passed and gave them the joyful assurance that nothing more would be heard in connection with the late tragic events. Both ladies were delighted.

"Poor Freddy," sighed Agnes, who had quite forgiven her brother now that he had paid for his sins, "he behaved very badly; all the same he had his good points, Noel."

"Ah, he had, he had," said Lady Garvington, the widow, shaking her untidy head, "he was selfish and greedy, and perhaps not so thoughtful as he might have been, but there are worse people than poor Freddy."

Noel could not help smiling at this somewhat guarded eulogy of the dead, but did not pursue the subject. "Well, Jane, you must not grieve too much."

"No, I shall not," she admitted bluntly, "I am going to be quiet for a few months and then perhaps I may marry again. But I shall marry a man who lives on nuts and roots, my dear Noel. Never again," she shuddered, "shall I bother about the kitchen. I shall burn Freddy's recipes and cookery books."

Lady Garvington evidently really felt relieved by the death of her greedy little husband, although she tried her best to appear sorry. But the twinkle of relief in her eyes betrayed her, and neither Noel nor Agnes could blame her. She had enough to live on—since the new lord had arranged this in a most generous manner—and she was free from the cares of the kitchen.

"So I'll go to London in a few days when I've packed up," said the widow nodding, "you two dears can stay here for your second honeymoon."

"It will be concerned with pounds, shillings, and pence, then," said Agnes with a smile, "for Noel has to get the estate put in order. Things are very bad just now, as I know for certain. But we must try to save The Manor from going out of the family."

It was at this moment, and while the trio wondered how the financial condition of the Lamberts was to be improved, that a message came saying that Mr. Jarwin wished to see Lord and Lady Garvington in the library. Wondering what the lawyer had come about, and dreading further bad news, the young couple descended, leaving the widow to her packing up. They found the lean, dry solicitor waiting for them with a smiling face.

"Oh!" said Agnes as she greeted him, "then it's not bad news?"

"On the contrary," said Jarwin, with his cough, "it is the best of news."

Noel looked at him hard. "The best of news to me at the present moment would be information about money," he said slowly. "I have a title, it is true, but the estate is much encumbered."

"You need not trouble about that, Lord Garvington; Mrs. Stanley has put all that right."

"What?" asked Agnes greatly agitated. "Has she made over the mortgages to Noel? Oh, if she only has."

"She has done better than that," remarked Jarwin, producing a paper of no great size, "this is her will. She wanted to make a deed of gift, and probably would have done so had she lived. But luckily she made the will—and a hard-and-fast one it is—for I drew it up myself," said Mr. Jarwin complacently.

"How does the will concern us?" asked Agnes, catching Noel's hand with a tremor, for she could scarcely grasp the hints of the lawyer.

"Mrs. Stanley, my dear lady, had a great regard for you since you nursed her through a dangerous illness. Also you were, as she put it, a good and true wife to her grandson. Therefore, as she approved of you and of your second marriage, she has left the entire fortune of your late husband to you and to Lord Garvington here."

"Never!" cried Lambert growing pale, while his wife gasped with astonishment.

"It is true, and here is the proof," Jarwin shook the parchment, "one million to you, Lord Garvington, and one million to your wife. Listen, if you please," and the solicitor read the document in a formal manner which left no doubt as to the truth of his amazing news. When he finished the lucky couple looked at one another scarcely able to speak. It was Agnes who recovered her voice first.

"Oh, it can't be true—it can't be true," she cried. "Noel, pinch me, for I must be dreaming."

"It is true, as the will gives you to understand," said the lawyer, smiling in his dry way, "and if I may be permitted to say so, Lady Garvington, never was money more rightfully inherited. You surrendered everything for the sake of true love, and it is only just that you should be rewarded. If Mrs. Stanley had lived she intended to keep five or six thousand for herself so that she could transport certain gypsies to America, but she would undoubtedly have made a deed of gift of the rest of the property. Oh, what a very fortunate thing it was that she made this will," cried Jarwin, genuinely moved at the thought of the possible loss of the millions, "for her unforeseen death would have spoiled everything if I had not the forethought to suggest the testament."

"It is to you we owe our good fortune."

"To Mrs. Gentilla Stanley—and to me partially. I only ask for my reward that you will continue to allow me to see after the property. The fees," added Jarwin with his dry cough, "will be considerable."

"You can rob us if you like," said Noel, slapping him on the back. "Well, to say that I am glad is to speak weakly. I am overjoyed. With this money we can restore the fortunes of the family again."

"They will be placed higher than they have ever been before," cried Agnes with a shining face. "Two millions. Oh, what a lot of good we can do."

"To yourselves?" inquired Jarwin dryly.

"And to others also," said Lambert gravely. "God has been so good to us that we must be good to others."

"Then be good to me, Lord Garvington," said the solicitor, putting away the will in his bag, "for I am dying of hunger. A little luncheon—"

"A very big one."

"I am no great eater," said Jarwin, and walked toward the door, "a wash and brush-up and a plate of soup will satisfy me. And I will say again what I said before to both of you, that you thoroughly deserve your good fortune. Lord Garvington, you are the luckier of the two, as you have a wife who is far above rubies, and—and—dear me, I am talking romance. So foolish at my age. To think—well—well, I am extremely hungry, so don't let luncheon be long before it appears," and with a croaking laugh at his jokes the lawyer disappeared.

Left alone the fortunate couple fell into one another's arms. It seemed incredible that the past storm should have been succeeded by so wonderful a calm. They had been tested by adversity, and they had proved themselves to be of sterling metal. Before them the future stretched in a long, smooth road under sunny blue skies, and behind them the black clouds, out of which they had emerged, were dispersing into thin air. Evil passes, good endures.

"Two millions!" sighed Agnes joyfully.

"Of red money," remarked her husband.

"Why do you call it that?"

"Mother Cockleshell—bless her!—called it so because it was tainted with blood. But we must cleanse the stains, Agnes, by using much of it to help all that are in trouble. God has been good in settling our affairs in this way, but He has given me a better gift than the money."

"What is that?" asked Lady Garvington softly.

"The love of my dear wife," said the happiest of men to the happiest of women.

THE END

Milton Keynes UK
Ingram Content Group UK Ltd.
UKHW040935171124
451301UK00016B/146/J